Ionia

Ionia

Land of Wise Men and Fair Women

Alexander Craig

MINT EDITIONS

Ionia: Land of Wise Men and Fair Women was first published in 1898.

This edition published by Mint Editions 2021.

ISBN 9781513291055 | E-ISBN 9781513293905

Published by Mint Editions®

 MINT
EDITIONS

minteditionbooks.com

Publishing Director: Jennifer Newens
Design & Production: Rachel Lopez Metzger
Project Manager: Micaela Clark
Typesetting: Westchester Publishing Services

DEDICATED
To
NAHUM EDWARD JENNISON
In acknowledgment of
valued counsel and encouragement.

Contents

A Note From the Publisher

While this is an exceptional and defining work of utopian fiction from the late nineteenth century, we would be remiss if we did not first call attention to the blatant anti-Semitism within the pages of this book.

We will present this text as it was originally published in 1898 because to do otherwise is to ignore that these prejudices did, and continue to, exist.

Mint Editions
Berkeley, CA

I

An English Village

The village of Chingford, in Surrey, is one of the prettiest in all England. Situated in a rich agricultural district, three miles from the nearest railway station, it is undisturbed by the bustle of industrial and commercial life, but its little community of five hundred souls pass their lives in such peace and contentment as seldom falls to the lot of those living in more enterprising and ambitious places. Its rows of handsome cottages, surrounded by well-kept gardens, betoken a standard of comfort and taste much superior to the ordinary level of rustic existence. It boasts a fine old church with ivy-covered walls, and has two or three modern edifices which are its special pride. One of these is the schoolhouse, built of stone from the designs of a celebrated London architect; another is Wolverton Hall, a two-story building of brick, faced with stone, dedicated to the instruction and entertainment of the people. It contains a library and reading room on the ground floor, while the second forms a handsome hall for lectures, concerts and other meetings. Here the village literary society assembles on Saturday evenings and discusses high themes of state and philosophy, and although the provincial accent of some of the speakers might provoke a smile from the undergraduates of Oxford or Cambridge, it is wonderful how the faculty of expression has been developed amongst these simple villagers. Some of the younger men prove themselves able to take an intelligent grasp of practical questions and their discussions are at least a great advance upon the pothouse talk of their forefathers. They are well known to each other, and divided in friendly rivalry into various groups; the interest they take in the subjects discussed and the delight of victory to the side which wins most votes at the end of a debate, is sufficient to furnish them food for thought and entertainment during the whole of the following week. Without the use of the library the literary society never could have had an existence, and the stimulus which the latter gives to mental exertion is seen in the large proportion of readers of solid works on history, biography, political economy and social science which are to be found amongst these humble villagers. The reading room is well stocked with the best weeklies, monthly magazines and reviews, and not an evening passes but its tables are surrounded by earnest students of both sexes, young and old alike. This is more particularly the case, of course, during the long winter evenings. In summer there are outdoor games on the village common for the boys and young men, while beyond the brook at the lower end of the village is a beautiful park with lawn and shade trees, bowling greens and croquet grounds where the elder and less active of the people take their ease and recreation.

Nearly in the center of the village is the public laundry, free to all the families living in the place, and with a separate room fitted up with swings and cots for babies so that the women may bring their infants with them and not be hindered in their work. The laundry is also the public school of cookery, where, at the end of the week, when the family washings are all completed and out of the way, practical lessons in plain cooking are given free of cost to all who choose to come, and the resulting dishes furnish a weekly dinner or supper to the families of the pupils in rotation. At the opposite end of the village from the park is situated the parish church, and hard by is the rectory where the good old parson, Dr. Wolverton, has lived respected and admired by the whole community for nearly fifty years. Beyond the rectory is the Grange, a property of some fifty acres enclosed by high brick walls and containing a wood of fine beech trees and a spacious park dotted with rare old oaks, some of which began to grow in the time of the Tudors. A wide driveway winds through grove and park up to a handsome mansion dating from the reign of Queen Anne, but recently renovated and fitted up inside with all the devices which modern ideas of comfort demand. Here resides the lady bountiful of the parish, Mrs. Helen Musgrave, daughter of the old rector. She has been for many years a widow, and I am her only son.

My father, David Musgrave, was the younger son of a neighboring squire, and having but a younger son's portion, he had been placed by his father in a London banking house, of which he became the head before he was thirty-five years old. Retiring at fifty with a large fortune, he had purchased the Grange and married the rector's daughter, expecting to spend many years amongst the scenes of his youth, enjoying the wealth which the best part of his life had been spent in accumulating.

But man proposes and God disposes. My father had no sooner settled down to a life of ease and enjoyment than his health began to give way. He had never spared himself in business, working early and late to raise himself to the top of the ladder, and he succeeded, but his success cost him dearly. He had been possessed originally of a powerful physique, and in the pursuit of business scarcely ever allowed himself a holiday or any kind of recreation, and nature took her usual revenge. Overwork had worn him out, and when at last he sought to recover health and energy by repose and a return to his native air, it was too late. No medical skill could help him, and he died about four years after his marriage, and when I was too young to remember him.

With the exception of a few bequests to various relatives all the wealth which he had amassed fell to be divided between his wife and child. My mother became sole owner of the Grange, with other property to the value of about seven hundred and fifty thousand pounds, while a like amount fell to my share, and as it was invested in the best securities and was to be allowed to accumulate until I came of age, it was no ordinary fortune that awaited me. Although my mother was only four and twenty at her husband's death, and very attractive in person and disposition, my father made no consideration as to remarriage in his will, and it was expected by all friends and neighbors that after a year or two of mourning she would make someother man happy in the possession of her hand and fortune, and after a time many a scion of the county families paid court to her, but she disappointed them all. She had made up her mind that her life was to be devoted to the bringing up of her son and to the improvement and happiness of the villagers amongst whom she had been born.

Chingford was then a very different place from what it afterwards became. The men were mostly agricultural laborers, whose wages were but scanty at the best, and a large proportion of them was spent at the two pot-houses which were the great curse of the village. The dwelling houses were in the last stages of dilapidation and decay; the women were slatternly and unkempt and the children for the most part ragged and vicious, given to robbing the henroosts and orchards of the neighboring farmers. The rector had labored earnestly amongst them, and had managed to induce a minority of the elders to attend church regularly on Sundays and their children to come to Sunday school, but as regards the majority he was in despair, and he often compared his parish to Nazareth, out of which nothing good could be expected to come.

It was therefore a difficult task which his daughter undertook when she resolved to make Chingford a model of industry and thrift, of cleanliness and respectability, but she set about the work with all the resolute determination of a high-souled Christian woman. She first bought up the two alehouses and demolished them, building a couple of neat cottages in their place. Next she built the schoolhouse and installed an energetic young man as teacher, with a couple of young lady assistants. There were plenty of scholars, for the place swarmed with children, and their mothers were glad to get them out of their way for the best part of the day. Evening classes were established for adults, which at first were rather thinly attended, but when the lady of the Grange went round to the cottages and personally entreated the attendance of the people who had grown up without schooling, none dared refuse the opportunity offered, and the teachers soon had their hands full. Very substantial prizes were offered to those heads of families who should make most progress in their studies. My mother announced that she had bought twenty acres of land adjoining the village on the west, which was to become the public common, with free grazing for animals owned by the people, and that at the end of the winter the twelve most proficient amongst the fathers or mothers who attended the night school should each be presented with a fine milch cow. To the children also many prizes were given for attendance and proficiency in their studies, which were of a more useful character than those usually given elsewhere, consisting of articles of clothing, boots and shoes, hats and caps for the girls and boys, with occasionally books for those who stood least in need of these necessaries.

A few months made a wonderful change. The suppression of the drinking places alone acted as a stimulus to respectability and self-respect. The men kept more steadily at their work; the women grew ashamed of their untidy habits and began to acquire a wholesome desire for decent apparel and the cottages began to lose their neglected and dirty appearance.

But Mrs. Musgrave was not content with inducing better habits amongst the people: she determined that the village itself should be rebuilt entirely and that its inhabitants should be in possession of homes which they could take both comfort and pride in, with sufficient ground to each for both kitchen and flower gardens. She bought up all the land, with the buildings standing on it, and engaged an eminent architect to make plans for the rebuilding of the whole with a view to picturesque general effect, but also and more particularly to comfort and perfect sanitary arrangements in each individual dwelling. A competent superintendent was put in charge of the work of construction, but the labor was done as far as possible by the villagers themselves, so that they should have the full benefit of the money which was being expended. It was a work of time, because no family could be asked to move before new quarters were ready for them, but as fast as the new cottages were completed they were occupied, and the ground cleared for the building of others; and care was taken to give the most industrious and deserving families first choice, in order that they might set a good example of order and neatness in the care of house and garden. In about two years Chingford was transformed from an assemblage of straggling and untidy hovels to a beautiful village of handsome cottages which excited the admiration of all who saw it. The people were no less changed, and had become worthy in appearance and conduct to be the dwellers in such an ideal place. There were, of course, exceptions, men who could not live without liquor and women who preferred dirt and disorder to cleanliness and comfort, but the unreclaimable ones migrated to other parts of the country where their bad habits would be less conspicuous, and their places were easily supplied by worthy peasants from the neighborhood.

The laying out of the village park and the erection of Wolverton Hall followed next, with various other improvements which furnished work for two or three years more. My mother dreaded the time when all these undertakings should be completed, for there had been evolved from amongst the rude laboring people of Chingford quite a little band of competent mechanics, for whom she feared it would be difficult to find suitable employment, but the difficulty vanished as the time approached. Some had saved up money enough to set up themselves as contractors and builders in the nearest towns and villages, others were offered good places by the architect or the superintendent, and those that remained were not more than sufficient for the work of keeping in order and repairing the village itself and the Grange and its appurtenances.

By this time the people had come to look upon my mother as a kind of providence, and young and old alike worshiped her. They always spoke of her amongst themselves as "Lady Musgrave," and although she reproved them so severely for doing so that they discontinued it in her presence, yet they could not understand why she was not more entitled to be called "my lady" than many of the titled dames of the county who could not be compared to her either in point of wealth or character. She was careful not to demoralize them by giving alms to those who were able to work, but the old people of the parish were never allowed to go to the workhouse, and if a poor woman were left a widow with a family of children, she furnished help in various ways and enabled them to tide over their misfortune until the children were old enough to work for themselves. She constantly visited the sick and furnished medical attendance free when necessary, as well as wine and other luxuries which the limited means of the stricken families could not afford. For years she kept a trained nurse constantly at the Grange, whose business was not so much to care for the patients as to teach the women of the village how to do it. Amongst the early lectures at the Hall were a series of addresses by eminent physicians on the preservation of health, and the people manifested such interest in these and the books on kindred subjects with which the library was well furnished that the position of village doctor soon became almost a sinecure.

While busy with these schemes for the reformation of her father's parish, my mother found plenty of time to attend to the education of her son. From the time that I attained the age of six until my eighteenth year I studied under tutors residing under our own roof and was hardly ever parted from my mother for an entire day. Being her only child she could not bear the idea of sending me to a public school, but in order that I should have the advantage of studying with boys of my own age she prevailed on my uncle, Sir Philip Musgrave, who resided about five miles from Chingford, to allow two of his sons to be educated with me. A carriage was sent for them every Monday morning and took them home on Friday afternoon, so that for the greater part of the time they lived at the Grange, and their schooling cost their father nothing at all, an arrangement which suited him very well, as he had several daughters to educate and his estates were very much encumbered.

Of the two boys Philip was the elder, being a year older than myself, and John about a year younger. They were fine, manly fellows and we were very great friends in the main, yet like all other boys we were liable to fall out and fight occasionally, but my mother treated us so impartially that our juvenile quarrels never lasted long, and the good feeling between the families was never interfered with in the slightest degree. Our teachers being selected with great care and with absolute disregard of monetary considerations, we made good head-way in our studies from the start, and the mental equipment of all three being nearly equal, our mutual emulation was of great service to us. In mathematics John was decidedly first, but in the acquisition of languages Philip and I showed greater facility. We made rapid progress in Latin and Greek, and by the time we were respectively fourteen and fifteen years old we could both read and converse in French and German with ease. In history I stood first and never tired of it, my memory being so tenacious that I scarcely ever forgot a name or a date which I took the trouble to fix in my mind. Most of our evenings were passed with my mother alone, for she did not care for society in general, but preferred the company of her boys. We sometimes read in turn to her and sometimes passed the hours in games of chess or whist, in which we became wonderfully proficient. The time never dragged with us, but I enjoyed those evenings best when, at the end of the week, my cousins had gone and my mother and I were together by ourselves, for from my earliest years I loved her passionately and looked up to her as superior to all other living beings. It was a great delight to me to read from my favorite authors with her alone for audience, or talk to her about my studies or the people of the village, or listen to her when she played or sang, and I was sure that no one else could sing so sweetly or look so graceful or compare with her in anyway.

Three or four times during each winter we had parties of young people at the Grange, to which the best families in the neighborhood sent their girls and boys, and the programme of amusements was so entertaining and varied that all looked forward to these occasions with unbounded delight and looked back upon them as among the brightest spots in their lives. In summer time the children of the village were invited to picnics in the Grange park, where all sorts of games were held, and I was encouraged to enter into the various sports on equal terms with the children of our poorer neighbors, who were made to feel perfectly at home with us, a privilege which they seldom abused. The pleasure they took in the great swings under the trees, the races and games in the park, and the grand banquet in the open air, at which they were waited on by all the servants of the Grange, was something to witness and remember. The years of my childhood passed swiftly away, and it was not without regret that I began to look forward at eighteen to a four years' course at the University of Oxford. My cousins did not accompany me there, for at this time they were both preparing to enter the army, in which they are now distinguished and rising officers, Philip in the cavalry and John in the engineers. I suffered severely from homesickness during the first three months at Oxford, never having been from home for any length of time before, but the distance by rail from Chingford was not great and I embraced every opportunity of spending a few days at the Grange. But I began to find friends amongst my fellow-students and gradually became reconciled to the new way of living, though my home remained as dear to me as ever. My mother began now to suggest to me that I should make choice of a profession or career in life, for she never entertained the idea that the possession of wealth formed any excuse for a life of idleness. I could see that the subject was a painful one to her, for she feared that I might adopt some vocation which would take me away from Chingford and thus permanently separate us, so I pondered over the matter long and earnestly and was in no hurry to make up my mind. One day during the long vacation after my second year at the university I said to her: "You are anxious to know what I am going to be, mother, and I can only think of one thing that would satisfy me."

"And what is that, my son?"

"To be prime minister of England."

My mother smiled and said: "Your ambition is rather exalted. Do you think you have the talents necessary to fill such a high station?"

"No, I do not," I answered, "for I have met many fellows at Oxford who are much cleverer than I am, and I have no doubt it would be the same in Parliament, so I am afraid I shall have to aim at something lower. I might possibly hope to be a cabinet minister some day if I gave my whole life to politics, but as nothing less than the premiership would suit me I think I shall stay out of Parliament."

"And what do you find so attractive about the position of the prime minister?"

"The power of doing good to his fellow-men. I know of no one who has done as much as you to benefit the people amongst whom we live, and it seems to me that the noblest ambition for your son would be to carry out your ideas of practical beneficence on a larger scale, and if I were premier I might institute reforms into our laws which would do much to ameliorate the condition of the working classes of the whole country."

"I am afraid," she replied, "that you would find the power of the prime minister much more limited in that direction than you imagine. He is bound by the ties of party, which prevent him carrying out his own ideas, and he cannot move in the direction of reform any faster than their convictions or their interests will permit. The first duty of the prime minister is considered by his followers to be to retain the governing power as long as possible and all other considerations have to give way to that. Far-reaching measures of reform would inevitably interfere with vested interests, which are always powerful and conservative, and the statesman who should deliberately defy them would be derided as a visionary and a theorist and would soon be swept aside by men of less elevated but more practical views. I am glad to know that you put such a high value on my efforts, but when you consider the smallness of the sphere in which I have labored you must be careful not to exaggerate the amount of good that has been done."

"But you have made a great many people happier and better, and if you are not proud of it I am, and if you can tell me of anyone who has done more I should be glad to know who it is."

"What I have done is not to be compared to the labors of others, if measured by the sacrifices involved. Think, for instance, of your grandfather's friend, the Rev. John Calderwood, who has given his whole life to the poor people of his parish in the East End of London, when, if he had listened to the promptings of ambition or worldly interest, he might have had high preferment in the church and might easily have attained to a bishopric by this time."

"He is a noble man," said I, "and I honor him for his devotion to what he considers his Master's cause, and yet you remember what he said when he was here last summer—that the visible results of his life's work were not a tenth part of what you had accomplished in this little village."

"I think in saying so his modesty caused him to underestimate his own work and his charity to overestimate mine, but while he has sacrificed comfort and health and every worldly advantage, I have made no sacrifice at all. I have had every luxury that wealth could buy, have lived in comfort amongst my own people, and the work I have done amongst the villagers has been itself the greatest pleasure to me. In the eyes of the Master my efforts are not to be compared to his for one moment."

"Well, mother mine, we cannot argue on that point, but I think your modest opinion of yourself does not detract from the merit of your achievements, and I think credit is due to results as well as to the means by which they are attained. How would it be for me to go and help Mr. Calderwood to do for his parish what you have done for Chingford? It would take a lot of money, of course, and you have never told me how much my fortune will amount to. The extent of it will have some influence on my choice of a career, and as I am now come to years of discretion I think you might safely trust me with that important secret."

"If I have not told you before it is partly because of the greatness of the wealth which awaits you, but I think it would be only right that you should know now, for it will doubtless influence you in the way you have indicated. As I have always tried to impress upon your mind that great wealth means great responsibility I trust you may prove yourself equal to the trust that will be imposed upon you on your coming of age, and yet I could almost wish the time were further off, for I cannot think of you yet as anything more than a boy, although I have to look up to you when you stand beside me."

"Well, mother, I see you are afraid to come to the point, but don't be alarmed, I promise you it won't turn my head if it should be a million."

"Your father left you seven hundred and fifty thousand pounds, all of which was very well invested, partly in stocks and partly in London real estate. The interest has been large and has been steadily added to the principal, till now it amounts to fully two million pounds."

"Two million pounds!"

I had just said that a million would not turn my head, but I had not bargained for two millions, and I confess that for the moment it made my head swim and took away my breath.

"Why, mother, that's positively awful."

"I think it is literally an awful sum, my boy, and I have prayed to God many a time that you would have the wisdom to use it rightly."

"Amen," said I, and for a few minutes I was silent, feeling absolutely miserable in the contemplation of the possession of such a load of wealth. All at once an idea came into my mind, and I said, excitedly:

"I'll tell you what I'll do, mother, I will really go and help Mr. Calderwood and make his wretched parish of St. Oswald's an oasis in the desert of East London, and when that is done we will begin upon the next and the next and drive away all the wickedness and the misery of it and set the people on their feet and make them self-respecting and self-supporting citizens just like your Chingford folks. Two million pounds! With such a sum as that we can abolish all the London slums and make tens of thousands of people happy."

My mother smiled at my enthusiasm, although it brought tears to her eyes, and, as she wiped them away, she said:

"God bless you my boy for the thought. There may not be so much virtue in two million pounds as you think, but it can be made to do a vast amount of good, and if you continue to feel about it as you do now, the possession of it will be a blessing to you instead of a curse, as it might easily have been in other hands. For the present I would not speak of it to anyone for you might change your mind before you are twenty-one, and I would advise you to think it over very seriously and learn more of what you would undertake before committing yourself to it."

"I should like to begin at once," said I, "next week if it were possible."

"Fortunately that is out of the question. Your fortune cannot be touched until you reach twenty-one, and if you will be guided by me you will not only finish the course you have commenced at the university but spend at least one year in traveling in foreign countries afterwards, so that you may know something of other lands before you begin any great work in your own."

"Well, mother, I am sure you know best, but I am also sure that this money which my father left me will be a great burden to me until I begin to spend some of it in relieving the distresses of some of my less fortunate fellow citizens."

And this idea which took such a sudden hold of me proved to be no evanescent youthful fancy. It seemed to me that the great wealth inherited from my father and the beneficent work of my mother combined to point out the path of duty clearly before me, and I believed myself destined by Providence to accomplish a great work amongst those of my countrymen and countrywomen who had been overtaken by poverty and misfortune. The east end of London offered a vast field for such efforts, and to it my mind constantly turned. I continued to pursue my studies at Oxford and endeavored to make as good an appearance at the examinations as possible, but all my spare time was devoted to reading works upon the condition of the poor in London and elsewhere. I corresponded with Mr. Calderwood and told him of the course I had resolved upon, and as soon as I was master of my fortune, sent him my first check as an installment of greater things to come.

It was only the earnest entreaty of my mother that prevailed upon me to postpone for a year the commencement of the work which had become the dream of my life. She consented to accompany me during the first month of my tour, and we had a very pleasant sojourn in France, Italy and Switzerland. There were with us a former tutor of mine, Dr. Reginald Godwin, and a maiden aunt of my own, Miss Virginia

Musgrave, my father's youngest sister. She was a person of great vivacity and good nature, and her presence added much to my mother's enjoyment of the trip. But no amount of persuasion could induce my mother to remain long away from her dear villagers, so we returned by the Rhine and Belgium to England and our native village. After a few days' rest Dr. Godwin and I set off again and visited nearly every country in Europe from Norway to Greece, and spent the winter months in Syria and Egypt, returning by Spain, Italy and Germany. Dr. Godwin was a delightful companion, for he had not only traveled much and made himself acquainted with all that was to be seen of historical and archaeological interest, but he had a very extensive acquaintance amongst the learned men of Europe, and at every university we visited he was sure to find some old friend who willingly did the honors of the place and showed us many things rare and curious that we should otherwise have missed.

While endeavoring to take full advantage of my opportunities to see and learn all I possibly could from the fine examples of architecture and painting which came in our way, as well as to improve my knowledge of history by studying the remains of ancient buildings to be found in all the different countries we visited, I never for a moment forgot the great work of my life, and made inquiry in all the large cities as to the condition of the poor and what was being done for their benefit. I was told of the building of hospitals and schools, of the founding of asylums for the aged and those who were afflicted with mental and physical disease, of charity doled out in driblets, but nowhere did I find any comprehensive plans in operation for the permanent raising of the poorest class to a self-supporting and self-respecting level in the way that my mother had followed in our own little village. When I told what she had done, wise men shook their heads and said that while her good work was worthy of the greatest praise, yet such a thing was only possible on a small scale and would be utterly impracticable in a great city, where the poverty and degradation of the lowest class was too vast for human effort to alleviate. The charitable labors of philanthropists might do good in certain individual cases, but the ranks of the destitute were continually being recruited from innumerable sources, and the great mass of hapless poverty remained practically unchanged from year to year. One great philosopher of world-wide fame expressed himself in conversation with me in these words:

"When we look backward over the history of mankind we find the condition of the world steadily improving. From epoch to epoch there is observed a constant upward tendency; there may be retrogression, but each step forward is always in advance of the last. In the earliest civilizations of which we have any record the condition of the poor was almost intolerable. The pyramids of Egypt and the Towers of Babylon were built by multitudes of slaves cowering under the lash of their taskmasters. Human life was of little account, and these great monuments were erected only through the suffering of myriads of poor wretches who toiled and died in misery in order that the glory of kings might be exalted. What a mighty advance we find in the joyous freedom and intellectual life of the Greeks! And yet even amongst them the larger proportion of the people were slaves. Wars were continually occurring, and the political situation was one of great instability. From the palmy days of Greece to the decay of the Roman empire and its disruption by barbarous hordes from the North was undoubtedly a great back-sliding, and yet the way was being prepared for the mightiest advance of all. From that time onward progress has been steady and sure. The art of printing has unlocked the fetters of men's minds and dispelled the ignorance which held them in bondage; slavery in all forms has been abolished from every civilized country; war itself has become civilized and is waged as between army against army rather than nation against nation; the red cross goes with the conquerors and robs the battlefield of its worst horrors; the poorest of men nowadays have opportunities which were denied to their ancestors, and the accident of birth debars no man from attaining to dignities, provided that he has the ability to contend with adverse circumstances. The condition of humanity today is vastly improved in comparison with the middle ages, but if we compare it with the lot of the masses living three thousand years ago it is like contrasting light with darkness.

"Now the cause of all this upward progress is not to be found in human effort directed consciously towards that end. The good that philanthropists and reformers have accomplished has invariably been local and temporary, and has been accompanied by counterbalancing evils. Christianity itself, which undertook to transform men into angels, could not prevent the lapse of civilized Europe into semi-barbarism, and the mutual persecutions of its various sects form a dark background to its doctrine of good will towards men. The fact is, that while humanity is weak, nature is strong. Evolution brought forth this beautiful green earth from the dark womb of chaos. Evolution has educed civilization from the savage state. Evolution will improve that civilization until the future inhabitants of this world will look back upon our era as one of barbarous ignorance and misery. The work may be slow; there may be periods of retrogression, but they will be only temporary. All human history and all cosmic history prove to us that the march of progress is irresistible. We cannot help it much; the most we can do is to endeavor not to hinder it. Whether we look forward or backward we find reason for supreme satisfaction in the inherent beneficence of nature; the evils we see around us will pass away and cause no uneasiness to him who looks at them with a philosophic eye."

This was cold comfort to one whose soul was glowing with enthusiasm in the idea of regenerating the down-trodden poor of his country, but it did not influence me much. I thought if that was all the help we could get from science and philosophy we must even get along without them and let them pursue their cold and barren path with whatever satisfaction they could find in it. I could not believe that humanity was so helpless as the great man seemed to think, and while failure was probable and success uncertain, yet there were thousands of earnest men and women whose efforts had left the world better than they found it, and I did believe that constant endeavor would at least clear the way for future laborers, and that at last the true path of progress would be found and humanity raised to a higher and nobler level.

It was therefore without any change of purpose or abatement of zeal for my self-appointed task that I returned home after my year of travel. I had seen so much of the poverty and distress of the great continental cities that I was perhaps a little less sanguine of good results, but at the same time I was more than ever convinced of the urgent necessity of the work to be done, and felt impatient to make a beginning. I remained in Chingford about two weeks, more to please my mother than from any need I felt of rest or recuperation, and then set out for the Metropolis to survey the ground and consider the plan of operations in consultation with the rector of St. Oswald's.

II

DARKEST LONDON

It was on a Monday afternoon early in June that I arrived at St. Oswald's intent on commencing what I sincerely believed had been marked out by Providence as the work of my life. We had been enjoying the most delightful summer weather at Chingford for the two weeks previous, but here it looked as if summer never showed itself. A cold northeast wind was blowing, a dismal canopy of cloud and smoke hung over the city and the steady rain had almost cleared the streets of passengers. Not a blade of grass nor anything green was visible, only dreary blocks of houses built of brick and so encrusted with the sooty deposit which rain and fog bring down in this part of the city that it was difficult to tell whether the original color had been red or white. The rector's parlor, whose windows looked out on the dismal street, was not much more cheerful than the view of the houses opposite. The small panes of glass, it is true, were whole instead of being broken and stuffed with rags like many of those which confronted it, but the threadbare carpet, the old-fashioned sofa and chairs with horse-hair upholstering, the faded wall paper and the feeble coal fire which smoked up the chimney, all betokened a lack of comfort which told of the ascetic life of its bachelor owner.

On being ushered into the room I found two persons present, one the Rev. John Calderwood himself, a tall man of sixty, with slightly stooping shoulders and scanty hair and whiskers of a sandy gray, the other was his curate, the Rev. Arthur Manson, a middle-sized, square-built man of thirty, with clean-shaven face of the bulldog type, massive jaws, coal-black hair and honest, clear, gray eyes. This was my first introduction to Mr. Manson, and I was well pleased with his appearance. He looked like one who would not shrink from difficulties or readily give up any undertaking to which he had once given his mind. We seated ourselves round the fireplace and Mr. Calderwood expressed his regret that my first visit to his parish should have been made on such a wet and gloomy day.

"Never mind that," I said, "the prospect is dark and cheerless just now, but before long there will be some sunshine upon St. Oswald's I promise you."

The old man smiled sadly and said, "See what a fine thing youth is! Here am I, old and pretty nearly worn out, with hope itself almost dead within me, and you come along with a young heart and fresh courage, and faith which refuses to be daunted by untoward appearances, and talking of sunshine when only dark and lowering clouds are visible. I trust your hopes will not be doomed to disappointment as mine have been, and I have faith enough left to believe that you may reap a harvest for which I have toiled in vain."

"I am sure," said I, "that you will help us to reap that harvest, nor do I think you should look so slightingly on your own achievements. You have saved many a soul from destruction and many a life from despair, and if the mass of misery and destitution around you seems as great as ever, it was simply because it was beyond the power of anyone situated as you have been to root it up. But I wish to know something of the nature of the evils we have to contend with, so if you please, I should like to hear from you what you consider the greatest difficulty in the way of reforming the wretched people of which your parish is made up."

"It is difficult to say whether ignorance or vice is our greatest enemy, ignorance which refuses to be enlightened, or vice which hardly recognizes itself as such, and neither believes in nor has any aspirations after virtue. Many of the people around us have inherited such depraved natures that even the grace of God seems powerless to change them. But there are others who are not naturally wicked who would lead moral and respectable lives if they could, and amongst these we manage to rescue one here and there. Of these very few remain here, they become disgusted with their surroundings and move to other neighborhoods where they can enjoy more of the comforts and decencies of life, and we never try to prevent them doing so. But their places are always filled up with others who are as bad as the people around them, and thus the parish remains at about the same level of wickedness and misery."

"Do those whom you persuade to try and lead better lives generally succeed in doing so, or is their reformation as a rule only temporary?"

"Alas! I am afraid we must admit that we are only partially successful in rescuing those even who are willing to be helped; there are dramshops and gin palaces at every corner, and many a man whom we have thought to be well along in the path of reformation has succumbed to some momentary temptation and fallen back at once into the slough from which it is more difficult afterwards to rescue him."

Mr. Manson, who had hitherto remained silent, now spoke with bitter earnestness, saying:

"That is the greatest curse of all! Those we have to deal with are either perversely wicked or miserably weak and the glittering gin palaces are constantly enticing the latter to their ruin. If we could only close up those that are within sight from the door of the church it would help us some."

"They shall be closed," I said.

"And then the houses are in such miserable condition; what with drafty doors and ill-fitting casements, to say nothing of broken windows and the utter absence of sanitary arrangements, the plague of rats and worse vermin, the over-crowding and the noisome smells, it is no wonder the poor wretches fly to the public houses for the comfort which it is impossible for them to find in their own miserable homes."

"That also shall be remedied," I said.

"I could give you thousands of instances," he continued, "of men who have endeavored to abandon their evil ways, but who have been dragged hopelessly down again by the sheer misery of their surroundings on the one hand and the allurements of the gin shop on the other, but one will suffice, for the story repeats itself in all. A man of the name of Wilkins, a brass-fitter, and an excellent mechanic, came to live in the court whose entrance you can see now from the further window, about six years ago. He was in the habit of getting drunk every Saturday and remaining in a state of intoxication as long as his money lasted. I spoke with him everytime I could find him sober and found that he was not bad at heart. He was thoroughly ashamed of his weakness, but had no confidence in his ability to conquer his appetite for drink. I induced him, however, to sign the pledge, and he tried hard to keep it. For nearly two years he never tasted liquor; he joined the church and endeavored to use his influence with others to follow his example, speaking at temperance meetings and taking a class in Sunday school. We looked upon him as thoroughly cured of his infirmity and felt little fear of his relapsing from grace, but his wife was a slatternly, untidy woman and his home never had any appearance of comfort, and in an evil hour he was tempted to cross the threshold of one of those wretched dramshops. It was probably only a momentary indulgence he proposed to himself, but the first glass of rum undid all the good that his two years of self-denial had accomplished, and he returned to his family in a state of maudlin intoxication. From that time his power of will has been utterly gone, and we have never been able to persuade him to another effort. He has a large family of children who live in starvation and rags and are growing up as thieves and worse than thieves, his wife has taken to drink, herself, to drown her sorrows, and there is no more hopeless, disreputable family in the whole parish. It is cases like this that make our work so disheartening, and we are glad to see those who try to lead decent respectable lives remove to other districts where their surroundings will be such as to elevate them instead of dragging them down even though our own parish should suffer by their absence."

"Then," said I, "it appears to me that the only hope of reforming the parish is by shutting up the gin shops and rebuilding the dwelling houses."

"That," said Mr. Calderwood, "would be transforming rather than reforming it. We should undoubtedly have a more respectable class of people living here, but they would not be of the class amongst whom we have labored."

"True enough," said I, "but you would still have abundant scope for your missionary work in the slums which lie beyond your transformed district. With your permission we will have this plan put in operation at once, at least as regards the four blocks which surround the church."

"It would be a very expensive experiment."

"I think," said I, "it would hardly be called an experiment. The removal of those miserable tumble-down structures and the erection of buildings fit for the abode of human beings would be a good work in itself, and the expense will be a matter of small consideration. But that will be a work of time, and I propose for the present under your guidance or that of Mr. Manson to make myself more familiar with the character of the people we have to deal with. I will accompany you in your round of visits amongst them and see for myself all the wretchedness and the misery of which I have so often heard you speak. I think perhaps four or five days in the week will be all I can stand of it at present, and I intend to retire to Chingford every Friday or Saturday and breathe my native air for a couple of days, returning with fresh energy each Monday. How you gentlemen can stand it day in and day out for years without breaking down is more than I can understand."

"With me," said the rector, "it has become second nature, but indeed there never has been a year when I have not taken a vacation for a week or two. You know how often I have been the guest of Dr. Wolverton, and I have many other friends with whom I have passed pleasant days in the country from time to time, especially of late years when my strength has not been so great as it used to be. But Mr. Manson has never left the post of duty for one day for five years, and I fear his health will give way under it unless he has some rest and recreation soon."

"Never fear for me," said the curate. "I am young and strong and in no danger of breaking down."

But even as he spoke I examined him more narrowly than I had hitherto done, and saw signs of exhaustion in the pallor of his face, and a certain yellow tinge in the whites of the eyes. He had a strongly built frame, but his clothes hung somewhat loosely upon him, and it was evident he stood greatly in need of toning up, and nothing but a good long holiday and complete change of air and scene would do it. So I said to him:

"Mr. Manson, I am going to ask a great favor of you, and that is that you should go away from here for a few weeks at least. Take a trip up the Rhine, or visit the mountains and lakes of our own country. Breathe the air of the hills and woods for a time and come back to your work the strong man that nature intended you to be. The charges shall be mine, and I will not hear of any denial. I said it would be a favor to me, but I will not ask you to do it on that ground. We are both now embarked in this enterprise of helping the poor and the unfortunate, and without health we can do nothing, so it is your manifest duty to accept this offer which is made in the interest of our common cause."

"Mr. Musgrave," he said, "I cannot find words to express my grateful sense of your kindness, but I fear it would be impossible for me to leave at the present time. The work of the parish is too heavy for the rector alone."

"That difficulty might be overcome," said Mr. Calderwood, "and I do not think you should allow any modest scruples to prevent you accepting Mr. Musgrave's timely offer, for I really think a change is absolutely necessary for you."

Then, turning to me, he said:

"Mr. Manson has a younger brother who has just taken orders and is without a charge as yet. He has taken great interest in our work here, and would take his brother's place most willingly and acceptably for a time."

"The very thing," said I, "and perhaps we may enlist him permanently in our cause. I want one or two zealous young men to act under my orders, and if Mr. Manson's brother is willing he shall be one of them. Now, Mr. Manson, are you married?"

"No," said he, "I am a bachelor."

"Have you a sister?"

"Yes, my youngest sister lives at home with my father and mother and my brother Edward."

"Well, take her with you. A man cannot always enjoy a holiday alone, and your sister will be company for you. Shall it be the Rhine or the Cumberland lakes or the highlands of Scotland?"

"Really, Mr. Musgrave, your kindness is too overwhelming."

"Never mind about that," said I, "it is a settled thing; you heard what the rector said. You just go home tonight and talk it over with your sister and make up your minds when you want to go. I am an old traveler and will be glad to help you to map out a route. And now, Mr. Calderwood, I must leave you for the present, but I shall report for duty tomorrow morning. There is just one other thing I wish to say, and that is, that I am determined to avoid giving alms personally in any case whatever, and as I feel that when I go with you or Mr. Manson amongst the poor unfortunates I shall feel as if my hand should be going into my pocket all the time to relieve their distresses, so I wish to ease my conscience on that score beforehand by asking you to take this check for five hundred pounds to be expended for the benefit of your parishioners."

"A generous gift," said he, "like many that have come before it, both from yourself and your noble mother."

On my way down to the east end next morning I called at my lawyers' and instructed them to go quietly to work and buy up all the property on the four streets surrounding St. Oswald's parish church and to secure options on other property in the immediate vicinity, and having thus prepared the way for future operations, proceeded to fulfill my appointment at the rectory. I found Mr. Calderwood awaiting me, and together we set out on a round of visitations amongst the parishioners. It did not take long to convince me that little good could be accomplished amongst them so long as they were compelled to live in the miserable rookeries which formed the habitations of the parish. The squalor and filth, the noisome smells, the dark, mouldy rooms, and the utter absence of all sanitary conditions were such as to preclude any idea of comfort and decency. The people themselves impressed me as being almost past redemption, loafing, blear-eyed men and women, many of them just recovering from a weekly debauch of gin; ragged, unkempt children swarmed about the courts and alleys. The scanty furniture of the rooms in which whole families lived together betokened the direst poverty, and in more than one case we found the wretched belongings of the tenants turned out into the street or court on account of unpaid rent, and the miserable inhabitants deprived of the wretched shelter which had hitherto protected them from the inclemency of the weather. Of sickness there was too much evidence, and many a haggard wretch we saw stretched upon a hard pallet or a heap of straw from which they would never rise again. Long before the day's work was over I felt sick at heart from the contemplation of the scenes of misery and hopeless depravity we encountered. Here and there we found families whom misfortune had overtaken and who were evidently struggling to keep up some show of decent living amid the most adverse surroundings. There were widows with large families who took in washing, men whom sickness long continued had rendered unable to earn bread for their children, and old persons who had outlived their strength striving by means of chores and occasional jobs of light work to keep body and soul together. For these my heart bled, and it was with difficulty I could resist the impulse to give money for the relief of their immediate necessities, but I adhered to my resolution and left all such cases to the good rector, who knew so much better how to deal with them.

I was glad when the day was over and I could betake myself to my rooms in Hoodwell street overlooking the Thames embankment, where I could breathe in comfort and revel in the spacious view and clear air of the river. I looked forward with dread to the repetition of days like that which I had just passed through, and felt overcome by a feeling of impotence in the thought of the hardened vice and stubborn depravity of the miserable wretches whom I had undertaken to reform. But I held on doggedly to the work; day after day, and week after week, I continued to play the part of auxiliary in the missionary work of the rector, and now and again we had the consolation of finding some who required but a temporary assistance to recover from the blows of unmerited misfortune. My weekly visits to Chingford and the encouragement and sympathy which my mother never failed to give me on these occasions put fresh heart and hope into me, and I invariably returned from the country with renewed determination to carry on the work. Meantime the curate's brother Edward had joined us and I had the satisfaction of seeing the elder Manson off on a trip to Switzerland with his sister, who evidently looked upon me as an angel in human form, so delighted was she with the prospect of a holiday such as she had never dreamed of in company with her brother, whose failing health she had been too well aware of.

Long before their return I was owner of a large part of the land and buildings in the center of the parish of St. Oswald's, and it was with intense satisfaction that we saw the work of tearing down the weather-beaten old buildings begun.

My plan of operations was now complete. I proposed to tear down the old buildings block by block, and replace them with substantial, well-ventilated apartment houses arranged for renting in suites of two to four rooms on terms so low as to make them within reach of people of the poorest class, and giving the preference to those who had previously lived in the neighborhood, so long as they were disposed to live decent, cleanly lives. The work could not be hurried, for I was averse to turning out one set of tenants before I had accommodation prepared for them, but as fast as one building was completed another was torn down and a new one commenced. I closed the gin shops at once in all the property that came into my hands. This was rather an expensive process, for there were leases to be bought up and the owners of these places looked upon me as their natural enemy and held out for exorbitant prices; but by employing a clever lawyer as go-between I managed to come to terms with them all without making any very serious inroad on my bank account. This step in itself relieved us of many of the worst characters in the district, for they very soon became tired of living in a place where they had to go several blocks to supply themselves with liquor. Still we had abundant applications for the new dwellings, and the difficulty was not to find tenants, but to retain sufficient accommodation for those whom we desired to help, and who showed themselves in any degree worthy by trying to help themselves. I proposed to keep myself as much in the background as possible, and having spent a whole month in going about with the clergyman and thus learning by personal contact all that was necessary of the character and situation of the people of the district, I resolved to engage three or four earnest men sympathizing with my views to visit them and endeavor to save from ruin and wickedness such as were not past redemption. Edward Manson was the first of my missionaries and he brought a warm heart and a strong will to the work. I soon found others who were willing to engage in it and selected two who proved able and trustworthy assistants. One was a man of middle age, who had been rescued from a drunkard's life by the rector himself. He had been a physician in good practice, who had resorted to stimulants to enable him to stand the strain of overwork and sleepless nights. The habit had grown upon him unawares and resulted in the loss of his practice and the death of his wife. He was apparently a mere wreck when Mr. Calderwood picked him out of the gutter, but temperance had restored his strength and manhood, and, although he could doubtless have recovered the ground he had lost in his own profession, he preferred to devote himself to the work of saving others from the vice which had brought him down so low. We found his help invaluable, for we had many cases where sickness was the sole cause of the misfortunes of poor families, and the doctor was very skillful and restored many a father and mother who seemed past human help and enabled them to start the world afresh. The third member of our staff was, like Edward Manson, a young man who had taken orders and had been engaged as curate in another part of London, but, hearing of the work which I had undertaken, he came and offered his services, believing that he could accomplish much more for the cause of Christianity by laboring amongst the poor than by assisting in the half-hearted worship of a fashionable congregation. He was a man somewhat of Mr. Calderwood's stamp and had very winning ways and great persuasive powers. He was much liked by the children, and through them brought many of their parents to amend their lives of idleness and wickedness.

These three, and a young man whom I engaged as agent for the property to collect the rents and see that the houses were kept in good order and repair, completed my staff, and in the course of twelve months we had everything in good working order. I was aware, of course, that even my large fortune would not be sufficient to root out all the slums of the east end of London and cover their sites with proper dwelling houses for the poor. It would hardly have been sufficient to rebuild the whole of Mr. Calderwood's parish, but I hoped that other people of wealth would follow my example and that the work thus begun would be continued indefinitely until London became in some respects a model city for the whole world.

We kept resolutely on, however, and my little staff of workers never got discouraged, although at times it seemed as if there was very little practical result from their untiring labors, but every now and again they managed to pull some poor wretch out of the mire and set him on his feet with fresh hope and courage for the battle of life, and many a poor widow was enabled to bring up her family to honest industry instead of drifting to the penitentiary and the street. So far my work had been a repetition on a larger scale of what my mother had done for the little country village, and in one other particular I resolved to copy her example.

I was providing good, comfortable, sanitary homes for St. Oswald's parishioners, and I determined to do something as well for their amusement and instruction. On the corner of the street facing the church I built the Musgrave Institute, named after my father, whose statue in bronze I caused to be erected over the main entrance. It is a handsome four-story building, designed to accomplish the same purposes as the Wolverton Hall at Chingford. The ground floor is a large, well-lighted restaurant, where wholesome food is provided to all comers at astonishingly low prices, but never below actual cost. The second floor is a library and reading-room, free to all respectable inhabitants of St. Oswald's parish. Above the library is a well-appointed gymnasium, to which all my tenants are furnished free tickets, and which is largely patronized by both sexes at different hours of the day. The luxuriant bath rooms, with which it is provided, have been a very great attraction both winter and summer. The fourth story of the Institute is a lecture hall, which is lent free of charge at all times to those having the good of the people at heart and willing to furnish them with a programme of wholesome entertainment or useful information. The expenses of the Institute were considerable, entailing the salary of a manager as well as the wages of caretaker and scrubwoman, but this provided places for some of our destitute people of the parish, and the benefits to the neighborhood were great beyond all proportion to the cost.

At the end of four years the streets in the immediate vicinity of St. Oswald's church were all rebuilt and presented a very different appearance from that which greeted me on my first visit to the rector. It was doubtless more of a transformation than a reformation, as that gentleman himself had said, but I am sure that he was delighted with the change, and glad to feel that in his declining years he could devote himself more exclusively to the proper work of the church and leave the slumming largely in the hands of my energetic little staff. The church was now filled at every service by a large congregation of respectable worshipers, whose spiritual wants required all of the rector's care and the curate's as well. The edifice itself had been improved by the execution of some much-needed repairs and the addition of a fine stained-glass window and a new pulpit and reading-desk, and the rector's house had been entirely rebuilt at my expense in order that it might be in keeping with its improved surroundings and afford to its occupant a little more of the bodily comfort of which he had formerly been too negligent.

I had now spent about half my fortune, and, although the results were meager in comparison with the hopes I entertained on beginning the crusade, I never regretted what I had done nor entertained the idea of withdrawing from the field. At the same time I resolved to pause for a time in my expenditures and for the present devote only my surplus income to the acquirement and rebuilding of lands and buildings. The rents of the tenements, although not always regularly paid, amounted to a considerable sum over and above the expense of keeping them in repair—sufficient, in fact, to cover all the ordinary expenses of our missionary enterprise.

I had now succeeded in getting everything into such perfect working order that my own presence was not an absolute necessity and I spent more time at Chingford than I had done at the beginning, and early in the fifth summer I took a vacation of several weeks' duration, which I spent with my mother among the lakes and mountains of Cumberland and the Scottish highlands.

III

A Visitor from Another World

Returning from my vacation, I found that my manager had given the use of Musgrave Hall for a meeting to be presided over by a certain Mr. Septimus Jones, of which the object, as announced in handbills widely circulated, was to consider "The condition of the working classes in England."

I had no personal acquaintance with this Mr. Jones, but knew him by reputation as a noisy and mischievous demagogue. I regretted that our hall should have been lent for such a meeting and intimated as much to the manager of the Institute, but he explained that the man was unknown to him, but came well recommended, and, being a glib talker, had persuaded him that his views were entirely in sympathy with ours. I said that we must make a point of being present at the meeting and find out about that for ourselves.

I was early on hand on the appointed evening and had to undergo the penance of shaking hands with the chairman and one or two of his clique. They invited me to sit with them in the front row, but I declined and took my seat at the back of the platform, where I could see and hear everything without being too much in evidence myself. The hall was soon filled, and, although I recognized a goodly number of our own people, the majority were entire strangers and among them a great many appeared to be foreigners—seedy-looking, wild-eyed men, whom I took to be anarchists from various parts of the continent.

The chairman opened the meeting by saying that he would make a short statement of the objects for which they were assembled together. He spoke rapidly for about half an hour, and his command of the English language (always excepting the letter H) proved that he had some claim to the title of "The people's orator," by which he was sometimes known. The burden of his speech was that, while the working people produced all the wealth of the country, the possession and enjoyment of it were in other hands. He denounced the capitalists, the nobility and the government as being banded together for the oppression and degradation of the honest poor, who, he said, were little better than slaves. But slavery was doomed the world over. The slavery of the blacks had been overthrown in America and he ventured to predict that the slavery of the whites would be terminated at no distant day in Great Britain, for the truth would make them free, and he was there to proclaim the truth that all men were entitled to the product of the labor of their hands and that, while they had the right to all the good things of life, they had also the might to seize them. They were many and their oppressors were few, and so soon as they recognized the justice of their claims and the strength which union could put into their hands, the working classes would sweep away with irresistible force the combination of tyranny and greed which had for untold centuries ground them under its iron heel. Loud applause followed the conclusion of his speech, but I was glad to see that our own people did not join very heartily in the cheering and hand-clapping, but that most of the noise was made by men whom I knew to be strangers in the district.

Three or four of the chairman's friends spoke after him, and what they lacked in eloquence was made up in strong denunciation of their betters, each of them being evidently determined to go beyond the chairman himself in bitter invective and wholesale charges of fraud and dishonesty on the part of the upper classes. I felt my face burn with indignation at the way in which my father's hall had been abused by such demagogues, and I could not make up my mind whether to protest against the sentiments expressed by rising and leaving the hall or to sit still in my chair and see the wretched business through to the end. One thing I was resolved upon at all events and that was that the manager of the Institute must in future obtain either my own consent or that of the rector to granting the use of the hall to outside parties. At about ten o'clock in the evening the fire of the professional agitators seemed to have burned itself out, and the chairman invited any person from the body of the hall to come up to the platform and speak on the subject before the meeting. As no one rose he repeated the invitation and said that it was intended to include all present, and especially if there happened to be any stranger present who, although not an Englishman, yet felt sympathy with the sorrows of the English poor and wished to speak, he promised him a fair and candid hearing. Upon this someone rose in the center of the hall and advanced towards the platform. I could not see him at first, but felt sure that we were about to hear a tirade from some exiled nihilist from St. Petersburg or anarchist from Paris, which was doubtless what the chairman anticipated, but if it were so he was doomed to a great disappointment.

As the stranger mounted the platform I perceived that we had to do with one who belonged to a different world from those who had hitherto spoken, for at a glance one could see that he was a gentleman. But that was not the thought which first came uppermost in my mind, for as soon as he came fairly into view my involuntary exclamation was, "Here is a man." His head was the head of Jove; a broad forehead with massive brows, under which shone a pair of lustrous black eyes; a straight, powerful nose; hair of iron gray, like his full beard, which was of moderate length and carefully trimmed; a deep chest and broad shoulders, with a figure straight and perfectly proportioned, made up an ensemble which would have attracted attention anywhere. My interest was awakened at once and I listened intently to hear what he would say.

His voice was deep and resonant, and at his first words a hush fell upon the audience, who seemed spellbound by his grand personality. He began by saying that he had not come to the meeting with any intention to speak, but that the chairman's urgent invitation seemed to apply particularly to him and he felt it would be inexcusable for him in the circumstances to remain silent. He went on to speak of the sorrowful lot of a child born to poverty in a large city; of the depressing moral and physical conditions which hemmed him in and prevented his development; of his multiplied privation and his meager and sordid pleasures; of the temptations to vice and crime, the lack of education which dwarfed his mind and the lack of fresh air and wholesome food which dwarfed his body. He traced the course of such a child to manhood and old age and premature death in such moving terms that I felt the tears spring to my eyes, and I saw that most of the women and many of the men in the audience were quietly weeping. But when he came to the remedy for the unfortunate state of things he had so vividly portrayed and began to talk to them of temperance, chastity, self-denial and thrift, the rougher sort showed signs of impatience, shuffling their feet and coughing loudly, and when they saw that their disapprobation instead of discouraging the orator, only caused him to speak more earnestly and emphatically on the necessity of raising themselves up by their own efforts, in place of trying to drag others down to their level, they began to mutter and to hiss. One shouted "Aristocrat," another "Spy." Many of the more disreputable-looking characters in the crowd rose to their feet and raised a clamor which compelled the speaker to pause, while threats of rough treatment were freely indulged in.

He was not to be coerced, however, but turned to the chairman to ask if it was not possible for him to obtain a hearing. Mr. Jones could not, of course, refuse this request, and, rising and holding out his right hand, was able to secure a moment's cessation of the tumult when he pointed out that the gentleman was on the platform by his special invitation and that, as Englishmen, they ought to allow even an antagonist fair play and that he hoped they would hear him quietly to the end. He had no sooner sat down, however, than the hubbub began again, and after waiting for a minute or two more the stranger bowed to the chairman and walked slowly down the platform steps and through the hall to the door. Those who had been making the greatest disturbance turned and glared at him as he passed, evidently sorry to see him retire without molestation, but there was something in his look and dauntless bearing which warned them to refrain from further insult, and when he reached the hall door no one else had moved from his place.

Before he had passed out of sight, I started up and quickly followed after him, for I felt to some extent responsible for the way in which he had been treated and would have been extremely sorry to let him go without explanation or apology. Catching up with him just as he reached the street, I explained to him that, while I was the owner of the hall in which he had been so grossly insulted, the meeting had been arranged without my consent and wishes, in my absence, and yet I could hardly forgive myself for being indirectly responsible for such outrageous treatment of a stranger, and especially of a gentleman who had given utterance to such noble sentiments as we had just heard from his lips. I would have said more, but he stopped me, saying:

"Mr. Musgrave, not another word of apology. There is no one to blame but myself. I knew that there were many men in the hall whose lives are spent in rebellion against established institutions and who would not listen to reason, and therefore I should have remained silent. But there is no harm done at all; on the contrary, it has given me the opportunity of meeting you, which I sincerely desired, for I have heard much of the great work you have done here and should be very glad to have a talk with you about it at anytime that would suit your convenience. My name is Delphion, and I am staying at present at the Hotel Imperial."

I held out my hand, which he grasped with cordial pressure, while I assured him that it gave me very great pleasure to meet him, and added that I had a carriage waiting, and if he had an hour to spare I should be delighted to have him come with me to my rooms in Hoodwell street, where we might have a quiet little chat over a glass of wine and a cigar.

He said that nothing would please him better, so we got into the carriage together and in a few minutes we cleared the noisy streets of the East End and were bowling rapidly over the asphalt pavements of the city.

Arrived at our destination, I led the way to my sitting room, where I had a large bay window commanding a fine view of the Thames. On this particular evening the scene was unusually fine, for the moon was full and the sky clear, and the lights on the embankment and the vessels in the river made up a very beautiful picture. My manservant having placed cigars and a bottle of my best Chateau Vergniaux before us, we settled ourselves in our chairs fronting the window and resumed our talk, which had been somewhat disjointed as we rattled through the streets in the carriage. My guest as yet had said nothing about himself, but plied me with questions in regard to all that I had done in St. Oswald's and the neighboring district, proving himself a very appreciative listener. Having heard my account of the four years' work he naturally inquired how it was that I had conceived the idea of devoting myself to the regeneration of the lapsed classes and I was led on to talk of the scenes of my childhood and the good work my mother had accomplished in our own village. It was now nearly midnight and Mr. Delphion rose to go, saying that he felt very much interested in all that I had related to him, and hoping that our acquaintance might ripen into friendship, asked me to dine with him at his hotel the next day. I happened to have an engagement for that date, but accepted for the day following, so he took a card from his pocketbook, wrote the name of his hotel on the bottom of it and handed it to me, bidding me a cordial goodnight. As soon as he was gone I looked at the card in my hand, on which was imprinted in handsomely engraved letters:

JASON DELPHION
Hooghley Diamond Co.,
Calcutta.

What a peculiar man! What could be his nationality? The name had a suggestion of Greek in it, but the Greeks produced no such men nowadays. I felt much puzzled and interested in my new acquaintance. Physically and mentally he seemed superior to any man I had ever met and I felt extremely curious to know a little more about him, but speculation was useless and doubtless he would take me into his confidence in good time. I had been remarkably frank with him, but no one could look into his face without trusting him implicitly, and I felt as if I had gained a friend for life.

At the hour appointed I arrived at the Hotel Imperial, where I found my friend occupying very pleasant quarters; having a suite of rooms which must have been the best in the famous hostelry. In one of these dinner was served, and such a dinner as caused me to conclude that the diamond business must be a prosperous one and my host no mean judge of good living. Yet he ate sparingly and of few dishes, and drank very moderately of the excellent wines which he had provided. He proved himself an excellent host, and whereas on our first meeting he had allowed me to do most of the talking, the positions were now reversed and I found that he could speak as well as listen. Indeed his conversation proved here so entertaining that when we left the dinner table I was surprised to find that nearly an hour and a half had elapsed since we had sat down to it. Having learned from me that I had traveled through Europe and the countries bordering on the Levant, he led the conversation in the direction of the various places of interest which I had visited, but whereas I had merely skimmed over the surface of things, he appeared to have made a thorough study of everything that could interest a student or an amateur in art. He not only knew all the picture galleries in Europe, but appeared to be familiar with every picture in them and knew the history of all the great painters down to the smallest detail. In architecture he was past master. I spoke of some churches and cathedrals which had interested me and he entered into details of the different styles of architecture, illustrated by description of ruins and chapels in out-of-the-way corners of Europe which would have made one suppose that he had spent all his life in studying them. Reference was made to the pyramids and the ruins of Baalbec, and it appeared that he had examined these with the skill and diligence of an archaeologist. He had theories of his own in regard to the dates of each of these ancient monuments, and in fifteen minutes it seemed to me that I learned more from him of the history of Egypt and Syria than I could have picked up by reading whole volumes of books.

Surprised at his fluent talk on such various subjects, I changed the theme again and again, but it made not the slightest difference; there seemed to be no subject which he had not mastered. I tried him on politics, but found he knew far more of the present condition of every European country than I did about England. I touched upon history, which was my own special study, but in this also I had to own that he was easily my master. And withal there was no ostentation about all this encyclopedic knowledge. He talked in an easy, pleasant way about everything, never taking for granted that I knew less than he, but bringing up the various points and incidents as if the subject in hand were equally familiar to both of us. At last I gave up the attempt to sound the depths of his knowledge and lay back in my chair and resigned myself to the enjoyment of listening, for whatever subject he touched upon seemed to be equally interesting. Perceiving my silence, he said:

"But I am afraid I bore you by talking too much."

"No," I replied, "on the contrary, you both entertain and instruct me, and I have seldom passed an evening so pleasantly in my life and I hope it will not be the last we shall spend together."

"Well," said he, "it will not be my fault if we do not see more of each other. The other night you were my host and you entertained me as I have endeavored to entertain you, and I am afraid you thought me rather inquisitive in regard to your personal history. You told me much of yourself and your family, whilst I have communicated to you nothing of my own antecedents, and, to tell you the truth, I am not at liberty to do so at present, but some day I may have that privilege, and in that case I shall have much pleasure in telling you all about myself and my people."

"I assure you," said I, "that I did not at all resent your friendly interest in my affairs, and I have no wish to learn more about you than you wish to impart. I am sure you are a good man and one of the most learned ever I met. There is only one thing I am curious about and that is your nationality, but I shall ask no questions about that or anything whatever that concerns you. I am delighted to have met you and trust we shall be fast friends."

"I am sure of it," said he, "but in regard to my nationality there need be no reserve. I am a Greek."

"A Greek! I should have taken you for an ancient Greek."

"More ancient, perhaps, than you imagine, but why do you say so?"

"Because in your personal appearance and your great powers of mind you seem more like one of the wonderful race which turned back the tide of Persian invasion from Europe and leavened the world with intellectual force, than of their modern representatives, who play so small a part on the world's stage."

"You flatter me very much," said he, "but it may be in my power some day to introduce you to many of my countrymen whom you will find worthy to rank with Homer or Pericles or Phidias."

This made me feel more curious than ever regarding the antecedents of my new friend, but after what had passed I could do nothing but wait until he saw fit to tell me more about himself. He promised to meet me at the Musgrave Institute on the following day, and from that time forward he was a frequent visitor there and took much interest in all that was going on, making from time to time very pertinent suggestions, which we adopted with good results. He was so moved with compassion by the tales of suffering and distress which my lieutenants brought in that he asked as a personal favor to be allowed to render pecuniary assistance in certain cases, requests which I could not well refuse, and in these instances he spared neither time nor expense in relieving the sufferers and placing them in a position to recover from their misfortunes. He spent many hours with us and when business kept him away for any length of time I missed him more than I could have thought possible.

We were both seated one day in my private office at the Institute, talking, as usual, of the people of the district and the efforts being made for their redemption. I was feeling rather despondent and confessed to him that the enthusiasm with which I had entered upon the work had become chilled by the amount of callous indifference with which it was viewed by those whom we intended to help and restore to respectability and virtue, and I asked him to give me his unreserved opinion of the possibility of saving the masses from their misery on the plan which I had adopted or by any other conceivable way.

He was silent for a little while and then said: "You have no reason to regret what you have done, although it has not come up to the ardent hopes which your youth and inexperience led you to indulge. On the contrary, you have every reason to congratulate yourself on the good that has been accomplished by your means. You have provided comfortable homes for thousands of worthy people who would otherwise have had to endure much discomfort or misery. You have put it into their power to live with some regard to the laws of health and given some attention to the cultivation of their minds. This alone is worth all the money it has cost, but you have done more. You have saved scores of people from giving way to the seductions of vice and intemperance, and I am sure that many a young person and many widows and mothers in this district have cause to regard you as their benefactor, and many a child will grow up into healthy, self-respecting manhood and womanhood who but for you would have succumbed to the influences of poverty and privation and disease. Therefore I say that you should not be at all discouraged, but rather be glad that you had the means and the disposition to help so many of the unfortunate. If the larger measure of success which you once expected seems beyond your power it is not you who are at fault, but rather the whole framework of society. Europe calls itself civilized, but what a wretched failure its civilization appears when we reflect that the masses of the people in all the countries you know of are steeped in ignorance and poverty, and are engaged almost from the cradle to the grave in a struggle for mere existence, and have neither time nor means to enjoy the bounties of nature or the treasures of intellect and art which human genius has created.

"We hear a great deal about human progress, and optimists endeavor to show that mankind is in the enjoyment of a high degree of happiness by pointing out the miseries of previous ages in comparison with the freedom and comfort of our own. Enjoying, as a rule, a considerable share of the benefits which wealth insures, they selfishly shut their eyes to the hideous inequalities of its distribution and try to make themselves believe that the proletariat ought to be content with things as they are, merely because in former times it can be proved that they were worse. But from the standpoint of the toiling millions the situation must seem very far from satisfactory. The many endure that the few may enjoy, and the few spend their lives for the most part in reaching out for gewgaws and baubles, social distinctions, glory and power, never reflecting that they live on sleeping volcanoes which may at anytime burst forth and overwhelm them.

"To my mind, the signs of the time seem to presage a plunge backward into anarchy and barbarism rather than a further advance in culture and civilization. Your modern society is like a creature having the mind of a child combined with the physical strength of a giant. It has made great strides towards the knowledge of the secrets of nature, but has not attained the wisdom necessary to a proper use of its discoveries. It is rapidly penetrating the mysteries of electricity; the power of steam has added tenfold to its might; chemistry has revealed many of its hidden wonders, and in dynamite and nitro-glycerine has disclosed forces which are terrible to contemplate in the hand of malice and ignorance. In other directions the most ingenious minds are working out problems which will evolve new powers for good and evil which as yet are hardly realized. Meantime the proletariat is becoming more and more dissatisfied with the unequal and unjust apportionment of the benefits which science and invention have created. Dynamite outrages have occurred in almost every country in Europe and are the terror of its ruling powers. In a few years at most another great invention will be added to the vaunted triumphs of the human mind. Men will construct ships which will navigate the air as safely and much more swiftly than any that sail the ocean. Think what a terrible opportunity that would give to the anarchist and the criminal. How would your soldiers or your police guard the heights and depths of the atmosphere? How would you prevent the plotter against the existing order of things from stealing along in his airship on a dark or foggy night and dropping a hundred pounds of dynamite over the parliament house at Westminster or the palace of the czar at St. Petersburg and shattering at one blow the whole machinery of the government? Think what a reign of terror such dynamite outrages as that would inaugurate! What frantic efforts would be made to stamp out disaffection! Wholesale reprisals would be the order of the day, and the innocent, in all probability, would be confounded with the guilty; liberty would come to an end and despotism and anarchy divide the field.

"On the other hand, private malice would adopt the same fiendish means of satisfying its ends, and no man could retire to rest at night without feeling that he might be blown to destruction with all his family before morning. Take the case of a strike in one of the large industries of this country. Suppose the workmen reduced to starvation and their children crying in vain for bread. Would not the temptation to wreak vengeance on a selfish and grasping employer, when vengeance would be so sure and swift, be too much for the scruples of the ignorant, and, perhaps, wronged and oppressed laborers?"

"Undoubtedly, but the man who cannot buy bread will not be able to provide himself with an airship."

"True enough, but those who foment strikes are never without means, and past experience shows that they do not stop at violence or crime to gain their ends.

"I should be glad to believe that the dangers which I have pictured are wholly imaginary, but they appear to me to be inevitable. Your philosophers who proclaim the belief that the world has at last entered upon a path of continuous progress, with the lamp of science to illumine its path and preserve it from the pitfalls and follies of past ages, are like the ostrich burying its head in the sand and persuading itself that there is no danger because it is unable to see it. If there were many rich men like you the case would be different, but for the most part those who are well-to-do are utterly indifferent to the wrongs and sufferings of those who are beneath them and their selfishness may well bring about the utter ruin of society.

"Assuming that the present state of European civilization expresses the highest point of development yet reached by the human race, it is easy to imagine Mother Nature taking her creature man to task in some such fashion as this:

"'I spent thousands of ages in preparing this world for your habitation, slowly but surely adapting it to supply your every want; its crust is stored with marble and stone, with coal and iron and all useful minerals in due proportion. I have covered its surface with rich soils and abundant vegetation; its animals and plants have been evolved from poor beginnings and brought with infinite labor to the variety and perfection which you find so admirably suited to your desires. I created the sea to be the highway of your commerce and have filled it with many kinds of creatures for your food. I have inclosed all with a soft mantle of air which tempers and reveals the glory of sun, moon and stars, and conveys refreshing showers to the thirsty ground; but on you I have lavished my most unwearying efforts. I have nursed and fostered you through infinite dangers and made you lord and ruler of all. I have guarded your childhood and brought you through endless trials not only unscathed but always stronger and better fitted for the proud position destined for you. And I have done all this with the rough tools at my command—blind forces you call them—working only in direct lines and crushing out remorselessly and inevitably whatever fails to conform to their inexorable laws; irresistible in their onward march and patient of results, for they have all I eternity for their work. But with you it is different; you belong to fleeting time; now is the day of your opportunity and it is for you to take advantage of it. You are a child no longer; you are full grown. I have given you an eye to see, a hand to work and a brain to contrive and design. I have done a mother's part by you and you are no longer in leading strings. Take the reins into your own hands and assume direction of the work which I have hitherto done for you. I am ready to aid you still: my almighty forces will help you at every step if you but move in the right direction. But do not imagine that you are indispensable to me. Although I have done so much for you yet your failure would not move me. I have other worlds to work in; infinite space is filled with suns and planets, and if you fail I have other children who will succeed. I have prepared and am preparing millions of far-off worlds for them, and could you visit these with me you would say of some, 'Surely this is paradise,' and of others, 'Truly this is little better than hell.' And I should bid you take warning, for either fate is in store for you, and it is for you to determine which it shall be. Of this, however, you can feel assured: I have done all for you that I have ever done for the most blessed world that swings through ethereal space, thrilling with the harmony of angelic life; and you have the means of making this earth the home of the noblest and best of my children if you will but wisely use the powers I have bestowed upon you.'"

He ceased speaking, and his face was filled with an expression of divine compassion, while a sensation of awe crept over me and half unconsciously I asked:

"Are you not of this world yourself?"

A pleasant smile reassured me, and he replied:

"I promised to tell you of myself and my people as soon as I had permission to do so. That liberty has been granted to me and I am about to tell you what has remained a secret to the world at large for centuries, and it is imparted to you because you have devoted yourself to the help of the suffering and the poor with a disinterested generosity which is rare amongst all men, but especially rare amongst those who are born to wealth.

"Before I tell you in what part of the earth my country is situated, let me state a few particulars in which we differ from all other nations.

"Our laws are few and simple, but admirably adapted to secure the happiness of the whole people. Crime is so rare amongst us that we have no police force and the legal profession is represented by half a dozen judges whose places are sinecures. Our wealth is abundant, but so equally distributed that want and the fear of want are absolutely unknown amongst us. We have no aristocracy, and the establishment of a plutocracy is absolutely impossible. The laws of health are so thoroughly understood and so carefully observed that disease of any kind is very rare, and the average duration of life is not far from a hundred years. Every child inherits a sound constitution and a vigorous mind from its parents, and the forms of the men are models of strength and symmetry, while the women are beautiful in face and figure beyond comparison with the fairest of their sex in any other age or country.

Beauty is with us considered the birthright of the sex and it would be considered almost a crime to permit a woman to be born without it.

"In all the refinements of civilization we are centuries ahead of the rest of the world. In agriculture and the mechanical arts we have made such progress that the material wants of the people are abundantly supplied by the labor of a comparatively small proportion of these for a few hours a day. In music, painting and architecture we have many masters who rank higher than the greatest of all time in the world at large. Our cities abound in noble edifices which are devoted to the use, entertainment and instruction of the people, anyone of which would become a world's wonder if it could be transported to London or Paris, while the ordinary residences of our farmers and mechanics are models of architectural taste, and perfect in their adaptation to comfort, convenience and health.

"While our standard of living would be considered luxurious by any other people, we are not given to the luxury of idleness. Every man has his vocation, and however wealthy he may be, it is his duty and privilege to contribute to the public welfare by the labor of his hands or his head until old age has diminished his ability; and with us a man does not begin to be old until he has reached the age of four score.

"Our government is a pure republic, but with all the advantages of a monarchy, for the administrative power resides with the chief magistrate, who is seldom changed except by old age or death, and the responsibility of office is seldom sought after, but is accepted only as a public duty and that often at the sacrifice of personal inclination. The public revenues are ample at all times, and are chiefly expended in the maintenance of roads and waterways, in the adornment of our towns and cities, and in the education of the young, the last item absorbing by far the largest portion of the public funds. In all cases our young people have the advantage of university training, and it is never necessary for a child to spend his years in labor before he arrives at the age of maturity. The two sexes are similarly educated in literature, science and art, and in the primary schools are taught in the same classes. In the universities they are separated, and while the young men receive a thorough course of instruction in such industry or profession as they are best adapted for with the view of fitting them to earn a living, the girls are taught those equally useful arts which make the homes of our people attractive and delightful. Every girl graduate is not only a thorough housekeeper and cook, but she is also an experienced nurse, and is so well versed in the laws of health that when she comes to occupy the place of wife and mother the services of the physician are seldom required.

"Our ancestry is Hellenic, but not without a slight admixture of other races, and while we take pleasure in the thought that our forefathers were the pioneers of European civilization, it is to our modern laws that we attribute our present advantages, and while your people were exploring the new world and founding colonies beyond the seas, ours were groaning under Asiatic tyranny and all but reduced to a condition of slavery and barbarism.

"Our country is a valley in the unexplored recesses of the Himalayas, which, with a few adjacent glens and forests, comprises about ten thousand square miles. It is absolutely inaccessible except to such as can sail on the wings of the wind, and air-ships are our only means of exit and entrance.

"We believe we have solved the problem of human living, and as a lover and benefactor of your kind you are invited to visit our fortunate country, which we call by the name of Ionia."

The feelings with which I listened to this marvelous recital can be more easily imagined than described, and I was at first at a loss for words to answer the extraordinary invitation extended to me. At length I found the use of my tongue, and said:

"You do me a great and I fear an unmerited honor, and if it lies in my power you may be sure that I shall avail myself of this great privilege. Am I to understand that it is the government of this wonderful country which honors me with so generous an invitation?"

"Assuredly," said he, "I am ambassador-at-large from Ionia, though not accredited to any other government. It is my duty to observe all that is going on in Europe, and send reports to the state, not only in regard to politics, but also with reference to all important inventions either in the arts of peace or war. I am expected to make note of the progress of science, the condition of the people in the various countries, and all that pertains to human affairs. I have occupied the position for ten years, spending most of my time abroad, but returning home annually for a period of rest and recuperation. In two months from now I return for good, and another citizen will assume the duties of my position, which is considered one of the least desirable in connection with our government.

"I may as well explain to you how it is that I introduced myself to you as a diamond merchant. The diamond, as you know, is merely carbon crystallized, and for over a hundred years we have been able to produce stones equal in brilliance and purity to the finest that are found in a natural state. The invention was purchased by the government, but as diamonds have no value in Ionia except in so far as they can be utilized in mining and other industries, there is no temptation for anyone to attempt the discovery on his own account. The person who occupies my position is furnished with a quantity of gems of large size and almost unlimited value which he exchanges for gold to defray his expenses, and these are left entirely to his own discretion. He is also permitted to retain for his own use and to bring into the country a sum sufficient to ensure him a respectable income for the remainder of his life. I am thus known to the jewelers in all European cities as the representative of a wealthy company of diamond merchants, but none of them suspects the stones to be other than natural or that I have any other function than that of a traveling merchant. You will admit that I practiced no deceit in introducing myself to you as I did, but on the other hand I have taken the earliest opportunity of repaying the candor with which you treated me on our first interview."

"You have done a great deal more than that," said I, "for I told you nothing but what all the world might know, while you have imparted to me the most stupendous secret in the history of the world."

"It is of course unnecessary for me to say that all I have told you is strictly confidential, and that until you have the express consent of our government, we shall expect you as a point of honor to refrain from divulging the secret of our existence and superior civilization, even should you consider that the knowledge of them would benefit humanity at large."

"I promise all that without hesitation or reserve, but there is one serious difficulty about my acceptance of the invitation to visit you. I have never had any secrets from my mother, and could not undertake so serious a journey without imparting to her a full knowledge of its scope and intention."

"Your mother," he replied, "must be no ordinary woman, and I think we can trust her as well as yourself. You will be able to communicate with her by letter and telegraph from Ionia, and she need have no cause for anxiety while you are away."

"Then, I think, there will be nothing to prevent my going with you, and I shall look forward to the trip with unspeakable delight. But you must come and make my mother's acquaintance and place the matter before her yourself. I hope you can spare us a week or two at the Grange before the time of your departure, and the sooner you can come the better it will please me."

"I have much to do before I return," he said, "and it is necessary for me to spend the next week on the continent, but if the week after will suit your convenience I shall be happy to be your guest for a few days."

So it was arranged, and about ten days afterwards I had the pleasure of introducing Mr. Delphion to my mother at the Grange.

My mother was delighted with her guest, and thought him so far superior to all other men whom she had ever seen that he appeared to belong to another race of men, and asked me to tell her all I knew about him. But I replied that Mr. Delphion would enlighten her on that subject before he left; that what I knew of him was imparted to me in confidence which she in good time would share, but which I could not honorably betray.

"Surely," she said, "there cannot be anything about such a man which it is necessary to conceal, anything I mean in the slightest degree dishonorable."

"If the archangel Michael came down from heaven to be your guest," said I, "there would be nothing dishonorable in it, but he would not wish anybody to know it."

"Well," she said, "I have heard of such a thing as entertaining angels unawares, but you cannot make me believe that such is the case with us, for I am sure that Mr. Delphion is a mortal man, although different in many respects from all others. However, I do not propose to seek to penetrate the mystery which, it seems, surrounds our guest, or ask you to betray his confidence by the slightest hint, so I shall endeavor to repress my womanly curiosity until he sees fit to indulge it."

"If you like I shall ask him to speak to you about himself this evening."

"Not for the world," said she. "My son's friend shall always be welcome in my house, and I would not have him think for a moment that he should present his credentials to me in order to stand upon the footing of the most honored guest."

"Well, mother, I believe you know that I never had a secret from you before, and I have already stipulated that you shall share in this one."

By this time it had begun to be rumored among the great folks in the district that we had a lion of no ordinary sort as a guest at the Grange, and we began to receive an unusual number of visitors, both ladies and gentlemen, who were all very much impressed with Mr. Delphion's appearance and conversation. They plied him with invitations to call or come and dine with them, but all such he politely declined, alleging the shortness of the time at his disposal as a sufficient excuse. Many of the ladies asked me privately to tell them who and what he was, and tried all sorts of blandishments to get some information from me, but to them all I gave but one answer—

"He is a visitor from another world."

And although this only piqued their curiosity it was all the information they could obtain, for I would tell them no more, and my mother, of course, could not.

Mr. Delphion seemed more inclined to cultivate the society of our humble villagers than that of the fashionable folks. He took great pleasure in inspecting all the improvements my mother had made, and at her request delivered a lecture in the hall on the different races of India, which was greatly appreciated by a large and enthusiastic audience. He also begged and received her permission to entertain the whole population of the village at an open-air festival on the commons. This took place on the Saturday afternoon following his arrival, and proved a grand success. He had a brass band down from London by a special train which brought also a company of caterers who laid out such a feast of good things as five hundred humble villagers had never seen before. Foot races and other athletic sports were rendered doubly interesting by a great variety of handsome presents provided for the winners. There was dancing for the lads and lasses to the music of the band, and seats were provided for the old folks to rest in and look on in comfort. When the sun set after a glorious afternoon the train departed with the musicians and the caterer's men, but the villagers seemed loth to break up and acknowledge that the festival which they had all enjoyed so much was actually over. There would still be an hour of twilight, and someone proposed that they should finish the day by a grand tug of war between married and single men. This suggestion was received with a shout of enthusiasm, and a strong rope was procured and twenty-five picked men on each side arranged themselves for the fray. Each one of the fifty took hold of the rope, married men on one side and bachelors on the other, with six feet of rope between the foremost on each side. Two stakes were set in the ground directly in the middle and the victory should belong to the side which first succeeded in hauling the nearest of their adversaries clear across the line marked by the stakes. They were nearly equally matched, but the younger men, being more supple, seemed to pull better together, and four times in succession they succeeded in drawing the foremost of their adversaries across the dividing line. They now felt sure of victory and indulged in a good deal of chaff and banter at the expense of the other side. Just before time was called for the fifth bout, an old grandsire whose three sons were on the losing side, stepped up to Mr. Delphion, cap in hand, and said:

"Axing your pardon, sir, may I be so bold as to ask if you be a married man?"

"Certainly I am," said he, "but why do you ask?"

"Nothing at all, sir, only I thought you would hate to stand by and see your own side beaten."

"You mean," said Mr. Delphion, "that I should take a hand and try to wrest the victory from the young men even yet?"

"Well, sir, it's not my place to be saying such a thing, but you do look as strong as any two on us."

Here my mother, who was sitting by watching the game, interfered, saying:

"For shame, Dobson! How can you be so impertinent?"

But Mr. Delphion, who seemed much amused at the suggestion, assured her that he should be delighted to take a hand in the struggle provided the bachelors would consent. This question was at once referred to them, and they having no fear of the result agreed to the proposition without hesitation, and Mr. Delphion took off his coat and assumed the position of captain of the married men. He made some changes in their arrangement in the line, and advised them as to how they could best apply their strength and throw their united weight into the tug, and then all took their places for the fifth and as the bachelors fully believed the last trial. But they found they had met their match at last. They tugged and strained and hollered, but all was of no avail. Mr. Delphion seemed rooted to the ground like an English oak, and when the young men had exhausted themselves he gave the word to his men, and slowly but surely they pulled their adversaries forward till the mark was passed, and the married men scored one point. The tables were now turned: the bachelors made some changes amongst their champions, turning out some of the lighter weights and putting likely young fellows in their places, but they did not score again, and at last the victory was declared for the married men, amid much cheering and throwing up of caps in the air. The bachelors looked quite crest-fallen and had little heart to reply to the thrusts of wit with which they were now assailed, but Mr. Delphion made them a little humorous speech which raised their spirits, and finished by proposing three cheers for the losers, which was heartily responded to, and the meeting at last broke up. On our return home my mother gently remonstrated with our guest for undertaking a task which she thought might well have resulted in serious injury.

"You and I," she said, "are not so young as we were, and cannot safely attempt what would have been easy to us at one time. Pardon me for classing you with myself as regards age, for I am an old woman, and you are still in your prime, but it alarmed me to see you entering upon a trial of strength with all those men whose frames are hardened by manual labor so that they can stand a strain which might be fatal to one of more delicate organization."

"But," said he, "so far from being at a disadvantage with these hard-working men, I was really in better condition than any of them to bring all my strength and weight into play, for whereas their labor stiffens their joints while it hardens their muscles, I take just sufficient exercise everyday to keep my strength up to the proper mark for any call that may be made upon it. I never travel without a pair of light dumb-bells in my valise, and practice with them at least an hour a day. In the matter of ages, although that is a delicate question when a lady is concerned, I have no hesitation in saying that I am old enough to be your father, for I was sixty-eight at my last birthday."

"Sixty-eight! Surely, Mr. Delphion, you are jesting."

"No, my dear madam, but in my country a man is still in his prime at sixty-eight. And I may as well take this opportunity of imparting to you what I have already told your son about myself and my country. Our existence is unknown to all the world, besides, and it is in the cause of philanthropy that I have taken him and am about to take you into my confidence, feeling sure from what I know of you both that the trust will never be betrayed. And then he told my mother of that strange, far-off country whose people have mastered the grand problem of human life, while all others have so signally failed. He wound up by stating that he had given me an invitation to visit Ionia in order that I might verify by actual observation the statements he had made in regard to the superior civilization of its people, so that I might be guided by what I there saw and learned, in any future efforts I might make for the elevation of the masses in our own country.

"His coming to visit us," said he, "will necessitate your being parted from him for a considerable time, and I know that your son is all in all to you, but he will be as safe with us as he can be anywhere, and you can correspond with him constantly, and whether any great good to the world will result from his visit or not it will certainly be both pleasurable and profitable to himself. He is too considerate of your wishes to answer my invitation before talking it over with you, and there is no need for any haste in deciding the matter. I do not leave Europe before the end of August, so you have plenty of time to think of it, but when the time comes, I hope to have Mr. Musgrave for my traveling companion."

My mother looked very grave at this, and while thanking Mr. Delphion for the kindness and consideration shown us both, said she would like to think over it for a day or two and talk with me about it, so the subject was dropped for the time. But before our guest left us it was all settled that I was to go with him, and I looked forward to the expedition with as much pleasant anticipation as if I had been contemplating a trip to another planet.

By this time the establishment in St. Oswald's was in good working order, and did not require my personal oversight. I requested the rector to assume my responsibility there for a time, and placed a large fund to his credit at the bank, so that he might be able to meet all contingencies.

By way of consoling my mother for my long prospective absence, I spent the last three or four weeks at home, except for two or three flying trips to London to see that matters were running smoothly there, and I found all my agents working so cordially and zealously under Mr. Calderwood's supervision that I felt satisfied that I should not be seriously missed.

IV

A FAR COUNTRY

Late in the afternoon of a day in the early part of September Mr. Delphion and I rode up the slope of a steep hill on the southern side of the Himalayas. The summit of this hill formed the site of an old stone fort called Benabra, dating from the early days of the Mogul empire. The country around is a barren plain without shade or sign of human habitation, the nearest village being ten miles away. The fort is the property of the Ionian government, and is used by them in their communications with the outer world, and is inhabited by an old Sikh and his family, a liberal allowance being paid them to keep the place in order and keep their own counsel in regard to what they know of their masters, which, however, is comparatively little. The old man's son had brought our baggage earlier in the day, but we preferred to wait till the sun was long past the meridian before undertaking the journey, and it wanted but an hour of his setting when we arrived in sight of the fort. Evidently we were not expected even then, for there was no sign of life about the place, but just as we dismounted from our horses a tall young man came through the gateway and saluted my companion in Greek, and then turning to me, grasped my hand warmly, saying:

"I am glad to meet my father's English friend, and I hope you will enjoy your visit amongst us."

He spoke quite fluently, but with a strange yet very agreeable accent. I replied that I was delighted to meet the son of my friend, and felt sure that my visit would afford me greater pleasure than anything I had ever undertaken.

Although rather taller than the average Englishman, I had to look up to this young man like a boy. I saw that he had his father's sparkling eye and grand leonine bearing. His face was clean-shaven except for the moustache, which was full and glossy black; his broad shoulders, deep chest and clean-cut muscular limbs made him a model of manly grace and beauty. He had much of the kindly expression which distinguished his father, and no one could look into his face without feeling that he was one to be trusted to the uttermost.

As I walked between these two grand men towards the interior of the fort I was overcome by a feeling of deep humility, like one in the presence of beings of a superior race, and I thought: if all the men of Ionia are like these two, what a puny race they must think I represent.

A few steps brought us to the interior court, the sight of which was very refreshing after our hot and dusty ride, for it was full of all manner of beautiful greenery. Palms and luxurious tropical flowers grew in great profusion, and a lovely fountain threw up showers of spray in the center.

"How is this," said I, "that you have water on the top of a hill in the desert? This seems like magic."

"But for the water," said Mr. Delphion, "the fort would never have been here. It comes, of course, from higher hills far away, and probably follows some subterranean channel of volcanic origin."

Dion Delphion now reminded us that the sun was sinking fast, and that we had a long journey before us, and led the way up a flight of stairs to a pleasant room overlooking the court, where we partook of a light refreshment of coffee, rice cakes, chicken and fruit; after which we repaired to the top of the fort, where I had my first view of an air-ship. The whole fort was roofed in with large stone flags, and as the ramparts were high, a small fleet of these vessels might have lain there without being visible from below, and doubtless this was one reason why the Ionians, desiring to pass to and from their own valley unobserved, had chosen the place for their solitary outpost. I approached the flying vessel with a great deal of curiosity, and found it very different from what I had imagined. There was nothing of the balloon about it, nor any elaborate apparatus of sails to make it float upon the wind. What I saw was like an enormous egg, at least twenty feet long, rather high in proportion to its length, and flattened at the bottom. It stood on four slender legs, made of double bands of elastic metal, which spread out at the foot like stirrups. Something that looked like a lady's fan extended underneath from a rod or shaft in the center, the broad end reaching to the stern. A similar fan-like device stood up perpendicularly behind, attached to a slender shaft protruding several feet from the body of the vessel. The surface of the ship was of a light sky-blue and beautifully enameled, showing neither seam nor joint except where a row of small port-holes ran round the sides and in front where there were two larger windows, one on either side, all of which were quite flush with the outer surface so as to reduce the resistance of the air to a minimum. There were also four or five small, round glasses in the bottom of the hull close around the shaft to which the fan was attached. This was all

I saw, and as the working of the vessel was still a perfect enigma to me, I asked young Delphion to enlighten my ignorance, which he readily undertook to do.

"You see this fan-like apparatus underneath," he said; "that is the elevator, and is used solely to raise the vessel when we take flight or let it down again when we wish to land. When we have attained sufficient elevation the sails are spread and the upright fan which we call the propeller is brought into operation and gives us our horizontal motion, and then the elevator is folded up again as you see it now. I shall take a little flight before you start with us, and you will understand the operating of the vessel better by seeing it from the outside."

He then went inside through a little door in the rear which I had not previously observed, on account of its close fitting, and left me with his father to see how the wonderful thing was managed. In a moment the elevator spread out its leaves (which were of thin, bright metal, making a complete circle,) and began to revolve with such rapidity that nothing could be seen but a whirling haze. Slowly at first, and then more rapidly, the ship began to ascend, till it was about a hundred feet above us, and then a number of long masts or poles shot out from the sides, and between these canvas was stretched until the vessel was surrounded by an immense spread of sail nearly horizontal, but inclining slightly upward towards the front. When this was accomplished the propeller began to act in the same way as the elevator, and the ship shot forward with great velocity. At the same moment another sail appeared in an upright position between the propeller and the hull, and the elevator folded itself up, and in a few moments the ship had disappeared, for the sun had gone down, and it was growing dark. I inquired what the upright sail was for, and Mr. Delphion informed me it was the rudder. Before I could ask anymore questions the vessel came fluttering quietly down and landed exactly on the place from which it started. Dion now opened the door and called to us to enter, which we did by means of a slender metal ladder which was let down from the inside, but once in I found it so dark that I could see nothing except the faint light coming in through the port-holes. In that latitude there is hardly any twilight, and as the sun had set some minutes before, it was now almost dark; I was led to a seat, however, and before I was conscious of any motion of the vessel itself I saw the walls of the fortress apparently sinking beneath us. I inquired if the whole journey had to be made in darkness, but Mr. Delphion assured me that we should have all the light we wished in a few minutes, but that Dion would have to get his bearings from the mountains ahead of us in order to shape his course. We appeared to be rising very rapidly, for from where I sat I could see nothing of the earth at all, but looking forward through the front windows I could distinguish a short stretch of twilight with the outlines of some dark hills between. It almost seemed as if we were rising out of the earth's shadow and overtaking the sunlight, but presently the motion changed, the sails were thrown out, and the propeller brought into play, and I felt the ship assume a forward motion; a number of incandescent lamps were lighted, and I found that we were in a very handsome and comfortably furnished saloon.

Mr. Delphion and I were sitting in two large arm-chairs side by side; behind us was the machinery enclosed in a glass-covered case, occupying a space of about three cubic feet, and behind that again sat Dion. Immediately in front of him was a long, narrow box, connected with the case which contained the machinery, and in this were arranged a compass and several gauges with two or three small wheels and levers, and by means of these he directed the course of the vessel, causing it to rise or fall, to swerve to the right or left, by an almost imperceptible touch of the fingers. Perceiving the ceiling overhead to be rather lower than I should have expected, I said to my companion:

"This saloon does not seem to occupy more than half the bulk of the vessel; how is the remaining space disposed of?"

"The upper portion," said Mr. Delphion, "comprising more than half of the hull, is a hydrogen chamber, which serves to diminish the total weight, and at the same time to give the necessary steadiness. Just as the ballast in a ship keeps it always keel downward, so our hydrogen chamber, being so very much lighter than the lower portion of the vessel, makes it impossible for any gust of wind to upset it."

"And what is the source of your power? I see nothing like a steam engine or any other device to control the machinery."

"Electricity," he said, "is the force which carries us through the air. No other force can ever be used to propel an air-ship, and although I once told you that we expect the outside world to arrive at the discovery of aerial navigation, they have to learn a good deal yet before they accomplish it. Their ideas of the storage battery are still very crude, and will have to be very much improved before they can travel as we are doing now. It would surprise your electrical experts to learn that we can store enough of the subtle force in this vessel to keep it moving for a week, and we not only do that, but we can draw upon the same stores to warm and light it as well. It is sometimes very cold when we get far away from the earth, and more electrical force is required to keep up the temperature to a comfortable point than to propel the vessel on its course."

"At what height above the surface of the earth do you usually travel?"

"That depends entirely upon the winds. If the lower current is favorable we may remain within two or three hundred feet of the surface, but if it is adverse we sometimes rise to a height of two thousand or even three thousand feet in order to find a breeze that will help, rather than hinder us."

"At what height are we sailing just now?"

Mr. Delphion turned to his son and asked: "How high are we just now, Dion?"

"About twelve hundred feet from the ground."

This seemed very high to me, and I asked if it was not dangerous to be so far from the earth.

"On the contrary," said Mr. Delphion," the higher we are the safer we are. For if anything should go wrong with the machinery when we are only two or three hundred feet up we might reach the ground with disastrous speed before we have time to put matters straight, whereas, if we are two thousand feet high there would be much more time to apply the remedy before any harm could befall. But as a matter of fact, the danger of any serious accident happening to our air-ships is almost infinitesimal, for the machinery which moves the propeller is quite independent of that which works the elevator, so if from any cause whatever the former should become disabled, the latter could be brought into operation at once, and thus the worst that can happen is a gradual descent to the ground before the journey is finished. Even such a slight misfortune as that is of very rare occurrence, for every part of the machinery is of the toughest metal ever made, and we overhaul it and see that everything is in perfect order before starting on a trip."

"What is the ordinary speed of your aerial flights?"

"Different vessels have different rates of speed, just the same as it is with sailing vessels and steamships. In a calm atmosphere the speed varies all the way from fifty to seventy-five miles an hour. The velocity of the wind has to be added to or subtracted from this, according to its being with or against us. We generally arrange to have it with us if possible, but this cannot always be done, and then progress is comparatively slow. Our country is so well sheltered by mountains that we seldom have winds blowing at a greater velocity than fifty miles an hour, so that the greatest speed ever attained by our air-ships is about a hundred and twenty-five miles in sixty minutes."

"At what rate do you think we are going now?"

"Dion can tell us exactly. How fast are we moving, Dion?"

"Eighty-five miles an hour at present."

"That is about what I thought," said Mr. Delphion. "The wind is with us, but it is a very gentle breeze; not more, I should say, than ten miles an hour."

Dion now suggested that before the moon rose I should go forward and take a look at the stars.

"Yes, you must do so," said his father, "for you will find it a very brilliant spectacle. The clearness of the air at this elevation has a marvelous effect."

So I walked forward to the front of the vessel, where were two plate-glass windows of considerable size, and so transparent that I could see as well as if I were in the open air. Dion extinguished the lights, and a scene of marvelous splendor burst upon my view. The heavens blazed with stars infinitely more numerous than ever I had seen before, and many times brighter. And what struck me as stranger still, they appeared not to be all set in the same equi-distant sky as with us, but the brighter ones seemed to hang in midair, while those of smaller magnitude looked as if removed to awful distances. The great multiplicity of stars at first prevented my distinguishing any of the constellations that were known to me, and I felt as if I were gazing at a new and more gorgeous heaven of stars. Right in front—in the northwest, but nearer, apparently, than any other—blazed an orb of regal splendor, which required no effort of the imagination to recognize as a distant sun; farther north, amongst a vast swarm of brilliants, were seven, conspicuously bright, which I presently made out to be the Great Bear, and that other splendid orb, the monarch of the sky, could be no other than Arcturus, but shining with tenfold his ordinary glory. Looking up toward the zenith, I caught a glimpse of Vega pouring down a flood of quivering light that outrivaled Venus at her brightest. Just then Dion said:

"I shall shut off the propeller for a minute so that you may hear the music of the spheres."

He did so, and an awful silence fell upon us. I could see nothing of the earth below except a vague, cloudy darkness, but above and all around were myriads of stars, glowing and throbbing with the intensity of celestial life. It was an awful thought that all those millions of suns and worlds were surging through space suspended in mere vacuity, and for the moment I could not resist the fancy that we, too, had left the earth and were wandering about amongst the eternal stars. The thought filled me with a sensation of horror, and I called out "Enough," and the propeller instantly resumed its chant and the chamber blazed again with light.

"I staggered back and dropped into my seat, and Mr. Delphion, looking anxiously at me, said, "What ails you, Mr. Musgrave? You look quite pale."

"You will doubtless think me very foolish," I replied, "but the idea came into my head all of a sudden that I was in the hands of the immortals, that you were Zeus, and Dion, Apollo, and that you were carrying me away off amongst the stars, and that I should never see the earth again."

Mr. Delphion threw back his head and laughed heartily. It was the first time I had ever heard him laugh, and there was such a genuine ring of human enjoyment in it that I should have felt reassured at once, even if the momentary fancy had taken a deeper hold upon me than was actually the case.

"Do you hear, Dion," said he, "how our friend flatters us?"

"I do not call it flattery," said Dion, "I should not like to think my father was such an unscrupulous old rascal as Zeus."

"I never thought of it in that way," said I, "but I am sure that you and your father might very well serve as models to a sculptor for these two gods."

"Now that is flattery, pure and simple," said the elder Delphion, "but let us talk of something purely human."

"With all my heart," said I.

"Well, then," said he, "I will give you some further information about the country you are going to visit, so that it may seem a little less strange to you when you arrive there, and that will be in something less than two hours from now. The principal part of our territory is, as I have already told you, a gently sloping valley, extending a hundred and fifty miles from east to west, averaging about forty in width. Through it flows the river Pharos, which is navigable at all seasons as far as the ancient capital, which is called Thalmon, situated very near the center of the valley. The river has many tributaries flowing into it from both sides, and these are connected by a network of canals, which have no parallel except perhaps in the Netherlands. All these streams have their source amongst the higher mountain peaks, and in order to regulate the water supply, a great number of large reservoirs have been constructed amongst the lower hills, and by this means we have a constant supply of water at all seasons without any danger of floods. The water is used for irrigation in the dry season, which extends from July to November, and every foot of land in cultivation can be flooded at will, so that a succession of crops is produced every season, and the country could support a much larger population than it is now required to do. We are about three millions of people, and we add to our numbers very slowly, for we do not consider a rapid increase desirable. The modern capital, Iolkos, has about five hundred thousand inhabitants, the city of Thalmon about half as many, and we have towns and villages of all sizes in various parts of the country. The rural population is large, for the farms are small, varying from twenty-five to seventy-five acres, and are always cultivated by the farmer himself, with the assistance in some cases of his son. Of farm laborers as a class we have none.

"The river Pharos flows from west to east, and empties itself into Lake Malo, which we shall pass over before arriving at our destination. This is a beautiful sheet of water about twenty-five miles long, and is discharged by the river Styx, which flows in a southerly direction through an impassable gorge, denominated the Gates of Hades, which in ancient times afforded an entrance to the valley; but the road was destroyed and rendered absolutely impracticable by our ancestors as a protection against a formidable foe, of which I shall tell you more at another time.

"The city of Iolkos is built at the mouth of the river, and commands a beautiful view of the lake and the vast ranges of mountains surrounding it. Although the chief seat of our manufactures, it is the cleanest and the quietest city in the world. The streets are paved with the hardest cement: all the vehicles which roll through them are propelled by electricity, and have rubber tires on their wheels. The roads throughout the country are paved in the same manner, and the spring rains clothe the hillsides with grass, so that no dust is formed anywhere. We have no coal and burn but little charcoal, for our heat as well as light and motive power is supplied by electricity, and thus our atmosphere is free from smoke as well as dust, and is always perfectly clear and wholesome in city and country alike. We have a great many beautiful edifices, and you will find a harmony of design in the architecture of our streets which is not to be met with in any European city.

"Our government is a republic, with a single legislative body called the senate, which is elected by the representatives of the people. Every man has a vote, which he casts annually for the magistrate of his district in the city or province where he resides. These magistrates elect the senators, who are apportioned strictly according to population. Their term is for three years, one-third of their number being renewed every year. A moderate salary is attached to every public office, not sufficient to form an inducement to aspire to the senator-ship or magistracy, and there is so little desire for the power of place amongst us that no man ever thinks of soliciting the suffrages of the people. On the other hand, it is held to be a public duty to accept office when one is elected, and in the event of anyone declining without good and sufficient cause, accepted as such by the judge appointed for such cases, he has to pay a heavy fine, and all the costs of a fresh election besides. This is a thing which very seldom happens, however, for there is a certain amount of odium attaching to such a dereliction of public duty.

"The chief executive officer is called the archon, who is assisted by a cabinet of six ministers, chosen by himself and responsible only to him, but theoretically impeachable by the senate. He has power to add to that number if he thinks necessary, but has very seldom availed himself of it. The archon is elected by the senate for five years, but is usually re-elected and often holds the high office for life.

"We have adopted many European customs, and our calendar is the same as yours, except that we divide the year into twelve months of thirty days, with one more in January, March, June and September, and one more in February in leap years. We have the week of seven days, with the first set apart for rest and recreation.

"We address each other in familiar intercourse by our individual names only. This will seem a little strange to you at first, but you will soon become accustomed to calling me Jason, my wife Helen, my daughter Leda, and so forth, and you must not be surprised to find yourself addressed simply as Alexander."

"I am sure I shall not mind what they call me, but until I become used to the ways of the country it will come hard to me to address your ladies by their Christian names without prefix or title. Have you no titles of any kind in Ionia?"

"None whatever. Even our first magistrate or archon is addressed simply by his name, Minos, nor does the dignity of his years and character suffer by what, amongst your people, would be unwarrantable familiarity. But now we are getting near to the Gates of Hades, the moon is up and the scene well worthy of your attention. You may not have another opportunity of seeing it, so if you will, we shall both step forward and find out where we are."

So we took our places by the windows in the house, and when Dion had turned out the lights I found we were amongst the most wonderful mountain scenery I had ever beheld. Right in front, and apparently about three hundred feet below the airship, was a chaos of rocks, tumbled together in shapeless masses, as if some mighty convulsion had broken up a range of mountains and thrown the fragments down pell-mell. We sped over yawning chasms which appeared to be bottomless, and past great mounds which rose up precipitously from the general debris, but for mile upon mile there was not a spot which could afford sustenance or even foothold for man or beast. Beyond this scene of desolation arose endless ranges of mountains, tier above tier, with snow-clad peaks which gleamed like silver in the light of the full moon. But presently we approached a great hill which shut out the distant scene, and when we had swept round it my companion directed me to look beneath, for we were right over the Gates of Hades.

Beneath us was a deep gorge, the sides of which were jagged precipices several hundred feet in height. The moon was not very high yet, so that only an occasional ray found its way to the bottom, but as my eye became accustomed to darkness I could distinguish a mass of foaming waters dashing past the cliffs and lashing themselves into spray against projecting rocks. Then followed a stretch of smooth, dark river, relieved occasionally by the white waves of some tremendous whirlpools. Again a half mile of rapids, boiling and surging more furiously than the first, filled the space from side to side with white foam. Gates of Hades was certainly no misnomer, and they would close swiftly on any unfortunate soul caught within their dreadful jaws. But now I saw that we were approaching the end of this fearful gorge. There was a wider space of light between the black walls of rock, and at last they disappeared from under us, and we were flying over a beautiful sheet of still water surrounded by the glorious mountain ranges we had seen in the distance.

And signs of human habitation came into view, vessels on the water, village lights on the shores, and a great airship, illuminated from stem to stern, and many times larger than the one we were in, flew past us like a fiery meteor, and in the far distance a luminous haze, becoming more clear at every moment, indicated our approach to a great city.

Every minute brought us nearer, until I could distinguish the lines of the streets and the forms of majestic edifices showing darkly against the light reflected from the streets.

"Why is it," I inquired of my companion, "that so few lamps are visible while at the same time every street seems so perfectly illuminated?"

"Because," he replied, "the lights, which are placed high up at every crossing, are covered with reflectors which throw down the rays at such angles that the streets are all equally illuminated, the lamps themselves being placed so high as not to trouble the eye with their glare."

And now we were within a few miles of the city, but instead of continuing in our course, which would have brought us directly over it, we swerved to the right and made for the angle of the bay which forms the head of the lake, and gives to the city a water front of about two miles in extent. We got a glimpse of the river, spanned by handsome bridges, and a view of the stately street which fronts the beach, the buildings being all on the further side, with stone steps leading down on the nearer side to the water's edge. Presently we flew past what seemed a city of palaces rising directly from the water, with a colossal statue of a man wearing a gorgeous crown, which towered high over all in the center and was brilliantly illuminated from below as if with the light of day.

Anticipating my enquiry, Mr. Delphion hastened to explain this wonderful spectacle.

"That Island is called the Acropolis, and contains the government buildings and the palace of the archon. The statue in the center is that of Timoleon, the great king whose memory is almost worshiped by us. The pedestal is made of immense blocks of granite, and the statue itself of pure silver with a crown of gold (said to be the only crown he ever wore), and it is set with diamonds, which in any other part of the world would represent a value almost incalculable."

Before he had finished speaking the Acropolis had passed out of sight, and we were approaching with slackened speed a row of handsome villas situated on the northern shore, and over one of them the ship paused and gently fluttered down till it touched the center of the level roof. We then made our way out, the sails and fans were all furled, and in a minute the vessel was fast moored to some large rings of metal built into the walls. I would fain have lingered to enjoy the entrancing beauty of the lake shimmering in the rays of the moon, but realizing that Mr. Delphion must be anxious to embrace his wife and daughter after his long absence, I made no demur when invited to enter with them what appeared like a summer house standing on one side, and found myself in an elevator which conveyed us down to the interior of the house. Arriving at the third floor, Dion invited me to follow him, and took me to a large front room, which he said was my bedchamber. Excusing himself for a moment, he left me to become acquainted with my new quarters and the impression produced was favorable in the extreme. The walls and ceiling appeared to be luminous, and they were painted by a master hand in representation of vines and flowers, so that I might have fancied myself in the center of a beautiful greenhouse. The floor appeared to be of oxidized silver, but I learned afterwards that it was of aluminum; it was covered, except near the walls, by a rug of velvet softness, the prevailing tint being a light salmon which harmonized delightfully with the greens and pale blues of the walls and ceiling. I was still puzzling over the source of the soft, pleasing light, which seemed to emanate from the walls and ceiling, when Dion tapped at the door, which I at once opened, and he came in, carrying my trunk and portmanteau, which he had fetched down from the airship, carrying one in each hand as easily as if they had been a pair of bandboxes. I began to apologize for giving him that trouble but he would not listen to me, saying it was no trouble at all, and as they had no man-servants in the country they did many little things themselves which would be considered beneath a gentleman's dignity in England, but which were right for a gentleman to do in Ionia, for there was no one else to do them. He then enquired how soon I should be ready to go down stairs to meet his mother and sister, and I told him to give me ten minutes to remove the dust of travel and I should be at his service. I could not help thinking that I should present rather a poor figure in my English clothes, compared with Dion's splendid form, clad in the graceful Ionian costume, but I made myself as presentable as I could and accompanied him to the story below, where we found the rest of the family in the library, a long, lofty room, lined with well-filled bookcases, and having many comfortable chairs, reading desks and globes for its movable furniture. All rose as we entered, and Mr. Delphion introduced me to Helen, his wife, and Leda, his daughter. I saw at a glance that these two women were more perfectly beautiful than any that I had ever seen before, but there was something also which impressed me more profoundly, and that was the expression of calm serenity, high intelligence, purity and goodness which their faces bore, and made me feel at the moment as if I were in the presence of two of the angels of heaven rather than of mortals. I therefore bowed profoundly to each, spell-bound for the moment and unable to say a word for myself, but the elder lady stepped forward and took me by the hand, saying:

"You are truly welcome to our home, Alexander, and I hope you will make a long stay with us. Jason has told us a great deal about you in his letters, and we think very highly of you. We wish you to consider yourself one of our family, and we are delighted to have you with us."

The younger lady also shook hands with me, saying that it was a new and very pleasant experience to have a visitor from another country in Ionia, and hoping that I should enjoy my stay amongst them.

I made my acknowledgments in the best way I could, and just then the door opened and another beautiful feminine form appeared, hardly as tall as the others, who were much above the average height of English women, but almost as perfect in grace of figure and loveliness of face and expression. She was dressed like the others, with exquisite taste, but wore a white apron, and I wondered if this adorable creature could possibly be a household servant. As soon as she appeared, my hostess said:

"Here is our cousin, Eurydice, come to tell us that supper is ready. She does not speak English very well, but knows French perfectly, which I presume you do too, Alexander?"

I said that I understood French pretty well, so I was introduced in that language to the charming cousin Eurydice, and then we all went down together to the dining room, and sat down to supper. Eurydice waited on us and then took her place at the table with the rest, and was treated so entirely as one of the family that as soon as she was seated, the conversation was at once changed from English to French, so that she might understand and take her part in it with the rest.

I learned afterwards that this was the universal custom in Ionia, the lady help, when there is one, being always called cousin, and treated as one of the family, a striking contrast to the custom in England, where the lady help is only different from a common servant in having harder work and poorer pay. In Ionia no kind of labor is considered menial or degrading, and no one is looked down upon for having to work for a living,—idleness only is considered unworthy and contemptible. The room in which this pleasant family party were assembled excited my admiration by the beautiful painting of the walls and ceiling. Slender pilasters of some white metal divided the walls, and the spaces between them were filled with exquisitely painted landscapes representing pastoral and hunting scenes; while the ceiling was painted like the sky, covered by a transparent veil of cirrus clouds. All the light in the room came from ceiling and wall, and every portion of it was clearly illuminated without glare or harshness. I expressed my admiration of the beautiful soft light, and asked my hostess, at whose right hand I sat, how it was accomplished.

"The lamps," she said, "are placed in front of the cove, which joins wall and ceiling, and if you look closely you will see that they are held in a frame which runs all round the room, the other side of which has reflecting surfaces, which diffuse the light equally, while the side nearest you, being in the shade and painted just like the ceiling, is but indistinctly seen. In this way we avoid the harmful effect of any strong light upon the eyes, and retain our powers of vision unimpaired."

"That is quite ingenious," I said, "and the effect is delightful. Do many of your people have their dwellings lighted in that way?"

"All," she said, "and our public buildings are lighted in the same way. We avoid glare in the streets also by having the lamps so high that no one can see them without looking directly upwards, which is very seldom necessary."

"That, also, is a very great improvement upon our method, for, since the introduction of electric lighting, the dangers of street crossings in London and other cities are very much increased, and the glare of the arc lights is not only disagreeable but injurious to the eye as well."

"I hope you will find other things to admire in Ionia, but should you find us deficient in anyway, you must be sure to enlighten us, and you will find us very willing to adopt any improvement which your larger experience of the world may suggest."

"My attitude here," said I, "shall be that of a humble learner, and I am sure I shall not have the presumption to assume the role of teacher in any department of human knowledge."

"And yet, Alexander," said the beautiful Leda, "you can teach us much if you will. In the matter of English speech, for instance, we know that we must be very defective, all except my father, for we have never heard a word of it pronounced by a native of your country before."

"But you all speak it very well indeed. I never heard English so beautifully spoken as here tonight."

"Oh, you must not flatter us," said Leda, "and we are not going to ask you to play the part of professor, either, but just promise to correct us when you find us going far wrong, and you will find us quite grateful."

"I promise," said I, "but my task will be an easy one, judging by all that I have heard so far."

"You have traveled in many countries," said the lady Helen, "while we have always lived in one, and there must, therefore, be many things familiar to you of which we are ignorant, so you will be able to instruct us in somethings while we shall be delighted to show you all that may be of interest to you here. And you have arrived in time to be present at our great yearly festival of the national games which are to be celebrated here next week."

"And what are they? Are they at all similar to the ancient Olympian games?"

"They are similar and they are different, but my husband can tell you better about that than I."

Thus appealed to, my host proceeded to explain:

"Our modern games are different in one important respect, for whereas the ancients admitted only the male sex to the festival, we admit both sexes, although only men and boys take part in the different contests. Hence our modern athletes are dressed similarly to your own, while the ancients wore no clothing at all. Something is, no doubt, lost of the beauty of the spectacle by covering the handsome forms of the supple and muscular youths who compete for the prizes in running, leaping, wrestling, etc., but much more is gained by the admission of their sisters, cousins and mothers to the entertainment. And we think too much of the ladies nowadays to debar them from the enjoyment of these great exhibitions of skill and strength. In other respects, our games are very similar to those of the great Hellenic festivals of old, except that in place of chariot races we have rowing matches, and flying contests between diferent classes of air vessels. The use of the horse has been almost entirely discontinued in Ionia, hence chariot races would be out of place amongst us."

"And so you are as much devoted as your ancestors to physical culture?"

"As much or possibly more. Our national games are attended by a larger concourse of people than ever the Olympian games were, and these were held every four years only, while ours is an annual festival."

"Moreover, every district of the country and every city and town has its annual games, from which competitors are selected to take part in the national races. Every school has its gymnasium, and physical training precedes the mental and accompanies it. The girls are trained as well as the boys, though not exactly in the same way. They become very expert in many athletic sports and exercises, but their modesty prevents them exhibiting themselves in any public spectacle."

"And how about the prizes?" I asked. "The ancients were satisfied with the honor of being crowned with a wreath of wild cherry. Does that custom still remain with you, or are more substantial rewards now given?"

"The wreath of cherry leaves is still the victor's only reward, except that in addition his name is engraved on the wall which surrounds the arena—a massive wall of granite one-third of a mile in extent,—and thus the victor achieves a kind of immortality which is very much sought after."

"And may I ask if the name of Jason Delphion is inscribed on that wall?"

"Oh, yes," said Leda, "in more places than one. And we hope to see Dion's name there, too, after next week."

"A hope," said Dion, "which is very likely to be disappointed."

"This is becoming very interesting," said I. "Of what nature are the contests you are to engage in?"

"I am entered for two races, one rowing and one flying. I hardly hope to win the former, for I have not practiced so assiduously as some others. As to the latter, much depends upon chance; one cannot foretell how the wind may blow at any particular elevation, and it is very easy to miscalculate. The flying race I am entered for is that of the skylarks, the smallest kind of air-vessel, carrying only one person, and a very slight puff of wind has a great effect upon them, so you see no one can have any certainty of victory, whatever may be his skill or the perfection of his vessel."

"May favoring winds attend you," said I, "but how am I to attend this great festival in these outlandish English clothes. Have I time to get myself fitted out with Ionian garments before next week?"

"Directly after breakfast you will be waited upon by a member of one of our tailoring firms, who will provide you with a complete outfit by noon, and before evening you can have as many suits as you wish."

"That will be delightful," said I, "and pray tell me at what hour you usually breakfast?"

"Eight o'clock is the universal breakfast hour in the city, and by nine everybody is at work; business men, artists, mechanics, professors in the university, and teachers in schools; all have the same work hours, which are from nine to three. Four o'clock is the universal hour for dinner, and these are our principal, and, with many people, the only meals, although a light supper before bedtime is not at all uncommon, and in this house we always have a little supper, and we like to linger over it, for there is nothing to do afterwards but retire to rest, and it affords a pleasant opportunity to talk over the events of the day."

I looked at my watch and found it was near twelve o'clock, and guessing rightly that they were up long past the usual bedtime, I pleaded fatigue after the events and excitements of the day, and said goodnight to all.

Dion took me up in the elevator, and as we went asked if I was fond of swimming.

"Because," said he, "my sister and I go for a swim every morning in the open air, and we should be glad to have you go with us."

"At what hour?"

"We rise at six and leave the house at about a quarter past. Fifteen minutes' walk takes us to the "Quarry," and we spend about an hour there, which leaves us ample time to get back to breakfast without hurry."

"Six o'clock sounds to me a frightfully early hour, and I have a good excuse for not going tomorrow in the lack of suitable clothing, but after tomorrow I shall be delighted to go with you, and I feel grateful to you for the invitation."

"You must not say that; it will be very pleasant to have you go with us. And now you must need rest, so I shall wish you goodnight and a sound sleep."

I felt too much agitated by the novelty of my situation and the recollection of the strange journey I had made to go to sleep at once, so when I had undressed and turned out the lights I pulled up the blind and sat down by one of the windows to see what I could of this new world by moonlight. The air was wonderfully clear and transparent, so that almost the whole extent of the lake was visible, hemmed round on every side by hills. Here a great precipice rose sheer from the water's edge, and there an arm of the lake or some tributary stream opened up a far-reaching glen, bordered by dark woods and romantic valleys, but in the background the mountains rose higher and higher, and distant snowy peaks were to be seen on every side. Away in the east towered one which dwarfed all the others, rising far towards the zenith, all I could see of it being of dazzling white, which showed its outline clearly against the pale blue of the sky. Between me and it lay the Acropolis, crowded with palaces sharply outlined against the mountain's snowy sides. They made a noble picture, and I could readily perceive that they were amongst the grandest efforts of human genius, but the grandeur of nature's handiwork in that stupendous mountain, towering in the distance against the sky, seemed to my eyes to dwarf them as the years of time are dwarfed when we think of eternity, and I felt crushed by a sense of my own insignificance. I had dreamed of accomplishing great things in the world, and possibly of making a name for myself that would long be remembered, but yonder awful peak had looked down upon the world millions of years before I was born, and would continue to do so for as many millions more after my bones had crumbled into dust, and beside it I was no greater than an insect creeping about an ant-hill at its base. I turned my eyes upon the city, sleeping in the moonlight, and it seemed like the creation of some magician's wand called into existence in the night, for not a sign of life was there. The lights were out, and not a particle of smoke hung over its chimneys; indeed, I could see nothing that looked like a chimney, but towers and domes innumerable, and many forms of architectural beauty, and every stone as clean and bright as if they had been put together yesterday. Over all reigned a silence so profound that it seemed as if I could hear the beating of my heart. Scarce a breath of air was stirring, and only now and again a tiny wavelet broke upon the beach below to emphasize the general stillness. The scene was very beautiful, but the extreme absence of sound and human activity made it seem unreal and dream-like, so I turned to my bed to seek repose as one turns to sleep again after being but half-awakened from a dream.

I awoke with a start in the morning, the sunshine streaming into my room through the window, which I had left uncurtained. I feared I might be late for breakfast, and I guessed rightly that the Ionians are a very punctual people, who, when they name an hour mean that time exactly, and not ten or fifteen minutes after it. But on looking at my watch, I was glad to find that I had plenty of time for my morning tub, and plenty of leisure for dressing afterwards. What a change the scene without presented from the night before. The great white mountain, which had filled my spirits with awe, now looked like a ghostly film in the distance, while near at hand all was life and motion. A gentle breeze covered the lake with golden, shining ripples; handsome boats and barges skimmed its surface far and near, and at least a score of airships could be seen cleaving their way towards the city at dizzy heights in the atmosphere. The city itself, shining in the morning light, had the same appearance of freshness that struck me the night before, being perfectly free from the grime and dust that discolor all European buildings, and yet I could see that some of the walls before me were mellowed by time, while others were as clear and bright as if the stones had been quarried the day before. And it seemed from my point of view to be full of splendid edifices, as if all the temples and choicest buildings of Europe had been massed together in one place. One street only I could see distinctly, and that was the one fronting the lake. The buildings were on one side only, with a broad street of smooth cement in front, and then a flight of wide stone steps leading down to the gravelly beach. The street was something more than a mile in length, and about the center appeared a handsome bridge of a single span, under which the river flowed into the lake. Six imposing buildings with ample spaces between filled the street from the nearest angle of the bay to the river. They were all of marble, but each of a different shade. Their architecture was different in style from anything I had ever seen, but very beautiful, and altogether they made a picture of such magnificence and splendor as infinitely to surpass anything I had ever seen before. The buildings on the farther side of the river appeared to be on the same scale of grandeur and beauty, but of course I could not see them so well.

A few pedestrians appeared on the street, and some carriages propelled swiftly along without either horses or steam, but there was no crowd or bustle; evidently the full tide of the city's life had not yet commenced to flow.

The only dwelling houses I could discover at first were those situated near the Delphion mansion, on the north shore of the lake. They were all built well back from the road, which ran parallel to the lake and about fifty feet from the water's edge. It was of hard cement, like the street on the city's front, with sidewalks of some darker material, and all as clean and free from dust as if they had just been scrubbed with soap and water. A continuous green lawn surrounded the houses, extending as far to right and left as I could see, with noble shade trees growing at intervals. Looking across the lake I could see a line of similar villas on the south shore, with others back of them on the lower slopes of the hills, and the transparency of the atmosphere was so perfect that I could distinguish the colors of the dresses of some people moving about amongst them at a distance of not less than two miles.

V

Amongst New Friends

When the family were assembled at the breakfast table, I expressed my admiration of their magnificent city and its glorious situation, but remarked that I could see nothing but public buildings, and that I could not understand where the people lived.

"That is very easily explained," said my hostess, "for most of the dwelling houses are on the other side of the river, and a majority of the public buildings and all the larger stores are on this side."

"And what is that splendid line of buildings fronting the lake between us and the bridge?"

"Those are the university buildings."

"Oh, the university! Magnificent! It must be an education merely to have such beautiful structures before one's eyes everyday. And they are very extensive, too. Do the young people of the whole country come to Iolkos to finish their education?"

"By no means; every district has its university,—there are five of them altogether, and the others are not far behind the university of Iolkos either in extent, beauty of architecture or excellence of instruction."

"Then I trust the youth of Ionia appreciate their unrivaled advantages. Would it be permitted to a stranger, like myself, to inspect these palatial halls? I mean the interior as well as the exterior."

"There is no public building in the country," said Jason, "which you may not enter unchallenged. As for the university, there is nothing to prevent you from attending any of the classes if you are inclined to do so, and thus learning something of our methods of education."

"That would be useless until I know more of the language than I do now. And my stay will hardly be long enough to enable me to profit by any course of instruction."

"I did not mean that," said my host, "and I should not for a moment entertain the idea that there is any need for you to become a pupil in any of our schools. But you have come here to find out what we are, and our system of education has much to do with what we are, so you will probably desire to know something about it. As for your ignorance of our language, that is not so great as your modesty would have us believe, and I have no doubt but you will be able to speak it in a few weeks as well as you read it now. But even that difficulty would not stand in your way in some of the class rooms,—those, for instance, where English, French or German literature are studied, for in these the instruction is given in the language which belongs to the subject of the course. In fact, a visit from you to the class of English literature would be hailed as an event of very great importance, and I think you could not very well escape without saying a few words to the students, who would naturally be anxious to hear how an Englishman speaks his own tongue."

"Then I am afraid I shall studiously avoid paying a visit to that class, for I am no speaker."

"Perhaps they would be content with a reading from Macaulay, or Gibbon, or say Milton?"

"That would not be quite so bad."

"That would be delightful," said Leda, "I should like to be there and hear it. But perhaps you will be so good as to read to us sometimes."

"I would gladly do anything," said I, "that would give you pleasure, but the truth is I am not much of a reader, either. It is true I used to take great delight in reading to my mother, but she was not a critical listener, and was always interested if she thought the subject interested me."

"Nor shall we be critical," said Leda, "nor very exacting, either, but it will be a great treat to us to hear an English classic rendered by an English tongue."

"Very well," said I, "I promise one reading at anytime you may wish it, but I think very likely one will be enough."

"And now," said my host, "I am about to pay my respects to our archon, and if it will suit your convenience, I shall be pleased to present you to him in the afternoon."

"I am entirely at your service," said I, "but I trust by that time I shall be outwardly presentable."

"You are entirely so at this moment," said Jason, "but as you are so sensitive on the point, you can rest assured that you will have it in your power to dress like an Ionian before my return."

Very soon after breakfast I received a visit from the tailor, a very handsome, gentlemanly person, not quite so striking a figure as either Dion or his father, but very well proportioned and athletic, his height being about six feet, which I found afterwards to be about the average stature of the men of Ionia. He knew little English, but spoke French very fluently, and like a well-educated man, as he undoubtedly was. He went through the business of taking my measurements from head to foot in a rapid, business-like way, and promised me a complete outfit in about three hours.

The interval I spent in the library, which I found a veritable treasure-house, one side of it being devoted to books in Greek, ancient and modern, and the other to standard works in all the European languages. They were all or nearly all printed in Ionia, and in typography, paper and binding superior to even the best productions of our English press. Every book had foot-notes in Greek, and I foresaw that it would be a great delight to me to renew the acquaintance of my favorite authors with the new light which these annotations would throw upon them. I went round from one case to another, glancing at a passage here and there without undertaking any serious reading, and in this way the time flew by very quickly, and I was perfectly surprised when the fair cousin, Eurydice, knocked at the door and informed me that a package had arrived from the tailor and had been taken to my room, whither I repaired without loss of time, as eager to try on my new clothes as a young girl with her first reception costume; but I took longer to get into that suit than ever I spent in dressing either before or since, for I had to find out the manner of adjusting and fastening each novel garment. At length, however, the task was completed, and I surveyed myself in the glass with considerable satisfaction, wondering, however, if my own mother would know me if she could meet me on the street in my new costume. My English trousers were replaced by a pair of knee-breeches of dark blue velvet, under which were silk stockings of silver-gray. A tunic of fine woolen stuff of the same color as the small clothes, shoes with silver buckles, a shirt of cream-colored silk, with a standing collar, stiffened by interior crimping and showing above the neck of the tunic,—these, with a chapeau of fine buff felt and picturesque fashion, completed the costume. The fit of every garment was perfect and there was a feeling of ease and snug comfort in them which made me feel that I should be very unwilling to don my stiff and heavy European garments again. Although well pleased with my general appearance, I yet felt a little shame-faced about venturing downstairs into the presence of my hostess and her daughter, and lingered unnecessarily long in putting the finishing touches to my toilet, so that I was surprised when Jason himself knocked at my door and inquired if I was ready to go with him. I opened the door, and inviting him in, asked him to tell me himself whether I looked quite ready.

"You are so completely transformed that your own mother would not know you, and you need not be afraid of any stranger taking you for a foreigner. But come and show yourself to the ladies, their opinion is worth twenty of mine in such matters."

"Well, I suppose I must undergo that ordeal, but I am afraid they will think me simply ridiculous."

"And why ridiculous?"

"Because I am such a pigmy beside you and Dion. If all the men in Ionia are like you two, I shall always be conspicuous by my diminutive stature."

"Oh, but you need have no fears on that head; we have plenty of men in this country who are under five feet ten inches in height, and that, I take it, is just about what you are."

"Five feet ten and a quarter," I said, proudly.

"Come along, then, you will pass muster in a regiment of us easily enough."

So we went, and the ladies were very kind, and even complimentary. Leda went so far as to say that I looked so perfectly like an Ionian that she almost regretted the change, for it was so interesting to have a real live Englishman in the house. Her father, she said, always looked like one when he came back from his travels, but they knew in his case it was only a disguise, and he always made haste to resume his ordinary clothing, and they preferred to see him in it, too; but with me it was the other way, the Ionian dress was the disguise, and it was so perfect that I might show myself on the streets or anywhere and no one be any the wiser.

I thanked her for the compliment, and set out with my friend without any further misgiving.

We walked about a quarter of a mile towards the city, and then found awaiting us at a small pier extending from the front street a very handsome barge belonging to the government, which had conveyed my friend from the Acropolis. The crew were two gentlemen in handsome uniforms, and I was introduced to them as a matter of course, and they very politcly wished me a pleasant stay in the country, and hoped they could be of service to me while I remained.

We had not far to go, the Acropolis being but half a mile from shore, and our handsome barge skimmed through the water very swiftly. The lake was alive with vessels coming from and going to the city, all propelled without steam or sails, although I saw one or two sailing yachts in the distance. The streets, so far as they were visible, were crowded with people and vehicles, but there was none of the noise we are accustomed to in our busy streets, the smooth pavements and rubber-tired wheels of Ionia dispensing with noise, and if I had but shut my eyes I might have fancied myself a hundred miles away from all human industry. But we were rapidly approaching the Acropolis itself, the splendors of which now engrossed all my attention. The island, originally irregular in shape, has been made into a parallelogram, six hundred yards long by four hundred wide, the rocks forming its surface having been leveled and used to change its shape as a site for the buildings of the national government. These are beyond all comparison the most magnificent structures ever designed by human genius, and rising directly on all sides from deep water, are seen to great advantage from every side. My feelings as I approached them for the first time were such as I cannot put into words, and speech failed me at the time. I took my hat from head and stood on the deck of the barge in mute admiration and respect. Then seeing Jason observe me with something like a smile on his face, for there were tears in my eyes, I grasped his hand, and said:

"My friend, I thank you for bringing me to Ionia."

"Then," said he, "you think I did not exaggerate when I told you we had edifices more splendid than anything that Europe has ever had to boast of?"

"You never prepared me for this," I said; "it seems like the work of gods, and not men. Our grandest cathedrals, the work of five hundred years, are but the bungling efforts of apprentices compared with this magnificent display of architectural grandeur."

"And yet," said Jason, "I can remember when there was nothing here but a barren and unshapely rock from which, as a boy, I have caught many a basket of fish."

"That makes it more wonderful still. I think, after all, you have carried me to the land of the gods. Human hands as I know them could not accomplish such wonders in so short a time or in any length of time."

Three canals form the entrances to the Acropolis, one each on the north, south and west sides. The east side, being farthest from the city, has none. We entered from the west under a magnificent arch of white marble adorned with splendid carving and with niches filled with statuary, both on the outer and inner faces. Passing swiftly through we found ourselves in a wide canal, bordered by the greenest, most velvety turf in the world to a breadth of twelve feet on each side; beyond this a wide stone pavement crowded with people moving swiftly to and fro, and on both sides the fronts of those splendid palaces which had filled me with such wonder and admiration: They seemed even grander from this point of view if that were possible. But I had little time for comparison, for in a few seconds our barge was gliding into the central basin in which all the three canals unite. The square inclosing this basin is some six hundred feet from side to side, and in the center of all stands the monument of the great king. A mass of the native rock rises some ten or twelve feet from the water; on this stands a massive pillar of polished granite, and upon this the colossal statue itself, the top of the crown reaching to a height of two hundred and sixty feet from the base. We had a magnificent view of the kingly figure as we approached, and I admired its fine proportions and perfect poise, and found grace and majesty in every line. Beyond the monument, and fronting the side from which we came, is the Hall of the Senate, which fills one whole side of the square, and is the largest building on the island. The other three sides being divided by the canals, are occupied by six buildings, the palace of the archon, the treasury, the land office, and the offices of the departments of education, irrigation and commerce. We landed on the steps leading to the Palace of the Archon, but Jason, seeing me inclined to linger, waited till I had feasted my eyes on the architectural splendors of the grandest buildings ever erected by man. The view of the Acropolis from the lake had seemed to me of unapproachable magnificence, and in the great mass of buildings presented to the eye it has a grandeur of effect that even this assembly of master-pieces could not surpass, and yet the splendor of each of these seven palaces of marble and the wonderful harmony of their different styles excited my enthusiasm to a still greater degree, and I felt that the genius of the architect had achieved in this square his highest crowning glory. We entered the palace and were conveyed in an elevator to the uppermost story, where the chief magistrate of there public spends his working hours, and he is said to be the hardest working man in the country. Being a bachelor, he has no family of his own, and regards the people at large as his children, and never tires of the labor of watching over their welfare. The palace is his official residence, but he has never lived in it, preferring a modest residence which he owns on the lake shore, not far from that of the Delphions. Minos has been archon for nearly thirty years, and at the age of ninety still presides over the destinies of Ionia with unabated vigor, and his name ranks in the estimation of the people as second only to that of the great King Timoleon.

We were not kept waiting long in the ante-room, and were ushered into the presence of the archon by a tall and handsomely dressed gentleman of fine presence and bearing. The room was very large and lofty, and lighted by four windows looking out on the central square, through which could be seen to great advantage the adjacent buildings and the colossal statue of the king. Minos rose as we approached, and hardly waiting for the ceremony of introduction, grasped my hand warmly, and said:

"Alexander, I am very glad to see you, and I bid you a hearty welcome to our country. You are the first Englishman to set foot in Ionia, and the first European we have seen for three hundred years. I am afraid we are not a very hospitable people, and we are so well satisfied with ourselves that we have no desire to have the rest of the world come and find out all the great things we have accomplished and admire them. On the contrary we should be very well content to go on living in our own way, and allow the rest of the world to go on its way without ever suspecting our existence. But we have an idea that the way of the world at large is a very bad way, and some of us have had rather an uneasy spot in our consciences in regard to our fellow-creatures on the other side of the mountains which guard our country so securely. While the outside world has been stumbling blindly on in the old, bad way of short-sighted folly, we have attained to a higher level of light and truth, and breathe a purer and diviner air. It is true that humanity at large accepts all its miseries as inevitable, and calmly lays upon God the responsibility of its sins and sufferings, but we know that these are not necessary elements of human life, which can be made wholly admirable, worthy and felicitous. And thus the question has often forced itself upon us whether we are justified in keeping to ourselves the benefits which our wise laws have insured to us, rather than risking our own well-being by proclaiming our existence to our fellow-men, and endeavoring to bring them round to the adoption of our laws and customs. During the last hundred years many of our citizens have offered to go out into the world as missionaries and teach men how to live, but our fore-fathers have refused permission to those who thus sought to make martyrs of themselves on the ground that the danger to our own well-being was infinitely greater than the prospect of benefit to those whom we in the fashion of our ancestors still call barbarians.

"But we feel the responsibility just the same, and my friend Jason and I have often talked of it, and he it was, I think, that suggested the middle course of finding in the outside world a man entirely devoted to the interests of his fellows; a man of intelligence and liberal ideas, and bringing him here to see with his own eyes what has been accomplished by following the dictates of reason and common sense. I gave the proposition my hearty acquiescence, and he has been seeking the man we wanted through every country in Europe, but seeking in vain until some lucky chance enabled him to make your acquaintance, and it did not take him long to decide that you were worthy of our confidence. He wrote me a long letter explaining the work you were engaged in, and the spirit which animated you, and without a day's delay I caused a telegram to be sent him authorizing him to bring you back with him.

"And so you can understand that when I tell you I am glad to see you, it is in no formal spirit of politeness, but spoken from the heart, and your arrival takes from me a burden which my old shoulders are weary of, and I am beyond measure relieved to have it assumed by you, who although you are so young, have already proved yourself wiser than many hoary headed sages of your country."

"I have no words," said I, "to express the greatness of the honor you have done me, nor do I underestimate the greatness of the responsibility you invite me to assume. Far be it from me to decline it, for it has been the dream of my life to deliver the less fortunate of my fellow-countrymen from the load of misery under which they have suffered. I am rejoiced to think that perhaps after all my dreams may in some measure be realized, but it may be that I am one of those fools who rush in where angels fear to tread, and I would ask you, Minos, in all reverence and respect, why it is that you in your ripe wisdom are so willing to place so great a trust in me, who am not only young and inexperienced, but up to this day, a total stranger to you?"

"Nay, Alexander, not a stranger. Although you do not know me, I know you very well, and while I know much that is good, I know nothing that is evil, and nothing that would render you unfit to be entrusted with this great responsibility. Although I have never been out of Ionia, I know a great deal of the world beyond. I have seen it with Jason's eyes, and heard it through his ears, and even if you were a stranger to me as you say, I rely on his judgment as if it were my own, and when he says, 'This is the man we have sought,' it is enough, and it would ill become me to put you through a course of examination as to the character of your aspirations or the extent of your learning. And so, Alexander, while I hope to become better acquainted with you before you leave us, it will simply be in friendship, and not in any spirit of criticism or uncertainty as to your fitness for the task we have imposed upon you. Jason's friend is above suspicion."

"I am afraid," I said, "you compliment me far more highly than my poor merits would warrant. I could wish no higher title than that of Jason's friend," and offering my hand to Mr. Delphion, I said: "I trust I shall never disgrace that title."

"You never will," said he. "And let me tell you that our archon is not given to flattery. I have never heard him praise a man so much as he has done you, but the greatness of the occasion warrants it. I have chosen you amongst all the men I have ever met as the only one fit to be entrusted with this great task, and it is well that you should know in what esteem you are held by us."

"It is a great responsibility, and although I do not shrink from it I fear that the consequences of it will weigh upon my spirits and interfere with the perfect enjoyment of my visit."

"This must not be," said Minos; "you are here as our guest, and your stay is to be a long one, and it would be a matter of great regret to us if you did not find it a time of unalloyed pleasure. Nor must you hold yourself as unreservedly committed to the work of reforming mankind on the lines laid down by our forefathers here in Ionia. It may well be that you will come to the conclusion that our laws and customs are too much at variance with the prejudices and superstitions of the modern Europeans and their descendants ever to be adopted by them. We could not blame you in such case, for it would merely show that you had reached the opinion which our own public men have always entertained. And if you should, after mature deliberation, come to such a decision, we have an alternate proposition to make to you, and that is, that you should cast in your lot with us, and we shall confer upon you the citizenship of Ionia.

"Therefore, I say to you that it is your duty to throw aside all care and thought of the future, and get all the pleasure you can out of the opportunity which Providence and Jason Delphion have thrown in your way, especially as it is one which no one else in Europe has ever had or is likely to have. Leave the future alone for the time being; the question of deciding about your duty may well be postponed for a few months, and we can talk about it when your season of holiday is coming to an end."

"I shall do my best to act entirely upon your advice, and for the present I thank you with all my heart for the kindness and the honor you have heaped upon me today."

We then took our leave, and returned by the way we came, except that we sailed through the southern canal instead of the western, and went round the island before returning; and from every point of view it appeared beautiful beyond all my past experience or conception.

The evening of that day I remember as the first of many pleasant evenings spent in the family circle of Delphion. We had two visitors and no more, and they seemed on such intimate relations with the family of my host that I saw they were almost looked upon as belonging to it. They interested me greatly from the first moment. One was a young man of herculean build, not quite so tall as Dion, but with such development of chest and muscle as showed him to be a man of extraordinary physical strength. His head was a mass of short curls of very fair hair, and his blue eyes and tawny moustache marked him as more of a Teuton than a Greek. His sister, a young girl of about twenty, was also a pure blonde, with a figure in which perfect grace showed in combination with a suggestion of the muscular strength which her brother possessed to such a remarkable degree.

When they entered the room my host introduced us, saying:

"Here are two of our friends, who might almost claim to be of your race, for their ancestors came from Holland. Your name is already known to them, and I have the pleasure of introducing you to Daphne Van Tromp and Leonidas Van Tromp." The lady graciously bowed, but Leonidas shook hands very warmly, and yet with extreme gentleness, for I felt that he could have crushed mine to a pulp with the slightest pressure if he had wished to.

"Since Jason has suggested it," said he, "I welcome you as a fellow-countryman. You at least know more of the country of my ancestors than I do, and I might say than I ever wish to know, for you have been there and can tell us that it is a land of fog and marsh, which would seem a very undesirable place to live in after Ionia."

"I have only been here one day, and yet I can assure you that any other country in the world would appear bleak and poor beside yours."

"We know that well," said the Gothic Hercules, "and you will find very few of us anxious to emigrate. And yet those Hollanders were good men and good patriots in the old days—that is, about the time that my forefathers emigrated. They made the first successful fight for political liberty in the modern world, and I am not ashamed to be called Hollander, but, indeed, we are all partly Hollander, and partly Hellenist, and our friend Jason has probably as much Dutch blood in him as I."

"How can you expect Alexander to believe that when he knows that your name is Van Tromp, and sees your Teutonic blood showing in your hair?"

"Oh, these are merely outward signs," said Leonidas. "There are other things to go by than these. For instance, I know and you know, too, that Jason can speak Dutch just like a native. Took to it just like a duck to the water, while I do not know a single word of it except my own name. That proves Dutch blood surely, if anything could."

"But I also speak Russian," said Jason, "and to be consistent you must hold that I am a Slav as well as a Hollander."

Leonidas made some reply, but I failed to catch its import, for I was absorbed in watching the pretty group on the other side of the room. Daphne sat between Leda and Eurydice, her bright golden hair and laughing blue eyes showing to the greatest advantage beside the darker tresses and eyes of her companions. They were in animated conversation, speaking their own language in soft, modulated tones, which sounded like sweet music. They represented three different types of beauty, but each of them seemed perfection embodied, and, if I had been called upon like Paris to determine which was the most admirable, I should have been quite at a loss for a decision.

Presently they ceased talking, and listened to my host, who was recounting some of his experiences in European capitals. He appeared to have met all the leading men in Europe, and to have much more than a newspaper knowledge of their characters. But his remarks were not confined to public men; he gave us many descriptions of private life in different countries, from Sweden to Spain, and from Scotland to Turkey, and depicted each with such absolute fidelity as made us laugh heartily at the idiosyncrasies of the different nations.

During a momentary pause the lady Helen asked him to tell us about his first meeting with me, and he gave a very vivid account of the meeting in Musgrave Hall. He told of the thread-bare garments and anxious looks of the people in the audience who had come there in the vain expectation of hearing something that would give them some hope of an improvement in their condition; and then he described the speakers and quoted verbatim from their grandiose orations. There was something laughable in hearing their high-sounding phrases repeated in cold blood, but I noticed that the effect produced on his hearers was that of anger and disgust. Leonidas especially seemed to boil over with indignation at the thought of such paltry demagogues swaying the minds of poor, ignorant men, his great fist was clenched on his knee, and the veins in his temples swelled like whip-cords, and if they had been within his reach, the people's orators would have been in a pitiful case. But Jason went on to tell of our meeting and the work I had done amongst the poor of London, and of our little country village, and of all that my mother was doing for the poor people there, and interested his auditors very much in the sayings and doings of our Chingford folk. When he had finished, the ladies expressed a great admiration for the character of my mother, whom they all said they would like to meet, and asked me if I could not bring her to Ionia. I assured them that I should like to do so above all things, but that I felt certain she could never be induced to make so long a journey, and, as she would consider it, one attended with so much peril, even if she could make up her mind to be away from her faithful villagers for a sufficient length of time, which I thought would be out of the question. "But, on the other hand," I continued, "if it would be possible for any of you ladies to visit her she would be delighted to reciprocate the hospitality which I am now enjoying."

The lady Helen replied:

"That would be a great pleasure to anyone of us, but unfortunately it is not within our power. It is one of the unwritten laws of the land, understood and acknowledged to be binding on all, that none shall leave Ionia without file consent of the government, and except for occasional hunting parties, none have ever crossed the mountains but those who go upon government business. For my part I have often thought that I should like to see Athens and Rome, Paris and London, but at the same time I have felt that the condition of the common people in European countries must be very distressing to witness, and I am satisfied that a visit to any of them would arouse so many painful emotions that there would be little pleasure in satisfying one's curiosity in regard to them."

"Pardon me," said I, "perhaps I do not understand you, but it seems to me that you would see but little to shock you unless you sought out the poor and the distressed with a view of affording them charitable relief."

"It may be difficult to make you understand our way of looking at these things," said my hostess, "but when you have been here some little time and have seen for yourself that the terms affluence and poverty have no meaning for us, you will see how the division of society into rich and poor appears to us a dreadful and unnatural state of things.

ALEXANDER CRAIG

That any considerable body of the people should have to toil throughout their whole lives for little more than suffices to keep body and soul together, indicates a condition so little better than slavery that it is hard for us to understand the difference. And that is just the state of things we should be compelled to witness in any part of Europe we might visit. Is it not so?"

"I am afraid it is," said I.

"Is it true," said Leonidas, "that many men in England work hard all their days and have to go to the work-house when they become old and infirm, and are at last buried in pauper's graves?"

"Such cases are not uncommon, but I believe they are now the exception, whereas I fear that formerly they were the rule among the rural laborers."

"That is a dreadfully unjust state of things," said Leonidas. "The man who works hard all his life certainly earns vastly more than a mere pittance; if he gets no more he has been deprived of the greater portion of his wages, and to treat him as a pauper at the end is adding wanton insult to injury. But I cannot understand why men should submit to it if they know anything about the earth they live in. Why do they not emigrate to new countries, where their labor will be of more value? I understand that these poor men marry and have families. Why do they not deny themselves of these luxuries for a time and work hard and live hard until they are able to betake themselves to Canada or New Zealand?"

"Because, in the first place, they know very little about the world at large, and in the second, their way of life does not seem to them so hard as it does to you. Their fathers and grandfathers lived just as they do, and their priests tell them that it is a virtue to be content with the lot to which God has called them."

"Then, apparently, the church is in league with the state for the purpose of keeping the poor people where they are, and preventing them from improving their condition. But I beg your pardon, Alexander; here am I vilifying your countrymen to your face before you have been twenty-four hours in Ionia. I am afraid that in respect of good manners you must already be of the opinion that there is at least one Ionian who would do well to go to England and take lessons."

"On the contrary," said I, "it was I who introduced the subject, and I am really anxious that you should tell me frankly what in your opinion are the worst features of our European civilization, for in that way my eyes may be opened to observe many points of difference that otherwise might escape me. You will, therefore, be doing me the greatest possible kindness if you will continue to criticize our English customs and institutions."

"Excuse me," said the blonde Hercules, "I am too impulsive, too apt to let my feelings run away with me. I would rather listen while you discuss this, matter with Dion or the young ladies."

As no one spoke, I proceeded to elicit opinions by questioning each, and first, turning to Dion, I asked him to tell me wherein he considered us most backward as a people.

"I have not given the matter very careful attention," said he, "but in reading books about the English, especially books written by themselves, one thing has always struck me painfully, and that is, the way in which those who are in high station are worshiped by all the others."

"Worshiped! Is that word not rather strong?"

"Not to my mind. They are addressed as 'My lord,' 'Your grace,' 'Your majesty,' and so on, and you will hardly find terms of stronger adulation in your prayer-book. Then the slightest movements and actions of these great ones are chronicled in your journals as if they were events upon which the fate of the world depended. Their births, marriages and deaths are recorded with fulsome details, and even their slightest movements, as, for instance, how they pass their evenings, where they ate their dinners, how they amused themselves afterwards, what dresses the ladies wore, and how they decked themselves out with diamonds and pearls, and so on, are all considered of sufficient importance to appear in public print. I do not speak of England alone, but of all the other European nations as well, and republican America is not a whit better. They have no lords or titled ladies there, it is true, but they worship their millionaires in just the same way, and every newspaper in its 'society' column proves the profound scepticism of the people in regard to the first article of their political creed—that all men are born equal. Your English author, Thackeray, writes very amusingly about this attitude of mind in his 'Book of Snobs,' but at the same time proclaims it as a universal failing, from which he allows that he is by no means exempt himself. I suppose it is an inevitable result of the inequitable division of wealth, which is so universal in the outside world, but it is nonetheless pitiful, both in those who give and those who receive such degrading homage."

"I am sure you are right, Dion, and yet I must confess it has never appeared to me in so very objectionable a light, for we are so used to the idea that the mass of the people must be not only poor, but badly educated and deficient in intelligence as well, that it seems very natural that they should look up to the lords of the soil as beings of a superior order to their own. I fear we have to accomplish a great reformation before there can be any great change in this particular, but please tell me of someother flaws in our social system; it is most interesting to know how these things appear to you, who are entirely free from our native prejudices."

"Ask the ladies," said Dion; "they have not spoken yet."

"Indeed," said his mother, "it was I who began this criticising which Alexander takes so graciously, but perhaps he would like to hear what the young ladies think of Europe."

"Indeed I should," said I; "if they will be frank and tell me the very worst. Leda, will you help me by saying wherein we show our barbarism most?"

"I should not think of using the word barbarous to such highly civilized people as the English, French or Germans, who have produced such splendid literature, and have advanced so far in science and art, and yet one cannot glance at any of your newspapers without seeing much that is distressing to think of, and astonishing when we consider that it exists, side by side, with much culture, wealth and refinement. For that reason I very seldom look at a European paper, although we have a number of the more prominent ones on file in the ladies' public library, but the other day I chanced to look over the 'Times' and noticed a statement there in regard to the school children of Vienna to the effect that a very large proportion of them were in a state bordering on starvation; that they were clothed in rags, and that they scarcely knew what it was to be warm, except when they came to school. Now it may be that this is an exceptional condition of things, and yet we are forced to believe that in all the cities of Europe a large proportion of the children are brought into the world without any provision for the tender nurture and education which, amongst us, is the birth-right of everyone. The thought of the helpless innocents enduring hunger, cold, and every other privation, is a very distressing one, and I am unable to understand how the people who are well to do can find any pleasure in comfortable surroundings when they know that such cruel suffering exists in their immediate neighborhood."

"I think, Leda," said I, "you have pointed out the greatest blot in our modern civilization. We have made much progress in many ways, and we have the poor always with us in undiminished numbers, and many children are crying for bread in cities of almost countless wealth. Much is done by private charity and government measures to relieve distress, and yet it never seems to be sensibly diminished. The truth is we do not know how to cure this great evil, and I am here in the hope of finding out how you have done away with poverty in order that we may, if possible, profit by your example.

"And now, Daphne, will you please give me the benefit of your thoughts?"

"After Eurydice," said she, "I will tell you; if I can think of anything sufficiently bad."

"Well, then, Eurydice, will you please tell me wherein you think us most imperfect?"

"There is one thing that has jarred upon my feelings in reading books by European authors, and that is, that some kinds of labor are looked upon amongst you as degrading. A man who works with his hands is supposed to be a common, uneducated, ignorant person, and no gentleman is supposed to earn his living in any but the learned professions. Now with us it is different; all work is equally honorable, and, although brain work is undoubtedly of higher quality than hand work, you will find that our mechanics are not looked down upon by artists or literary men, for the simple reason that they are just as likely as not their equals in general intelligence. If you attend any of the receptions given by the mayor or the president of the university you will be sure to find groups of ladies and gentlemen discussing some difficult problem of astronomy or biology; and of the principal speakers you will find that one is a professor of natural history, another a carpenter, and a third may be the man who steered your boat today to the Acropolis. This question touches me personally, and that is why it has occupied my attention more than any other in reading European books. If this were a European household I should be entirely out of place in the family sitting room, my place would be the kitchen, and Jason and Helen, instead of being like a second father and mother to me, would be my master and mistress, and I should be simply their servant, which means little different from a slave."

"What you have said, Eurydice, proves to me more than anything else how vast is the difference between our civilization and yours. For the fact that so few professions are open to gentlemen amongst us simply shows what a miserable minority our gentlemen, taking the word in the sense of men of culture, are, compared with the bulk of the community. If your mechanics are able to hold learned discussions with your professors, then I am sure that our savants could sit with advantage at the feet of the undergraduates, and it is almost discouraging to think that we are so very far behind in intellectual progress. Nevertheless, I thank you for pointing out this essential point of difference, which shall have my most careful attention, and if you are almost infinitely in advance of us it will give us the advantage of a higher standard to aim at, and our progress ought to be correspondingly great.

"And now, Daphne, you see I am far from sinking under this load of condemnation, and we shall be glad to hear what you have to add to it. Do not spare us, I beg of you."

"It is an ungracious task you have imposed upon us," said the lovely blonde, "but as you ask us to be perfectly frank and candid, I may say that what appears to me to be the most appalling of all the disadvantages you labor under is the continual presence amongst you of disease in its most dreadful forms. I understand that in your large cities such fearful diseases as typhoid fever, scarlet fever, diphtheria and even small-pox are always present in greater or less virulence, and that they spare neither old nor young, rich nor poor, and the consequence is that you do not, on the average, live half your days. Consumption appears to find its victims everywhere, and cuts off young men and women by the thousand in the very bloom of their youth. Nothing can surely be sadder than to see youth or maiden droop and die just when all the brightest hopes of life are blossoming, unless it be to see little children carried off by agonizing sickness just when they have wound themselves most tightly round the affections of their parents. I understand that a large proportion of the children born in Europe die before they are two years old, and it makes me wonder whether it is the ignorance of the parents or the incompetence of the doctors or the callousness of the governing powers that is most to blame."

Daphne's expression as she spoke was one of infinite tenderness and compassion, and I remained silent for a minute before undertaking to reply. At last I said:

"All you have said is true, but I never realized the unspeakable sadness of it before. Whatever we are accustomed to seems natural, and we become indifferent to it. In a time of war men become used to seeing their comrades fall around them, and their appetite for the next meal is unimpaired. In a plague-stricken city people see the bodies of their neighbors carried off in the dead cart by day or by night, and become indifferent to the horrors around them until their own turn comes. So we in Europe know that children are being constantly stricken down under the eyes of their parents, mothers taken away from their babes, husbands from their wives, and youths and maidens from their families, and so long as the fell destroyer keeps aloof from our own hearth and home we think nothing of it, for it has always been so. Jason has told me that in this land of yours these things do not happen, or only in exceptional cases; if it is the rule that men and women die only in the fullness of their years, when they have tasted all the sweets of life, and fall asleep only when the fountain of their existence is exhausted, then yours is, indeed, a blessed land, and I shall be able to make all men's ears tingle with the tale."

"I have never known a young person die," said Daphne. "Accidents do sometimes happen, but they are very rare. No one has died under ninety years old in our family for generations, and almost everyone you meet will tell you the same about their own. That seems to us the natural state of things, and it is difficult for us to understand why it should be so very different elsewhere."

"Nor can I explain it to you. Doubtless our ignorance is at the bottom of it all. You spoke of ignorance on the part of the parents, apathy on the part of the ruling powers, and incompetence on the part of the medical profession. The first two causes may certainly be credited with a large part of the responsibility, but as for the last, I had supposed that our physicians and surgeons were very learned and skillful. I should like to hear what our host has to say upon that point."

"From personal experience," Jason said, "I am not in a position to speak, for I have never had occasion to consult a European medical man at anytime. I have met some of them personally and found them very intelligent, well-bred gentlemen, but I have seldom known them to save a life in danger, and I have known them to fail in many cases where I thought they ought to have succeeded. They are banded together like the members of a trades' union, and whether the patient lives or dies they are very careful to collect their fees whereever it is possible to do so. I may wrong many of them in saying this, and one would gather a very different impression from reading some of your foremost authors.

"They tell us of large-hearted men of wonderful ability and learning, working day and night for the good of the community, and that with an absolute indifference to monetary reward. Unfortunately I have never personally known of any such cases, but on the contrary, I have sometimes been disgusted with the grasping spirit of practitioners who limited their fee only by the extent of their client's supposed fortune. For instance, I have a friend in Paris, the head of a large jewelry firm named Lapointe and Company, whose little daughter was taken sick about two years ago. The operation of tracheotomy was performed, and the child speedily got well, and M. Lapointe, who loved her passionately, would gladly and gratefully have paid a good round fee to the surgeon who had undertaken the case. But when he received a bill for fifteen thousand francs, his feelings were changed, and he flatly refused to pay it. He was no millionaire, business had been dull for a year or two, and fifteen thousand francs was more than he could well spare. In a weak moment he allowed the question to be arbitrated by a jury of physicians, and they unanimously decided that the fee was just and proper, and ought to be paid; and it was. When the physicians carry on their work in the full glare of publicity, as when the head of a nation is stricken, they show themselves as helpless as so many children, but this does not prevent their trying to enrich themselves by charging enormous sums for helping the patient to die. Their fees would be many times too large if they had saved their patient, but it is the opportunity of a life-time, and they seize it like bandits when they have a prince to ransom.

"Were the salvation of Great Britain intrusted to my hands with the powers of absolute dictatorship, the first thing I should do would be to summon all the doctors and all the lawyers, and at least nineteen-twentieths of the clergy to London, and ship them off to the antipodes. I should give them land and seed and agricultural implements, and a supply of food for a few months, and let them shift for themselves. Then I should set to work with some hope of success with the people accustomed to work for an honest living.

"Without the doctors' pills and potions they would be able to live in health and die in peace; without lawyers to foment their differences they would avoid civil disputes or settle them quickly by arbitration; without the clergy to stir up theological strife they would forget their religious differences and work together in harmony for the general improvement.

"The vast sums which these professional gentlemen have drawn from the resources of the people would support all the poor people who were too old to work, as well as all the orphans and incapables, and educate the children in a thorough and practical way, and leave a large fund besides for much needed reforms; and in two generations at most the millennium would dawn upon England."

"What an opportunity the English people lost when they let you come away," said Leonidas.

"Why did you not ask Queen Victoria to resign?" said his sister.

"And then I might have been an empress," said the lady Helen.

"And I a princess imperial," said Leda.

"I wonder how it would feel to be Prince of Wales?" said Dion.

"And you could not have done less than make me a duke," said Leonidas.

And so they went on while Jason said never a word, evidently well pleased that they should have a little fun at his expense, but when their sarcasm exhausted itself, he turned to me and said, gravely:

"I was wrong, Alexander, entirely wrong. As dictator I could manage the people of England well enough, but my unruly family would bring my gray hairs with sorrow to the grave in less than six months."

At this Leonidas sprang to his feet, and assuming a tragic pose, said, in a voice that sounded like distant thunder:

"And so perish all tyrants!"

"Amen, amen!" cried all the rest.

"And thus you see," continued Jason, "how demoralizing is the effect of exalted station on people who are not born to it, for these young persons, ordinarily most dutiful and affectionate, are so carried away by the thought of it that they are gloating in imagination over my untimely death. But let us talk of something nearer to us at present than the British Empire. I mean the national games. I have yet to learn who are to be the contestants in the principal races, and Alexander will doubtless wish to know a little more about the great celebration in which he is to assist as our most honored guest."

But our hostess suggested that it was time for a little supper, and so it was at the table that the coming festival was discussed, and that with such lively interest that I began to catch a little of the true Hellenic enthusiasm for physical beauty and manly sports. The ladies seemed to look forward to the great event as eagerly as the gentlemen, and I thought how fortunate were the young men who carried away the prizes under the admiration of such beautiful eyes.

VI

A Model City

Remorselessly at six o'clock next morning Dion called me and intimated that it was time to dress for the early swim, and although I responded immediately to the summons I could not refrain from the liveliest regrets at my consenting to be roused at such an untimely hour. But when we were once outside, the glorious beauty of the scene and the freshness of the morning air made me feel that the sacrifice of a little sleep was already repaid. The "Quarry" was just a little way off on the other side of the hill, which rose behind the row of houses where my friends live, and we walked along at a rapid pace, Leda chatting gaily with her brother and myself, and looking, if possible, more divinely beautiful than ever in her exquisitely simple morning dress. A number of swiftly moving barges were crossing the lake towards the canal or stream which communicates with the quarry, and the air was filled with the sound of the talk and laughter of the passengers with which they were crowded. Young people they were mostly, though not without a sprinkling of gray beards, and the handsomest, happiest looking crowds of people I had ever seen. A very few minutes' walk brought us to our destination, a sheet of water about a quarter of a mile in extent, beautifully clear, so that one could distinctly see the bottom of white marble rock, except where the precipitous sides were reflected as in a mirror. The walls were very high, and just as the quarrymen had left them, except that to the height of forty feet they had been cut into galleries supported by Doric columns, behind which were the dressing rooms, hewn out of solid marble. In the center rose an island of the native rock, on which was a miniature temple, adorned with finely executed statuary. The road we followed was considerably above the water level, and landed us at the second gallery, from which at this point, steps led straight down into the water. Already a great many people were disporting themselves in the crystal element, and although their dresses were more modest than those to be seen at our sea-side resorts, especially those of the males, yet it seemed to me that I had never seen such grace of form and motion as was exhibited by these splendid swimmers. We separated here from our fair companions, the ladies' dressing rooms being on one side, and those of the gentlemen on the other. As I followed Dion along the gallery, I was quite absorbed in watching the motion of the bathers below, who seemed to be in their natural element: practicing every variety of stroke, and diving below the surface like ducks. My attention was suddenly arrested by a couple of strange looking monsters coming straight down the center of the pond at an enormous rate of speed.

"What are those strange creatures, Dion?" I exclaimed. "They look like seals, but what are they doing here?"

"They are men," said he, "in racing suits. They are rather out of place here, and are only allowed early in the morning. After half past six they must retire in favor of those in ordinary bathing dress, and as it is close upon that time they are taking their last spin. Let us stand here a moment, and if they come as far before turning you will be able to see them distinctly. You see they are on their backs, and have a rubber hood which fits tightly on the head and shoulders to enable them to cut the water like aquatic animals. Now before they turn look at their hands and feet. You see they have elastic edges which open out with the stroke and hold the water like a hollow vessel but making no resistance to the return. On their lower limbs are flounces an inch deep, three of them between the ankle and the knee, which open just far enough to take a hold of the water as they shoot their feet out, and close against the leg as they draw them back. These devices render the limbs of a man equal in purchase to the fins of a fish, and enable him to rival the fish in speed. But as I was saying, this is not the place for racing; the open lake is the place for that."

Before he had done speaking the two strange looking figures had almost disappeared. They had turned just about opposite us, and gone back the way they came, cleaving the water with astonishing speed, not less, I should say, than ten miles an hour.

Walking a little farther, Dion showed me a dressing room which I could use, and requested an attendant to furnish me with a suitable bathing suit, and in a few minutes we were ready for the plunge. Descending by the nearest stairway, we dived at once into deep water and found it deliriously cool and exhilarating. By this time the water was so full of swimmers that I wondered whether we should be able to find Leda amongst them all, but she had been before us, and had already crossed from the other side, and almost as soon as we came to the surface she had joined us, and we shaped our course for the central island. I swam my hardest so as not to keep them back, but they made no effort to distance me, although I knew by the easy way in which they made their strokes, chatting with each other as they went, that they could easily have left me far behind if they wished. Presently we arrived at the island temple, and landing on some steps in front, we passed into the interior, which was adorned with handsome statuary, representing gods and heroes of ancient Greece. A stairway on one side led to the top of the walls, and thither we followed some of the other bathers who had preceded us. The temple was built without a roof, and on three sides it rose perpendicular from the water to a height of some thirty feet. From this height most of the bathers dived as soon as they reached it, and Dion asked me if I could do likewise. I said I could not, but would be glad to see him and Leda do it. And this they did without hesitation, flying through the air as gracefully as a pair of eagles swooping down from the sky; then when they had turned themselves in the water they joined hands, and with light, graceful strokes slowly swam to the surface, which they reached about eighty feet away. It was a lovely sight to witness, but I had no mind to emulate their example, and by the more inglorious way of the staircase I reached the steps again where I found them awaiting me.

Leda now proposed a visit to the cave of Poseidon, which she said was only a hundred yards off and well worth a visit. So we swam to the opposite side, and through a low, but wide archway, into what seemed to me a place of utter darkness, and if Dion had not given me his hand I should have been utterly bewildered. In a few moments, however, when the sunlight left my eyes, I began to see the outlines of the place. It was a long, vaulted cavern, with a watery floor, and on each side were steps, extending the whole length of the cave and reaching to the bottom of the arch of the roof. On these a number of the bathers were seated, and we took our place amongst them on one of the upper steps near the farther end. I now saw that what light there was proceeded from the water itself. Below the surface the walls were perpendicular, and a row of electric lamps ran round the bottom, so that while the upper portion of the water was comparatively dark, the lower part was perfectly illuminated. The great feature of the cave, however, was immediately beneath us, and consisted of a representation of the golden temple of Poseidon. Twelve statues, representing twelve of the ancient Grecian deities, stood in a circle on the floor, supporting a richly carved entablature, and in the space enclosed sat the sea-god on a car drawn by dolphins, his trident upright in his right hand. All this was exquisitely carved in white marble and brightly illuminated with a flood of rich yellow light from cunningly concealed lamps, so that the effect was really that of a temple of gold. In and out through the twelve openings swam and floated living forms as graceful and perfect as those of sculptured gods and goddesses.

I looked on this wonderful sight in silence and admiration for a few seconds, and then, turning to Leda, said:

"I owe you a thousand thanks for bringing me here. I never saw anything so ravishingly beautiful before."

"It is indeed lovely," said she. "Almost worth coming from England to see,—is it not?"

"But there are Leonidas and Daphne. Will you not bring them here, Dion?"

And her brother dived swiftly into the water, and for the moment disappeared. I stood up to see if I could distinguish our two friends amongst the amphibians below, and there stood Leonidas grasping the trident to steady himself, while his other hand held one of Daphne's. His figure showed to no disadvantage beside the massive form of Poseidon, while Daphne might have been taken for Venus herself, about to rise from the sea, except that there was more of drapery about her than the goddess is usually supposed to wear. Presently Dion was beside them, but by this time they had been a good many seconds below, and were under the necessity of coming to the surface to breathe. Daphne gave her free hand to Dion, Leonidas let go his hold of the trident, and the three floated gently upward out of the illuminated space into the darker water above, where we lost sight of them, but presently they came up the steps and joined us.

There were probably fifty or sixty people in the cave, but the perpendicular walls at the ends echoed every sound so sharply that there seemed a perfect babel of talk going on, as if thousands of people were gathered together in the comparatively small space, and everyone talking his hardest to everyone else. There was no shouting or screaming, but a confused, low murmur, which neither gained nor diminished in volume, but suddenly there was a shrill bugle call from the other side, and midway between the two ends. It was only a human voice, but the imitation was so perfect that I thought the sound came from a brass instrument. Everybody stopped speaking, so that the bugler might have it all to himself, and as the sound of these voices died away and the echoes caught the bugle notes and repeated them again and again, it seemed as if a whole company of buglers were playing together, and each trying to outpeal the others. When the voice ceased, the echoes gradually became fainter and fainter, as if withdrawn to distances more and more remote. When they had altogether ceased, the same voice, or another equally clear and resonant, commenced singing a kind of a chant, which sounded pleasant enough, but had very little melody. The tones of it, however, must have been skillfully arranged, for before three lines had been sung, the echoes furnished the most harmonious chords as an accompaniment; the effect was very fine, and filled the cave with a weird, unearthly kind of harmony. This was also allowed to die away into silence, the last whispering notes seeming the sweetest of all, and then the singer gave vent to a loud "Ha," which, being echoed rapidly from end to end, had all the effect of a peal of laughter so natural as to be contagious, and forcing the audience to join in real laughter almost in spite of themselves. This was the signal to go, and everybody took to the water and swam out in swift procession to the open air. As our time was up, we all made for the points from which we had started, but all the way down Dion and Leonidas kept gamboling like a pair of dolphins, now under the water and now on the surface, playing all sorts of tricks, and seemingly able to live without air for a surprising length of time, for they never came up panting, and would dive again after a breath or two just as if the water were their natural element.

On the way home, I asked Dion if all the people in Ionia were expert swimmers, or if those I had seen this morning were the exception?

In reply he said:

"Every person in Ionia above the age of six or seven can swim. It is part of our education, and one of the first things that are taught us. Everywhere there is abundance of water. Those parts of the country that are far from the lake have the river or the canals, and every city and town has large open-air swimming baths like the one we have just been enjoying ourselves in. Every school has shallow tanks for the use of the young children, and it is impossible for anyone to grow up amongst us without acquiring the art of swimming. Our climate is favorable to it, too, for open-air bathing is enjoyable for nine or ten months in the year, and as it is a very healthful exercise, it is neglected by no one, and the result is, as you have seen this morning, we are not far from being amphibious animals."

"It appears to me," said I, "that you can turn yourselves into aquatic animals altogether when you please, for those two men we saw this morning in the racing suits, as you called them, seemed more like seals than men. Is that kind of swimming much in vogue amongst you?"

"It is practiced only by a few, and does not add very much to the pleasure of swimming, for it is very fatiguing until one becomes used to it, and makes diving almost impossible. The choice of positions is very limited, as you must swim either on your back or on the right or left side. On the other hand it is very safe, for the hood is inflated with air, and those who are accustomed to it can accomplish long distances in a short time. It is no unusual thing for a party of two or three to leave the city in the morning, swim the whole length of the lake, and, after a little rest and refreshment, start on the return trip and finish it before night."

"Well, it is a wonderful accomplishment to beat the fish in their own element but I think the ordinary swimming is good enough for me. I feel much refreshed by the morning exercise, and I mean to repeat it if you do not find me in the way."

"On the contrary, we are delighted to have you with us, and you swim like one of ourselves, so you must come every morning until the cold weather sets in."

"You flatter me too much, Dion, but I mean to take advantage of the opportunity and try to improve by your example."

As soon as breakfast was over that morning my host intimated to me that his chief business for the present was to make me better acquainted with the people and the country, and if I felt inclined, he proposed that we should go for a ride through the city and see some of its chief thoroughfares and buildings. In this I, of course, readily acquiesced, wondering at the same time what kind of carriage we should ride in, as I had not as yet seen any of their vehicles, except at a distance. When we were ready to start, he took me to the coach-house in the rear portion of the grounds, and there showed me no less than eight handsome carriages of various sizes, made to carry from two to six persons, some open and others covered. They were of light construction, beautifully painted, and all as bright and clean as if they had just left the carriage factory.

"What handsome vehicles these are," I said. "You must have an excellent coachman to keep them in such splendid order."

"We have no coachman, and need none. There is no dust nor mud on our streets, and the carriages need no more attention than the furniture in the house. But choose which one you will ride in."

I pointed to one of the smallest, which seemed very comfortable for two, and my friend asked me to step in, and he followed and sat down beside me. Then, at the touch of a lever, the carriage backed out, turned, and bowled away over the lawn to the road below. The wheels having rubber tires, a carriage-drive was unnecessary, as they made very little impression on the grass. There was a graceful elegance about this little vehicle, with its finely-moulded front, which made it suggestive of the pretty barges I had seen on the lake, and I smiled as I thought of the clumsy contrivances our horseless carriages are at home, which always look as if they were meant to have horses before them to give them a finished appearance. It was more like sailing, too, than riding on land, for the motion of the pneumatic tires over this perfectly smooth pavement produced neither jar nor noise.

We passed first along the front street, with the lake on our left and the superb buildings of the university on the other,—buildings which I should have said were peerless had I not visited the Acropolis the day before. We turned to the right when we reached the river, and here a scene of extraordinary bustle and activity presented itself. The broad streets and the bridges, which seemed innumerable, were full of vehicles and foot-passengers; the river was covered with boats and vessels of all sizes, moving swiftly up and down, but the din and roar of city streets as we know them was absent, a subdued murmur of human voices and the gentle sound of the tiny waves breaking on the beach behind us were all that could be heard. The soft tires of wagon or carriage made no noise on those immaculately smooth streets, and the vessels, propelled by the same electric force, made no noise in moving up or down the stream. It seemed like enchantment to be in the midst of such a busy scene, and yet be surrounded by almost perfect silence, and I had to rub my eyes more than once before I could persuade myself that I was wide awake, and not dreaming.

"Jason," I said, "you must speak to me, or I shall think I have gone suddenly deaf."

"How so, Alexander? What put such an idea into your head?"

"It seems so unnatural to be in the very heart of a city, with all its active movement going on before your eyes, and yet not hear the roar of business."

My friend laughed and said:

"To tell you the truth, it always seems strange to me, too, when I come back from Europe. But you will soon become accustomed to it, and when you go back you will find the hubbub of London's streets noisy and unpleasant for a time."

"I have no doubt but you are right, and the silence is not at all disagreeable, only I feel as if I were dreaming all the time, and to dispel that idea I want you to keep on talking, and tell me all about what we see. What are those beautiful bridges made of? They look so airy and light that it is hard to believe they are strong enough to bear the traffic which is now passing over them."

"They are of aluminum, which with us serves all the purposes of iron and steel, and a great many other substances besides. You know that it is one of the lightest of metals, and we have found out how to make it hard and tough like finely tempered steel, and its lightness enables us to obtain strength and solidity, with a great saving of material. Iron is a scarce mineral in our mountains, which seemed a great hardship in the early days of our separation from the rest of the world, but ultimately proved the greatest boon, by forcing us to find out how to extract this infinitely more serviceable metal from the rocks and the soil, which contain it in inexhaustible quantities."

"I never saw such handsome bridges or such a magnificent street as this. Palaces on either hand as far as the eye can see, and so many handsome domes and towers rising far and near. What are those splendid structures opposite to us?"

"Those are the city public buildings."

"And these on this side, which are only a little less magnificent?"

"These are mostly hotels and banks."

"And where are the stores, and the workshops, and the dwelling-houses of the people?"

"I shall show you them all before the day is much older. We shall turn to the right at the next corner, and we shall be in Mercer street, where the ladies do a large part of their shopping."

But when we arrived there, I could see nothing resembling our retail shops,—no display windows, no flaunting signs, nothing that I could see to indicate that goods were offered for sale. The street was wide and filled with handsome carriages, the buildings were high and stately, with large plate-glass windows, and on each side were handsome trees, which afforded a continuous shade to pedestrians on the sidewalk, but not tall enough to obscure the light of the windows even of the first story.

"Well," said I, "this is a very pretty street, but where are the stores?"

"All these buildings are stores, and judging by the number of people passing in and out I should say they are doing a very good business."

"But they have no signs out, and no display windows—nothing to attract customers."

"If you look carefully, you will see the merchant's name and business displayed over each door, but the goods inside are the attraction, and the customers will come where they are most satisfactory. In this country we spend very little money in advertising, and it would not pay if we did. Our people do not believe in bargains, but are willing to pay a good price for a good article. We thus save the immense sums which go to support your far too numerous newspapers, as well as the money which is spent in disfiguring your streets and public conveyances. Our wholesale merchants do not keep up an army of commercial travelers or flood the postoffice with lying circulars, and in this way they can do business on a much smaller margin, and the community at large is the gainer to an enormous extent."

"But I do not see how new goods or new business houses can be brought before the public in any other way."

"New lines of goods can easily be introduced by old-established merchants if they are of real value, and of that they are, perhaps, the best judges. As for new business enterprises, they will always be supported if they are required, and if not, they had better be left alone. You are aware that amongst your merchants failure is the rule and success the rare exception, amounting only to some five percent, of all those engaging in business. With us it is the reverse, and such a thing as bankruptcy is almost unknown. Our people are not in such a hurry to get rich as to embark in any undertaking without forethought or the means of compelling success, which are,—capital, experience and good judgment. In this way, we avoid the loss which results from bad debts and from commercial panics, which are impossible in such a community as ours."

"Do you mean me to understand that your merchants and business men enjoy uninterrupted prosperity, and that they never know what dull times are?"

"I mean that they do not encounter the extreme fluctuations in business that your merchants have to contend with. The periods of depression which result in the closing of factories and the swamping of large numbers of commercial houses are caused by lack of confidence in the ability of debtors to meet their obligations, but where there is no inflation of credit there can be no lack of confidence. Now, in Ionia, cash payments are the universal rule, and no one asks or could obtain more credit than what is necessary for the convenience of business. In retail trade, cash payments are the rule for each transaction, and in wholesale business accounts are settled monthly, and if the buyer is unable to liquidate his account on the usual day, his credit is at an end: he can buy no more goods, and must go out of business. Everyone knows this, and therefore it is that no one embarks in trade with the idea of being carried along by credit obtained from the bank or the manufacturer, but first provides himself with sufficient capital to pay his way under all circumstances. Thus you see that such a thing as 'panic' cannot exist, for the soil of credit or financial dependency in which it grows is altogether too limited amongst us for it ever to take root."

"Have you no such thing as joint stock companies?"

"Yes, but their stock is seldom for sale, and is, therefore, not used for speculation. Nearly all our large business houses are joint stock companies, but the shareholders are generally those who are engaged in carrying on the business. Not only the managers but the bookkeepers, clerks and salesmen, and in manufacturing business the foreman and mechanics very commonly own more or less of the stock. The privilege of purchasing it is one of the rewards of zeal and ability, and the result is that there is hardly any such distinction amongst us as employers and employes, for all except those least skilled or competent are interested in the success of each undertaking, and each contributes his best endeavors to produce the finest results."

While giving these explanations my friend had turned our noiseless carriage westward, and we were pursuing a course parallel to the river, and had traversed the entire district devoted to retail trade, which embraced a great many handsome streets. Those we were now entering had a different appearance. The private carriages were fewer and their occupants mostly of the male sex, and large wagons loaded with merchandise came and went in all directions. Yet all this movement was accomplished without noise or confusion; every vehicle of whatever description had wheels provided with pneumatic tires, and, keeping to its own side, was propelled with great speed by electricity. On approaching crossings, they invariably slowed down considerably, and the rules of the road were so well understood and acted upon that there never appeared any danger of collision or blocking of traffic or any occasion for the chaff and bickering which goes on so continuously with our London drivers.

There were a great many magnificent buildings in the streets we now passed through, some of the warehouses occupying whole blocks, and built to last for ages, but always with an eye to artistic effect, and I would fain have lingered to examine at leisure some of those palaces of commerce. But Jason requested me to defer this to another visit, as his intention on this first day was to give me a general idea of the plan of the city, and that would occupy all the time at our disposal. At this point commenced a series of canals communicating with the river, and running at right angles to it alternately with the streets. In this way all the warehouses backed on alleys, which were wider than the streets themselves, each with a navigable canal running through its center. It was here that the business of receiving and shipping goods was done, and the number of vessels which lined the wharves showed how large a part the waterways sustain in the commerce of the country.

The bridges were all of similar construction to those which crossed the river, and seemed so light and fragile as to suggest a doubt of their solidity, but the great volume of traffic which was then passing over them without jar or perceptible vibration, proved them to be as strong in reality as they were airy in appearance. They are constructed entirely of the metal aluminum, and the carriage-way is polished by the passing of vehicles so that it shines like silver.

A few minutes' ride brought us to the manufacturing district, and there, for the first time since we set out on our ride, my ear recognized sounds such as we are wont to call the hum of business.

"Now, at last," I said, "the spell of enchantment is broken, and I can perceive that this is no phantom city. I can hear the whirr of wheels and the beating of hammers, and I am sure that I am wide awake."

"Is there nothing lacking now to make it all seem like perfect reality?"

"Yes; there is the smoke, and grime, and dust. This clear, crystal atmosphere seems out of place in a manufacturing district, and those splendid edifices of stone,—which look as fresh as if built yesterday,—are they really factories?"

"Everyone of them."

"I cannot understand how you manage to carry on all this business without accumulating dirt?"

"The secret lies in electricity, which gives us heat, and light and mechanical force, without smoke and the other waste products of combustion."

"But," said I, "it is not only the earth and the air that are so spotlessly clean, but the water also? The very canals which we cross are full of pure, clear water, and I can see numbers of fishes swimming in their depths."

"The reason of that," said Jason, "is that they are filled with living water. They are fed from a higher level of the river, and there are always currents flowing through them. Stagnant water is always more or less detrimental to health, and we do not suffer such a thing in Ionia. Nor do we allow any impurities to be drained into canal, river or lake. The factories have to dispose of their waste products in someother way, just as the towns and cities do of their sewage, and the community gains not only in health but in wealth as well, for all the waste material is ultimately returned to the soil, which is thereby enriched and made more and more productive."

We had now arrived at a part of the city where the land seemed to occupy less space than the water, for we found ourselves amongst a perfect network of canals and basins. The quiet of the business portion of the city had given place to a babel of sounds produced by the clang of hammers and the buzz of turning-lathes pertaining to the industry of ship-building. Jason stopped the carriage at the door of a handsome office building of granite, and saying that this was the establishment of our friend, Van Tromp, he took me inside, through the countingroom, where several clerks were busy with their ledgers. To one of these Jason spoke, asking if Leonidas was to be seen, and this gentleman conducted us to a large apartment in the rear, where we found the young Goth himself, busy with a number of drawings spread over a large table. Leonidas greeted us warmly, and offered to take us over the yards and show us how ships were built in Ionia.

I said I should be delighted, if it were not taking up too much of his valuable time.

"My time," said he, "could not be spent to a more laudable end, and my work will not suffer, for I always manage to keep abreast of it and never let it get behind. And first," he said, "let me show you some of these models, of which there are, as you see, several hundred in this room."

So he showed us all the different descriptions of sailing craft which he had built,—barges and passenger boats for the river, fishing boats, yachts and larger vessels for lake navigation. Every model seemed perfect of its kind, with exquisite lines for swift sailing and sumptuous cabins for the accommodation of passengers and crew. I noticed that only one or two of the pleasure yachts were fitted with masts, and he explained that sails were only used by a very few who fancied that kind of pastime. All the vessels used in the country were propelled by electricity, and neither masts nor smoke-stacks were required. The bridges over the river would not allow of such useless encumbrances, and the great majority of all the vessels in use, either for passengers or freight, had to pass under these bridges almost daily.

He then invited me to come and see some of the vessels now under construction, and we visited a number of ships, and inspected at least a dozen vessels of various sizes in all stages of progress. I remarked that none of them were very large, and Leonidas reminded me that the voyages they had to make were very short, and that it would hardly pay to build ships which would take longer to load than it would to make their whole trip. The largest vessel we saw was for passengers: it was of about a thousand tons measurement, and was for the lake service, leaving the city each morning and calling at all the principal ports, and returning the same day. Leonidas pointed out that all the vessels were constructed with double hulls, with air spaces between, and that the keel and the ribs divided these spaces into a vast number of air-tight compartments, so that the piercing of the hull in several places would not cause it to sink. In fact, he assured us that it was impossible to sink one of these vessels, even if the water poured into the hold through several large holes, provided the cargo were not of unusually heavy material and greater than the vessel was warranted to carry.

The inner and outer shells were formed of thin plates of aluminum, and I remarked that they seemed of rather weak material for the purpose. For reply Leonidas took up a large sledge-hammer, and, swinging it several times round his head with one hand, struck the side of the vessel by which we were standing a blow which would have shattered an ordinary boiler-plate, but the only result was that the hammer was thrown back with great force by the elasticity of the plate, which showed scarcely any mark from the blow. I took up the hammer itself, which was of bright, white metal, and found it so heavy as to require the strength of both my arms to raise it as high as my head.

"What makes this hammer so heavy?" I asked. "It seems to be made of aluminum, like everything else, but it is much heavier than iron."

"It is aluminum outside," said the ship-builder, "and tempered in a peculiar way, so that it is as hard as glass and tougher than your finest steel, but it has a core of lead, and that gives it the weight required to strike an effective blow."

"I had no idea that it could be so heavy when I saw you swing it with one hand just now, and after that exhibition of your strength I should be very sorry for any man who would be rash enough to quarrel with you."

Leonidas looked very grave at this foolish speech of mine, and said:

"Surely you do not think I would take advantage of the strength of my muscles to hurt anyone! The man who would get into a fight in Ionia would be forever disgraced. We never have any opportunity of fighting, except with bears or tigers in the Indian jungles when we go on our hunting expeditions, and you must join us on the next one we undertake,—that is, if you would find any pleasure in such a thing."

"I did not know that you ever left the country for such a purpose."

"Oh, yes; we do frequently. We go in our air-ships, and accomplish the journey by night to avoid observation. Our aerial mode of traveling enables us to penetrate to parts of the jungle where no other human being ever set foot, and we always find plenty of game."

"I should much like to go with you as a spectator, but I am no sportsman, myself."

"Very well; I will see that you have the opportunity at no very distant date."

"I thank you for that," said I, "and for your valuable time this morning."

"On the contrary," said he, "it is I who have to thank you for honoring my establishment with so early a visit, and if you would but stay a little longer, there are other things about the yards which I might be able to interest you in."

"Someother day, Leonidas," said Jason. "I promised our guest a general view of the city today, and we have not crossed the river yet."

"In that case, I must not hinder you," said Leonidas, "and I hope you will have a pleasant day."

So we left the ship-yard, and, riding eastward, crossed the river by one of its innumerable bridges. We were still surrounded by workshops and factories, the busy hum of which enabled me to realize that I was surrounded by members of my own species, although the architectural magnificence of the various buildings we passed suggested the idea that we were surrounded by the workshops of the gods.

A few minutes of swift riding brought us to a different kind of scene, in which I felt spell-bound, as in the morning, by silence.

We were in the residence district. Wide, straight streets extended in every direction, with breadths of smooth, green grass and rows of handsome shade-trees on each side. Each block was occupied by one great building, with entrances at the corners and in the center of each side. No two blocks were alike, but with a general harmony in height and design, there was great variety in style and material, so that each one as we passed it seemed more perfect in beauty than those that had gone before. After a few minutes of silent admiration, I asked:

"Are these great palaces the residences of your millionaires?"

"Oh, no," said Jason, "this is where our mechanics, and clerks, and all people of ordinary incomes, have their abode. Each family occupies only a suite of rooms, of course, and they find it more economical and convenient than having separate houses. Your English people make a great mistake in spreading your cities over such a vast extent of territory."

"It is a mere prejudice, no doubt," said I, "but an Englishman's house is his castle, and he does not believe in sharing it with anybody else."

"That is all very well when he lives in the country, but in the cities it is the height of folly. The inhabitants of London could have much better habitations than they have now, on a quarter of the space at present occupied. The street architecture and the paving of the streets might be infinitely better, with only half the outlay. The cost of gas and water mains, of street lighting and of transportation would all be reduced to a quarter of what they are at present. The same might be said of the cost of your police department,—a thing of which we in Ionia know nothing about, for we have no police force, and, happily, no need for any. One other advantage you would have in the economy of space, and that is that you would be able to devote more ground to parks and places of recreation for young and old. You have some noble parks in London, but there are too few of them, and they are too far away from the dwellings of those who need them most. Here in Iolkos, you will find one within a mile, at the farthest, of any dwelling-house. We are just coming to one of these play-grounds now, and you will see how much they are appreciated."

While Jason was speaking, I became aware of a lively sound of children's voices like what we hear when a large school sends forth its hundreds of children from the decorum of the class-room to the freedom of the play-ground. In a few seconds we were in the midst of a park occupying four ordinary blocks, and divided in two by the street on which we were riding. Each half of this space was surrounded by trees, and shrubs, and pretty beds of flowers, affording shady walks and comfortable benches for old people, and mothers with young children in their charge. The center of each was a large well-kept lawn, where the youths of both sexes disported themselves in all kinds of games and exercises. One side was reserved for school-children, and the other to young men and women old enough to attend the university. The day being Saturday, and the schools closed, the number of those engaged in play was much larger than it would have been on any other week-day, and we stopped a few moments to enjoy the lively scene. The beautiful forms and faces of these young people, their handsome dresses and their extraordinary agility in the various games made up a picture which the older people about evidently enjoyed very much, and which I felt loath to leave behind, but Jason reminded me that we had still far to go, and that we would find the same scene repeated at many points of our drive. We continued on our way through streets similar to those we had already passed, and soon came to another park like the first, except that in the center was a large building with a beautiful dome, which I learned was a public library, one of many which the city contained, and which were scattered over the city so as to be easy of access to the people of each district. Another of these parks showed a building like an ancient Greek temple of the Doric order, which Jason said was a picture gallery, open to the public everyday in the year. We passed a good many magnificent public buildings, all of which were in the center of parks, or occupying squares free of other buildings, so that their full beauty could be seen and appreciated from all sides. Continuing our course mainly in a southerly direction, we arrived in a district occupied by the houses of the wealthier citizens, each standing on its own grounds, which were beautifully adorned with shrubs, and flowers, and statuary. The houses were the most costly in material, and the most elegant in design that I had ever seen, and there seemed to be no end of them, mile after mile of such streets and residences, showing the wealth of the city to be vastly greater than that of any other in the world. We returned by the drive along the lake front, which was filled with carriages—public and private. It was past three o'clock, and the citizens were returning from the labors of the day; some were wealthy merchants, some more humble—mechanics and clerks,—but so far as appearance or dress was concerned, it was impossible for one to distinguish which was which. There was not one amongst them all but would have attracted attention in any city of Europe as a remarkably handsome and distinguished-looking man.

VII

A DAY OF REST

The next day, being the first of the week, was a day of absolute rest from almost every kind of labor. We sat out on the verandah after breakfast, reading the weekly journals, which are published on Saturday night and devoted to literature, science and art, rather than to what we call news. To the Ionian the various moves and feints of the European game of politics are absolutely devoid of interest, and if a murder had been committed or a train wrecked anywhere in Europe or America, he would rather not hear of it, and such things do not occur in his own country. Hence there is little demand for daily newspapers, and, although one is published at government expense, and containing all official announcements and proclamations, it is but little read, and its circulation is very small. The Ionian is content to take his current history of the world in weekly installments, and, even so, it must be condensed into a few short paragraphs.

As we sat reading that morning, with the most beautiful scene in the world spread out before us,—blue water, purple mountain and gray city all luminous in the clear air and warm September sun,—it seemed to me as if I had never seen the idea of a Sabbath so perfectly realized. Now and again a vessel, full of passengers for the country, passed from the river and sailed away down the lake, but there were no other boats about, no vehicles were moving on the street, and pedestrians few and far between. It was the day of rest for all, and the citizens were observing it thoroughly, as is their custom in regard to everything they undertake. I made a remark to my host on the delightful feeling of repose produced by the absence of noise and movement, and he replied that it was intended that the first day of the week should be one of complete cessation of labor, but that if we were on the other side of the city, where the majority of the people reside, I should find abundance both of noise and activity. From nine o'clock in the morning the parks and public play-grounds are lull of young people, engaged in sports and exercises, and as it would be no rest to them to keep still, they make it the busiest day of the week.

"What about the museums and picture galleries? Are they closed today?" I asked.

"They are all open in the afternoon and evening," he said, "and if the weather is fine, most of the people turn out into the streets and enjoy a promenade or a visit to one or other of these institutions."

"And have you no churches or places for public worship?"

"We have temples of music in every district of the city and the country, and it is the custom for most of the people to spend a couple of hours there on the day of rest. Come with me today, and you can judge for yourself whether they are places of worship or not."

"I shall be delighted, of course. At what hour are the services held?"

"They commence at noon, and it is nearly time for us to go now."

So we all set out together, and as the distance was not over a mile, we walked, Jason and his wife and I in front, while Dion followed with Leda and Eurydice. As we came near the place, we found ourselves amongst quite a throng of people, all going in the same direction, and a few minutes' walk brought us to the entrance of the temple, which is a very fine example of the Corinthian order, having double rows of massive columns on all four sides, and no windows or other openings in the walls, except the doors at one end. Having entered, I found we were in a large hall with a beautifully arched roof, pierced by many windows, so arranged that the light was thrown upon the walls, and that not a single ray could reach the floor directly. The walls were covered with magnificent paintings, on which the eye was compelled to rest, owing to the dim lighting of the interior space. The softly-carpeted floor was taken up with seats like the pews in a church, except that each individual seat had comfortable arm-rests, so that there could be no possibility of overcrowding. A large number of people were in the place before we arrived, and in a few moments every seat seemed to be occupied, and the doors closed. The younger members of the family seemed to have got separated from us in the throng of people, for when we had taken our places I found only the lady Helen and her husband near me. I would have asked what had become of them, but an absolute silence reigned in the building, and I feared to break it, even by a whisper, lest I should transgress the etiquette of the place, so I held my peace and occupied myself in examining the beautiful paintings which adorned the walls. My attention became riveted upon one which was on my left front near a platform slightly raised above the floor, and adorned by statuary, and palms, and flowering plants. The picture itself was brightly lighted from above, and represented an ocean bay, with woods and meadows on one side and a vast stretch of mountain-land on the other; in the foreground, the half-naked figure of a savage stood on the beach beside a canoe. The back of the man only was visible, and he seemed to be waiting for the sunrise, which was evidently just at hand, for there was a silver streak on the sea where it joined the sky in the center of the picture, and some fleecy clouds which floated higher up were already tinged with a faint rose-color, while between them was a broad belt of sky glowing with pale amber light. Unconsciously I began to expect the rising sun in sympathy with the figure in the foreground, and fell into a reverie in which I seemed to see the colors change in these gauzy clouds as the coming of the sun sent his search-lights through them, exhibiting glorious and ever-changing harmonies of crimson, and green, and purple, and gold; the hill-tops caught the first rays of rosy light as they started upwards; the silver rim on the sea spread and widened; the dawn was changing today; a moment more, and the sun himself appeared in a blaze of splendor which dazzled my sight. I passed my hand across my eyes, looked again and realized that I had been dreaming, though awake, for the picture was exactly as I had seen it first, but the air was filled with the music of many instruments in glorious harmony. I felt conscious of having listened to the music for sometime, but the beginning of it had been a series of sweet chords, coming in soft whispers, which had translated themselves in my mind into the most gorgeous sunrise I had ever seen on land or sea. But now the gentle zephyrs of harmony had given place to loud-swelling chords, suggestive of the full splendor of the risen sun pouring its floods of light and life upon a newly-awakened world. The source of the music was unseen, and I felt glad that there was no see-sawing of fiddle-bows or frantic movements of a conductor's baton obtruding the mechanical element in the production of those divine harmonies, and neutralizing the exalted feelings which they inspired.

The symphony came to an end all too soon, but was followed by a space of delightful quiet, unbroken by whispering comment or murmuring gossip, and the aftertaste of the music lingered pleasantly in the brain.

Again the hall was filled with the sweet sounds of the instruments rehearsing a most delightful melody, and then a new note was sounded which thrilled me to the soul. It was a woman's voice, but such a voice as I never heard before, so velvety soft and sweet, so rich and full, filling the hall with its glorious tones like sunshine in a deep, clear river. It began with a succession of slow, clear, ringing notes, and then burst into a melody of joy and gladness sweeter than any sky-lark ever caroled. I could not distinguish the words, the language was not sufficiently familiar to me, but no words were needed, for the song told its own story. It told, as no words can tell, of the ineffable joy of living in a world where all things are beautiful, day and night, sunshine and shadow, flowers and stars, mountain and lake, verdant plain and flowing river, all combining to delight the eye of man and ravish him with infinite variety; and it told of human joy, too, sweet affection and brotherly love, and noble deeds and splendid achievements.

All this and more did that wonderful song suggest, and in listening to it I felt inspired by new hope and confidence in the final triumph of right over wrong on this old sinful world of ours.

It came to an end at last, and I listened in vain during the service for another strain from that heavenly voice. But there was much more of exquisite music, in which many voices joined, and when, after two hours, it was over, and we all walked home together, I told my friend Jason that of all the religious services I had ever taken part in this was not only the most delightful, but also the most soul-inspiring and elevating.

The whole family sat down for a while to rest in the shade in front of the house, and enjoy the beauty of the scene and the delicious cool air that came in gentle zephyrs from the lake. The talk ran upon the music we had been hearing, and I mentioned the strange effect produced on my mind as I looked at the picture of the rising sun and listened unconsciously to the music, and Jason said:

"You are not the first that has had that experience. It was the sunrise symphony that was being played, and the first notes of it are so soft and low that if your eyes were riveted upon the picture it was perfectly natural that you should fall into a dreamy state in which the suggestions of the music seemed to come through the eye instead of the ear."

"It was a very beautiful dream," said I, "but that noble song which followed was the most entrancing music I ever heard. I have heard all the great singers of Europe and thought I knew all that the human voice was capable of, but that song was a new revelation to me. The voice was absolutely perfect and unapproachable; to listen to it was the most unalloyed delight, and there is nothing I wish for so much as to hear it again."

My friends seemed much amused at my enthusiasm, and were all smiling except Leda, who blushed like a rose. Her father said:

"That wish will not be very difficult to gratify and perhaps no farther off than this evening. What do you say, Leda?"

The truth now dawned upon me, and I exclaimed: "What, Leda! was it you who sang so divinely? Accept my heartfelt thanks and homage."

And kneeling on one knee I touched the fingers of her right hand with my lips, whereat they all laughed heartily, Leda herself appearing as much amused as the rest. Recovering her composure, she said:

"I am very glad, Alexander, that my singing gave you so much pleasure, but there are many who can sing better than I, and that you will find out for yourself before you have been in Iolkos much longer."

"Give me leave to doubt that, Leda; it is your modesty and not your judgment that speaks. Besides, what you say is impossible, for your singing was absolutely perfect, and could not be excelled; indeed, it is difficult for me to believe that you have an equal. I leave the question to your father."

Seeing that I looked to him for an answer, Jason said:

"Perhaps none of us here are in a position to judge this matter impartially. There is no one whose singing I like so well as Leda's, but that may be because she is my daughter, and there are many others whom I think you will find superior to the professional vocalists of Europe."

"And have you no professional singers here?"

"No, we have no need for them. Those amongst us who have the talent are glad to exercise it without fee or reward, and they would consider it beneath them to appear on a public stage to be stared at by an audience while they sang."

"And to what do you attribute the immense superiority of your people in this respect?"

"In the first place to the perfect health which they enjoy from the day of their birth, whereby the vocal organs are always in the best condition and capable of the highest training. In the second place it is partly due to the purity of our atmosphere, which is free not only from excess of moisture, but also from dust and smoke.

"A third reason for the excellence of our musicians is found in our system of education, which provides, not a uniform training for all scholars, except as regards the minor elements of learning, but rather a development to the highest degree of the particular talents which each child possesses. It is the business of the teachers to find out what those talents are, and to see that every opportunity is provided for their cultivation, without neglecting such general instruction as is fitted to produce intelligent, well-informed men and women. In this way every kind of natural ability is developed to the utmost extent, and there is little chance for any of our people to go through life without finding their true vocation, and the precious years of youth are not wasted in studies for which the pupil is not naturally fitted."

"Then what you have said holds good doubtless in regard to painting, sculpture, architecture, and all the mechanical arts, as well as music."

"Most certainly, for with us education covers the whole field of human activity, and is not supposed to be completed until the pupil is thoroughly trained to play his part in life in the sphere to which he is best adapted."

"Fortunate youth," said I, "to be born in such a country. The more I learn of your institutions, the more barbarous do those of my own country appear by comparison, but I cannot hope to understand what is going on around me here until I become more thoroughly acquainted with your language. I presume you can recommend me to a teacher?"

"We must think about that," said Jason.

"I would make a suggestion to our friend," said Dion, "and that is that he should spend some of his time on the public carriages of the city, where he will hear nothing but Greek spoken, and thus be learning the language unconsciously. Most of the drivers can speak either English or French and would be glad to give him all the assistance in their power. I know one, for instance, whose French is perfect, and who will be glad of the opportunity of learning English, and I shall be glad to introduce you to him. He will take it as a compliment, and you will find him a very intelligent, agreeable companion—what do you think of it?"

"I think it is an excellent plan, and I shall be delighted to give it a trial. But I must make it my first business tomorrow to change some English gold for the currency of the country, so that I may be able to pay my way."

"You can do that, of course, at anytime, but you may not have any opportunity of spending money for sometime. You must be careful not to offer any to my friend the driver, for that would hurt his feelings very much. It will be a course of mutual instruction, with advantages on both sides, and no financial obligation on either."

"But at least I must have money to pay the fares on the omnibus or car or whatever you call it."

At this Dion looked a little puzzled, and his father hastened to explain.

"There is no charge for riding in the public conveyances of the city. All transportation of passengers within the city limits is done at the cost of the municipality."

"That seems strange, but it must be very pleasant for the people who ride, although it must be an enormous expense to the city."

"On the contrary, it is the most economical plan. The people have to pay the cost in any case, and when it is done at the public charge all the expense of collecting fares and keeping account of them is avoided. But that is only one of many things which the city provides for—heat, water and lighting are all furnished without charge."

"But surely the taxes must be enormous to cover all these expenses."

"No indeed, they are very light and consist only of the small annual rent paid for ground occupied. All the land covered by the city is owned by the municipality, or what is the same thing, the city has a perpetual lease of it on payment of a moderate rent to the government, and thus all increase in the value of the land is enjoyed by the people at large instead of going into the pockets of speculators. This house is mine, but not the ground on which it stands; for that I pay a fair, but very moderate rent, which represents all my share of the expense of the municipality. In this way the city is in receipt of an enormous revenue, which it finds some difficulty in spending, but which is raised without injustice or inequality, and at very little expense for collection."

"I find," said I, "that you manage everything better than we do, and I feel myself like a new-born child in a world in which he has everything to learn."

But at this point my education was interrupted by a summons to dinner, and it was not till sometime afterwards that I learned the history of the single tax system in Ionia. In the evening of that day I enjoyed the first of a series of concerts by the members and friends of the Delphion family, which I am never likely to forget. On that occasion there were present besides the family only three visitors, Leonidas and his sister Daphne, and a gentleman of the name of Theseus, music master and composer. He had taught Leda all she knew of music and singing; he was professor of music in the university, and conductor at the temple of music and composer of several of the magnificent pieces I had heard performed there in the morning. He was tall and thin, with white hair and beard, a high forehead and piercing black eyes, in which the fire of genius burned with unmistakable lustre. The music room, which I had not seen before, was on the same floor as the library, and similar in size. It contained a piano and an organ, instruments of the violin order of all sizes, flutes and many others which were new to me. The floor was of dark, polished wood, and almost covered with rugs made of the skins of various animals of the chase, amongst which were those of the lion, the leopard and the tiger, and others, including one which had belonged to a polar bear of the largest size.

While the tuning of instruments and other preliminaries were going on, I asked my host if he had brought these skins with him from Europe.

"No," he replied, "I shot most of the animals myself. Dion killed the tiger on whose skin your feet are, and the lion, whose coat you see under the piano, and someothers; between us we are responsible for the deaths of all these noble animals, whose furs help to furnish our chamber of music."

"But the polar bear, surely you did not shoot that?"

"Indeed I did," said he, "and close by the north pole, too. That was many years ago, when I was quite a young man. An expedition was sent from Ionia to the pole, and we reached it, too, but the dangers and difficulties were so great that it has never been repeated. Twelve air-ships started, but only six came back. The winds were so contrary and so violent that it took us ten days to get there, instead of five, and our provisions were almost exhausted. Six of the ships were more or less disabled, and we left them there under an immense cairn of stones, and if ever your explorers reach the pole itself they will find its position so marked, and if they have the curiosity to remove the stones they will find the remains of the air-ships with an intimation that some Greeks have been there before them, but as we carefully avoided putting any date to the document we left sealed up near the top of the cairn, they may come to the conclusion that it has lain there from the time when Athens was in her ancient glory."

The music master here intimated that all was ready, and requested Jason to play the violoncello part.

"But I was in hopes," said Jason, "that you would allow me to assist Alexander in the part of audience. It is not often you have such a distinguished listener, and he might feel lonesome if I did not stay and listen, too."

"I am in hopes," said Theseus, "that he will do us the greater honor of assisting either with voice or instrument."

"Of that," said I, "I regret to say I am quite incapable. I have no musical ability or training, and although that very circumstance may render me a poor critic, it will not prevent me being a most delighted listener, and that must be my part."

So Jason was excused for the time, but by and by his services were required, and except when solos or duets were being performed, I was sole auditor.

And never was so rich a feast of music served up to a king as I enjoyed that evening. Such wonderful melodies and such exquisite blending of voice and instrument; it was the music of the gods. Leda sang for me again and again, and each song seemed the most enchanting ever I heard. And the other voices were scarcely less wonderful. Daphne's rich contralto, Dion's pure and powerful tenor, and Leonidas' grand basso were each a joy and pure delight to hear. The lady Helen proved herself a consummate pianist; Theseus played now the organ and now the violin with the touch of a master, and the others played each several instruments in turn, with equal skill. For over two hours they held me spellbound, and when the concert seemed to be ended I thanked them for the exquisite pleasure they had given me, and said further: "Your music expresses the happiness which seems to be a distinguishing characteristic of your life in this fortunate valley, and while I feel as if I could enjoy listening to it forever, and would not wish the character of it changed in the slightest degree, I cannot help remarking that there was not one note of pathos or of tragedy in it all. You are to be congratulated in the absence of melancholy themes in your music, for doubtless it means that your lives are almost free from mourning and grief."

"It is true," replied Leda, "that when we sing, it is natural for us to use the music of mirth and gladness, but if you would like to hear something of an opposite character, the master can play you a dirge which will almost break your heart, and Daphne can sing you a song fitted to draw tears from a marble statue."

Hearing this, Theseus, who was still at the organ, played a few bars of a funeral march, which seemed to express the grief of a whole people prostrated with woe, but he broke off short and requested Daphne to sing the song of Niobe, which she did with such melting tones that I was forced to put my handkerchief to my eyes to wipe away the tears which would flow in spite of me. I caught Leda smiling at me, but the effort was too much for her, and she finished by fairly sobbing aloud.

When the song was finished, I said to Daphne:

"You have fairly conquered us with that beautiful song, so beautifully rendered, and, yet I am glad to observe, that you had to go back several thousand years to find a subject so pathetic. How fortunate it must be to be born amongst a people where sorrow is a plant of alien growth."

"It is even as you say," said Daphne; "few of us have any sorrows of our own, and we have to borrow a little trouble even to make a song of, but let us not end our music on such a melancholy key. Theseus, will you not dispel the sadness which we have both helped to create?"

And the master played the prelude to the song of the king, a kind of anthem in praise of Timoleon, in which all joined; a chorus of glory and triumph, which so carried me away, that I could barely help rising and shouting aloud myself.

VIII

The Ionian Games

The scene of the national games of Ionia is situated on the southern shore of Lake Malo, about three miles below the city of Iolkos. The ground rises directly from the water's edge in the form of an amphitheater, on the slopes of which a million spectators could be accommodated. In front of this is a space of artificially made ground extending into the lake, and bounded by wharves of granite. This forms the arena on which most of the races and other athletic sports take place. It is nearly circular in form, rather more than a quarter of a mile in diameter, and covered with a thick sod of fine grass, which is carefully cropped and rolled and watered, so that at a distance it looks like a carpet of green velvet. The inner boundary of the arena is a wall of marble which curves from shore to shore, attaining a height of seven feet in the center, and sloping down to the points where the wharves commence, which are marked by two statues in bronze representing Apollo and Hercules. The height of the wall on the outside is about two feet, and all round it, tier above tier, are placed the seats for the spectators. These are strong, wooden benches, which are stored away during the year, and brought out and placed in order during the week before the games. They are furnished with spikes which pierce the turf and hold them firmly in place, and are arranged so that everyone has a perfect view of the arena while comfortably seated, and the spaces between the rows are so ample that the audience can take their places or disperse in a very few minutes. The front seats are, of course, the best, but as everyone of the spectators is provided with a powerful field-glass there is no rush or crowding, and all take the lowest seats vacant as they arrive, without distinction or preference, except that the front row is reserved for the Archon and his ministers and other dignitaries, with the members of their families.

A large proportion of the spectators are from the country, and of course the hotels are filled at this time, and many find accommodation with friends or relatives residing in the city, but a vast number are provided by the government with tents, pitched like the encampment of a great army on a table-land above the amphitheater itself.

Being attached to the family of a minister, I had the privilege of sitting in the front row, and had the most perfect view possible of all the magnificent sports, but the view of the audience itself was to me one of the most interesting features of the entertainment. There is always something imposing in the appearance of a great multitude of people, and nowhere else had I seen at one time a tenth part of the number that were here assembled. But the marvel was that every face here was radiant with beauty and intelligence, and beaming with enjoyment and good-will. Of all the men, women and children seated in that amphitheater there was not one that a painter would not have delighted to take for a model, or that could have failed to rejoice the eye of a sculptor. I looked amongst them in vain for a woman who could by the severest critic be reckoned as homely, or a man whose face was not noble and attractive, while the children were perfect models of grace and beauty. All were handsomely and richly dressed, which of itself was an exquisite charm, while their behavior was the perfection of courtesy and good breeding. Of course there were no very young children there, for it was no place for them, but I saw numbers of school children of ten years of age and upwards, who comported themselves in such a way as to prove them perfect little ladies and gentlemen.

The games occupy four days, from Tuesday to Friday, leaving Monday and Saturday for the arrival and departure of visitors. The hour of commencing is ten o'clock, and the sports are continued till three, with the interval of an hour at noon for social intercourse and refreshment. In the evening all the picture galleries, museums and libraries are open and thronged with visitors from the country, the residents of the city remaining at home on these occasions to avoid over-crowding. Thus the festival is especially a season of pleasure to the city's guests, but it affords the most unbounded enjoyment to all who take part in it, and the exuberance of good spirits is so infectious that I felt myself losing my English indifference to all forms of entertainment and entering into the enjoyments of the time with the enthusiasm of a child.

The program for the first day consisted of running, leaping, throwing heavy weights, wrestling, etc., and while I do not propose to quote any of the records made, lest they should seem incredible, I will state that they were far in advance of anything ever achieved by the best of English athletes. The runners appeared to fly over the ground so that their feet barely touched it, and in leaping, both as to height and distance, their feats were such as I should have deemed impossible if I had not witnessed them with my own eyes. There was a race in which the course was a mile in circuit, with a large number of hurdles of a height of six feet placed at intervals. All these had to be cleared at a bound, and although there were twenty competitors, not one of them failed to clear each hurdle, and that without any apparent effort or the slightest relaxation of speed. The forms of the young men engaging in these races were marvelously graceful and symmetrical, and impressed me with an idea of masculine beauty that was altogether new. I could not tell which to admire most, the supple and beautifully moulded limbs of the runners, or the great chests and iron muscles of the wrestlers and others who exhibited feats of strength later in the day. They all wore clothing similar to that worn by our own athletes, but not sufficient to disguise the perfection of form and motion which the exercises called forth. Our friend Leonidas, who had been champion wrestler at the previous festival, had some worthy successors in those who struggled with each other in the arena that day, and when I saw their wonderful feats of strength and skill my admiration for one who had come off winner in such a contest rose to a very high pitch. The first day passed very pleasantly, and the results of the various contests seemed to give general satisfaction, but as I was unacquainted with any of the competitors I felt no personal interest in them, but on the second day both Dion and Leonidas were to take part, which made it much more exciting for the members of the family whose guest I was. Dion competed in the forenoon in a splendid rowing race for individual scullers, but failed to carry off the prize after an exciting contest, in which he came in a close second.

Leonidas competed in the last event of the day, which was a three-mile swimming race. The course was triangular; from the end of the wharf enclosing the arena northeast to a buoy moored a mile off, then west to another buoy at the same distance, and back to the wharf again, making an equilateral triangle, of which the sides were each exactly a mile long. Smaller buoys were fixed at intervals to indicate the straight course, and in the interior of the triangle half a dozen skiffs, each managed by two men who were accomplished swimmers and divers, accompanied the competitors in case the strength of any of them should fail and necessitate assistance. Chairs were placed on the wharf for the judges, and the government officials with their families, but the majority of the spectators retained their usual places, and could see the race quite distinctly by using their field-glasses.

There were thirteen candidates for the prize, all men of splendid muscular development, and apparently about twenty-five to thirty years of age, all except one young fellow, who seemed not more than twenty-two, but whose long, clean-cut limbs, muscular thighs and well-developed biceps marked him as a very formidable competitor. I asked Leda, who sat next to me, if she knew the youngest of the swimmers, and she said she did not, but referred the question to Dion, who occupied the seat next her on the other side. Dion said his name was Orestes, that he came from Thalmon, and was considered quite a prodigy amongst swimmers in that part of the country. Meantime the competitors had taken their places on the end of the wharf all ready for the plunge. They were dressed in woolen attire, each having a distinctive color; the arms were bare and the legs also below the knee, and as their figures appeared outlined against the lake they formed a magnificent group, which could not have been matched elsewhere for perfect physical development and manly beauty. The signal for starting was given by the firing of a gun, and the swimmers dived into the deep water simultaneously. When they came to the surface Orestes was leading by several feet, and swimming at a tremendous rate of speed. Most of the others made great efforts to overtake him, but he kept his lead, and steadily increased it. Such a pace evidently could not be kept up long, and it seemed as if most of the swimmers would be exhausted before the first turning point was reached, unless the speed were reduced. Leonidas was now behind all the others, and he did not seem to be making any effort to get to the front, but swam steadily on his right side with a slow but powerful stroke, evidently husbanding his resources for the distant home-stretch. As he was very well known, and was looked upon as the champion of Iolkos, several remarks were made about his lack of speed, and one young fellow hazarded the assertion that he was out of the race, but he was immediately corrected by an old patriarch, who told him that if the others did not speedily relax their efforts Leonidas would be the only one to swim over the course. All this, of course, was said in Greek, and I had to listen attentively to make out the meaning of the words, but I understood, nevertheless, and mentally thanked the old gentleman for Leda's sake, but as he was a friend of the family and knew that she was betrothed to Leonidas, I had a suspicion that he spoke for her encouragement as much as from real conviction. However that may have been, the foremost swimmers soon began to ease off a little, and Orestes, finding himself a long way in front, settled down to a more steady stroke. And now Leonidas began to forge ahead, and at the end of the first mile he had passed about half of the competitors. At the end of the second mile there were only two ahead of him, and he speedily gained the second place. At this point a number of those who were farthest behind gave up the contest and climbed into the attendant boats, but some half a dozen of them swam doggedly on, apparently without any hope of winning, but either trusting to an accidental turn of fortune or making it a point of honor to swim over the entire course.

The last half-mile was marked by a white buoy with a red flag, and at this point Orestes still appeared to be about fifty feet ahead of Leonidas, but the latter for the first time quickening his stroke, gained upon him rapidly. The young fellow now realized that the race was not yet won, and began to make the most strenuous efforts to retain his position, but the length of the course and the great exertions he had made at the beginning told on him fearfully. His strokes were rapid and nervous, but they had lost their vigor, and foot by foot the gap was closing up. I could not help feeling sorry for the young fellow, who doubtless had been counting on an easy victory; it must have been terribly exasperating to know that this tireless pursuer was pressing him so hard and the goal so near, and that while his own energies were failing his competitor was only now putting forth his full strength. Leonidas lay now on his left side, and at every stroke of his powerful right arm the foam flew before his head, which was buried in the water at every sweep. At length they were side by side, yet Orestes would not surrender without a struggle, and putting forth all his remaining strength, he managed to gain a few inches. But the effort was too much for his exhausted condition, and with a sudden cry he disappeared below the surface. Without a moment's hesitation Leonidas dived after him, and for many seconds that seemed like minutes, they both remained under the water. Leda had risen from her seat, and as the moments passed and her lover failed to appear her face assumed a look of horror and distress that was most painful to witness. I kept telling her that there was no cause for alarm, that Leonidas was so strong that he could not fail to master the young man even if he struggled, and that he would come up in a moment more. Dion was saying the same things to her in their own tongue on the other side, but I doubt if she heard a word spoken by either of us. She was as pale as death, her mouth drawn in agony, and her eyes almost starting from their sockets as if they would pierce the depths of the water in search of her lover. I was on the point of giving up hope myself when at last a golden ripple broke the surface and Leonidas' close-cut, curly, amber locks rose up, followed by the darker head of Orestes. Leonidas was swimming with his left hand free, while with his right he held the body of his competitor, both arms pinioned to his sides. Evidently there had been a struggle, and it was well for our friend that he had the strength of a giant, for without it he could never have reached the surface alive. Meanwhile the third swimmer in the race continued calmly on the course, but Leonidas did not relinquish his charge until two of the attendant divers had him safely between them. He then easily passed the other man, who indeed made no effort to win, evidently feeling that he could not do so honorably in the circumstances. When Leonidas reached the goal, the whole multitude rose and cheered lustily. The women waved their handkerchiefs, and the men their hats, and the cheering continued as long as Leonidas was in sight. The sound had something of the majesty of nature's mighty voices—the thunder, or the waves dashing on the shore in a storm; it was not so deafening as one would have expected, on account doubtless of the distance at which the great majority of the individuals joining in it were necessarily situated, but the vastness of multitude was there, and it inspired a feeling akin to awe by the consciousness of its far-reaching volume. Few indeed are the men who have been honored with such a spontaneous and magnificent triumph, and most would have had their heads turned by it, but Leonidas walked straight to his tent apparently unconscious that all this uproar was being made on his account. He was not allowed to enter it at once, however, for several of the managers of the games interposed and insisted on his acknowledging the ovation. He turned around, apparently with great reluctance, walked a few steps forward, bowed gracefully to the archon, who was standing in his place and clapping his hands enthusiastically, another bow to the people on the right and one to the left, and then with quick strides he disappeared through the door of his tent.

Meantime Leda alone of that great assembly had resumed her seat, her handkerchief pressed to her eyes, which rained tears of joy. I expected to see her faint when the cruel suspense of that terrible half minute was over, but fainting is an accomplishment in which the ladies of Ionia are not very proficient. She had remained standing until Leonidas was actually out of the water, and then sank into her seat and wept silently until the cheering subsided. She then calmed herself with a great effort in order to avoid attracting attention, but remaining very quiet, and dared not trust herself to speak all the way home. When the family met at the dinner table she was quite herself again.

That was a very happy evening at the Delphion's. Leonidas and Daphne, of course, were there; Dion's failure was entirely forgotten, and all the ladies seemed bent on petting the hero of the day. Leonidas persisted in talking on every subject but the one that was uppermost in their minds. Being forced at last to say something about it, he declared that it was one of the most unpleasant experiences of his life.

"You must have had a dreadful struggle with Orestes below the water," said the lady Helen; "we began to think you never would come up."

"Oh, that was nothing," said Leonidas; "I had some trouble with him, for he did not know what he was doing, and tried to wrap all his limbs around me as soon as I grasped him by the arm. I soon had both arms fast, but it took me a little longer to free myself from the clutch of his legs, and all this time we were sinking till we actually touched the bottom. But you know I was stronger than he, and never had the slightest doubt about the result, although I had been exerting myself considerably and was very glad to be able to breathe again when we came up. Yet I have been through something of the kind before and did not think much of it, but the idea of all that crowd shouting themselves hoarse over it and my being compelled to acknowledge their plaudits, as if I had done something great! I feel ashamed when I think of it."

"But you know," said my hostess, "the voice of the people is the voice of God, and it never spoke more unmistakably than it did today. And I am sure there are many people speaking of it in Iolkos tonight."

"Well, it shall not be so here if I can help it, and I'll tell you what will be done to prevent it. Since you ladies appear to think I am deserving of so much honor, you cannot refuse to grant me a boon if I ask it, can you?"

"What is it?" they all asked in chorus.

"That you four ladies shall give us a concert of vocal and instrumental music, and Jason and Alexander and Dion and I shall be the audience, and you must entertain us until supper time."

This modest request could not be denied, and all the four exerted themselves to furnish music worthy of the occasion. But Leonidas only partially succeeded in serving his purpose of diverting attention from his gallant feat, for the ladies found a great many pieces in honor of heroes of the past which they made apply to him by turning their eyes upon him while they sang, and although he affected not to see it he could not help blushing several times, greatly to our amusement. They reserved their most effective piece to the last. It was supposed to be a chorus of Spartan maidens, sung in praise of the immortal three hundred of Thermopylae, and as the name of Leonidas occurred in it again and again, and was held up as the greatest name amongst mortals, we felt that the ladies had gained their point, as they always do, and their crowning effort was rewarded with much applause and laughter. Leonidas himself laughed with the rest, but said he never liked that piece, for the words were positively silly, and the music only second rate.

The trials of speed between various classes of air-ships came off on the following day. The race of the dragons was a magnificent spectacle. These are the largest class of aerial vessels, and one condition of the race was that each should carry at least a hundred men including the crew. Each city and district was represented, and the ships were all magnificently painted and decorated, but that of the mining town of Laureion was the most gorgeous, literally blazing with crimson and gold. It was understood that the miners were determined to wrest the prize from the capital, whose ships had carried off the honors for five successive seasons. The people of Laureion are very wealthy, and very proud of their city, and they had spared no expense in preparing for this contest. They had purchased ships from three or four of the most celebrated builders and had subjected them to repeated tests in their own neighborhood, in order to find out which was the most speedy and trustworthy. The one they finally selected was said to be the fastest that had ever been built, but as much depends upon the crew as upon the vessel, and there was considerable difference of opinion as to whether they would be able to carry off the prize from the skillful navigators of Iolkos.

Directly north across the lake, at a distance of twelve miles from the race grounds, there is a snow-covered mountain peak, known as Parnassus, and the course for the dragons was from the tableland back of the amphitheater straight to the peak, around it from the east side, and back again. We could not see the vessels as they started, but a few seconds would bring them all into view and then we should have them all clearly in sight with our field-glasses over the whole course, except for the short time required to go behind the mountain. Precisely at the hour appointed the signal gun was fired, and in an incredibly short time we saw fifteen magnificent vessels flying over our heads and sailing grandly over the lake. The wind was blowing straight towards

Parnassus; where we sat it was merely a gentle zephyr, and it did not seem as if it could make much difference one way or the other, but as the vessels rose higher they seemed to catch a stronger breeze, for those which attained the greatest height were seen to be making the greatest speed. The men of Laureion and those of Iolkos were the first to take advantage of this circumstance, and were well ahead of the rest, but the others soon rose to the same level and followed the leaders in a row, looking to the naked eye like a flock of wild geese sailing away to their northern haunts in triangular order. The lines were soon broken, however, for the Laureion crew took their vessel higher yet, and it became impossible to tell which was first, but the Iolkos rounded the mountain first, which was the signal for a cheer from the people of the capital, and still another vessel had disappeared behind the mountain before the Laureion reached it. The miners gained the peak at last, and being very near the top made the turn in a much shorter time than the others. And now they took a widely different course from the rest, for while the Iolkos kept as low as possible in order to meet with the minimum resistance from the wind, the Laureion soared higher still, evidently seeking a countercurrent of air, and they apparently found what they were seeking, for they soon began to move towards us with enormous speed. When the Iolkos reached the opposite shore it seemed to be almost touching the water and skimmed over the surface like a duck. I thought the race was theirs, till suddenly the Laureion swooped down from the sky with such enormous velocity that I feared to see them fall into the lake, but the crew knew their business too well for that. Making a beautiful curve, they reached the level of the table land, shot over our heads like a cannon ball, and touched ground fifteen seconds ahead of their nearest opponents. The whole time of the race was about fourteen minutes, which was considered very fast for such large vessels. The last race of the day was that for the Skylarks, carrying only one man, and it was especially interesting to us because Dion Delphion was one of the competitors, and he had not made any secret of the fact that he had set his mind much more strongly upon winning this than the rowing race in which he took part. The course was the same as for the larger vessels, with this difference, that instead of going round the mountain they were required to bring back some of the snow from its sides, scooping it up in a vessel of metal about the size of a two-quart measure, with a long chain attached, which was furnished to each competitor before starting.

When the signal gun was fired most of the little vessels sought to attain the level of the stronger breezes by mounting upward perpendicularly before directing their vessels forward, but Dion and one or two others adopted a more slanting course, and this proved the wisest, for they reached the mountain before the others. Dion's vessel was of a pale, delicate green, and as all the others were of different colors, we were able to follow it all the way with our powerful glasses, although even with these it appeared in the distance no larger than a bee. He went much higher than any of the other aeronauts, who steered mostly for the lowest point of the snow-line, hoping thereby to save half a mile or so of the distance. All at once I lost sight of the little green speck and turned to ask Leda if she still had it in view, but I saw that she, too, had lowered her glass.

"Where has he gone to?" I asked.

"He has gone behind the mountain," she said.

"And why should he do that?"

"I am not sure," she said, "but let us watch for his reappearance."

I put up my glass again, and in a minute more the green point reappeared, headed straight for the camp.

Meantime all the other skylarks had arrived at the mountain, and we could see them skimming back and forth over the snow, evidently trying in vain to fill their pitchers. A full minute passed from the time of Dion's reappearance before the first of the others started in pursuit, and by that time he must have been fully half a mile ahead, after allowing for the greater distance he had to travel. None of them could make up that lead, and he landed a full half minute ahead of the next man, and received hearty cheers for his decisive victory. We could not quite understand how he had managed so completely to out-maneuver all his competitors, but he made it very clear to us later in the day.

He reminded us that we had enjoyed a succession of sunny, cloudless days for a week or more, and said he felt sure that the snow on the southern slope of the mountain exposed to the full blaze of the sun must have been partly melted and frozen many times, and the surface must be covered with a solid coating of ice, so that if there was any loose snow anywhere it must be on the northern side under the shadow of some high rock. He found such a spot without difficulty and filled his pitcher at the first scoop, whereas the others were obliged to land and fill theirs by hand, after vainly trying to scoop up the snow on the wing. The conditions of the race were not announced till just before the start, so there was no opportunity of a previous examination of the mountain, and Dion was allowed to have won solely by his superior skill and judgment.

The fourth and last day of the race was taken up by the competition of orchestral societies from different parts of the country, and from the cities. There was no limit to the number of orchestras from each place, and the capital was represented by no less than five, Thalmon by two and Laureion by two, the total number competing being twenty-five. The audience was much smaller than on the previous days, for many of the visitors who were not devoted to music spent the day in the art galleries, which were crowded from morning till night. This enabled those who were left to arrange themselves in more compact space and hear the music to greater advantage. I never saw an audience so attentive or so thoroughly delighted with what they heard, and the music and the rendering of it were such as I am very sure has never been heard in any other part of the world. I think I enjoyed this last day most of all, and that is saying much, for the whole festival had been a season of unalloyed pleasure.

But the crowning spectacle was still to come: in the ceremony of awarding the prizes. This took place on the evening of the fourth day.

An hour after sunset was the time appointed, and the audience was greater than ever, so that almost every seat was occupied. During the afternoon a great change had been accomplished in the arena. Between the center of it and the middle of the great wall, a platform had been erected and covered with a handsome carpet. On each side were seats for about a hundred persons, arranged in a semi-circle, in rows rising upwards from the floor, all richly upholstered, and having a background of flowers and palms and other tropical plants. On the right side sat the victors in the different games, who were to be crowned with wreaths of wild cherry. On the other side were the archon and the ministers of state, the city councillors and the representatives of any of the other city or district governments who happened to be present. In front of these sat thirteen beautiful maidens, and in the center of the row Daphne Van Tromp, in a graceful dress of white silk, while the others, who were all brunettes, wore dresses of similar make and material in delicate shades of blue, pink, primrose, etc. On Daphne's right sat Leda, and on the left Eurydice, all the rest being friends and former fellow-students chosen to support her in the ceremony of crowning the victors. It is the custom for the archon to select some young lady from amongst the families of his friends for this honorable service, and she has the selection of the twelve who are to occupy the seats of honor by her side. Leda had been the crown-giver at the previous festival, and then Daphne had sat at her right side; next year someother maiden would occupy the place of honor, for the same one is never chosen twice by the archon. The crown-giver is free to select whom she will to support her, but they must be unmarried, and not over twenty-five years old.

When all had taken their places the lights were turned out over the amphitheater, which brought into brilliant relief the distinguished companies on both sides of the platform, on whom a flood of light was poured from lamps placed a hundred feet above them, and shaded so that their direct rays could not reach the audience. The handsome, bearded seniors on the one side, with the row of lovely maidens in front, in contrast with the lithe figures of the young athletes opposite, who were dressed in a uniform of blue and white donned for the occasion, and well calculated to display their fine proportions, their uncovered heads and clear-cut faces showing to great advantage in the brilliant electric light,—all this formed a picture of human beauty which of itself was a feast for the eyes of that artistically educated assembly, and they showed their appreciation of it by cheers and applause, which overpowered the music of the orchestra below. There were two bands of music placed respectively on the hither and further sides of the platform; one of these was a local orchestra, and the other was the one which was victorious in the contest of the early part of the day. These played alternately during the whole of the crowning ceremony, and although at any other time their splendid performances would have been listened to with the closest attention, the cheers which greeted each of the victors as he came forward to be crowned, prevented us from hearing their strains, except only at short intervals.

It being impossible to announce the names of the prize-winners vocally so as to be heard by so many people, this was not attempted. The names of each and the titles of the races they had won were displayed in letters of gold by some electrical device on the dark background beyond the platform. As each name appeared the fortunate youth rose from his place, crossed the platform, and knelt on a cushion in front of the crown-giver of the year, and Daphne, standing up and receiving the wreath from the hands of the lady next her, placed it on his head. The victor then rose, and with a graceful bow, returned to his place, to be succeeded by the next, whose name appeared after a moment's interval on the invisible canvas between us and the lake. The prizes for those contests in which numbers took part, such as that of the dragons and the rowing races of eight oars, were not wreaths, and the victors were not crowned like the individual winners. They were rewarded by the presentation of a trophy of gold of great value and artistic beauty, of which they were allowed to retain possession for the year, or until it was wrested from them by a different crew. There were seven of these splendid works of art, and they were displayed on a table covered by a snow-white cloth which stood on the platform in front of the ladies, on the right, or the side nearest the audience, the wreaths being placed on a similar table on the left. Both tables were profusely decorated with flowers. The trophies were too heavy for a woman's strength to lift, so when the races to which they belonged were called, they were lifted by two stalwart attendants and placed on the cushion in front of Daphne. She then placed her hands upon the trophy, the captain of the winning crew did the same, and thus received possession. It was then replaced on the table to be taken away later on by its temporary owners.

Each victor, as he appeared, was greeted with applause by the audience, which he acknowledged with a bow as he crossed the platform in returning. Some were greater favorites than others, and were received with louder cheering, but when it came Leonidas' turn to be crowned, the audience, remembering his heroic rescue of Orestes, treated him to a repetition of the ovation given him on the day before, which so mortified him that he privately resolved never to take any active part in the games in future.

Dion was the last of the victors to be crowned, and he also received an unusual amount of applause, partly because he was a favorite and partly, no doubt, because he was the last. As soon as he had returned to his place a signal gun was fired, and in a moment a dozen of the largest air-ships or dragons appeared in view, brilliantly lighted from stem to stern. They were hovering over the lake near the shore, and as all had been dark in that quarter but a moment before, it seemed as if they were phantom ships created by some stroke of magic art. And now they commenced a series of beautiful evolutions, wheeling in columns and in line, crossing each other's bows and sailing over and under each other with the perfect order and precision of an army corps going through their drill. This splendid spectacle continued for about fifteen minutes, and then they separated into two squadrons and went through the form of a sham-battle, bombarding each other with shells and rockets so that the air was like a tornado of fire, and I marveled that the vessels were not injured, till it was explained to me that every part of their exterior was fire-proof, so that the bursting of a shell or a rocket in contact with any part of them was as harmless as so much water. These missiles, harmless though they were, exploded with loud detonations, and it was difficult to realize that we were not witnessing a terrific and destructive action in aerial warfare. The firing of a great gun on the shore gave the signal for the turmoil to cease, and the twelve vessels then formed a hollow square, above the water's edge.

The festival was now over, but the great audience remained seated until the archon and the other prominent personages had taken their departure. Daphne and her twelve attendants moved off first, escorted by the victors, wearing their wreaths. Minos and the high officials who had occupied the seats of honor followed next with the members of their families, from the front row of seats amongst the audience. Two barges carried all these persons, of whom I had the privilege of being one, two more held the bands of music, and the fleet of four moved off in stately procession, escorted by the twelve air-ships of war formed in a square above us, so that we occupied the space beneath its center. This formation was maintained all the way to the city, and the air vessels kept up a continual discharge of rockets on the outside of the square so that we seemed to be moving between walls of fire. Carriages were in waiting at the landing-place to convey us all to our homes, and the aerial fleet sailed away over the lake with a thunderous parting salute.

IX

TIMOLEON, THE LIBERATOR

During the next few weeks I spent my time partly in learning the language of the nation whose guest I was, and partly in studying the geography of the country and becoming acquainted with its towns and villages, and the manner in which its agriculture is carried on. Jason placed himself entirely at my disposal, and several times a week we made aerial excursions to different points of interest, in the course of which the land was spread beneath us like a map, and every detail could be observed with a minuteness which no other mode of traveling could approach. Every rood of the land between its mountain ramparts is cultivated like a garden, and every part devoted to the products to which experience shows it to be best adapted. The slopes at the foot of the northern hills are mainly occupied by vineyards and the raising of silk worms. The lower hills are covered with sheep and the smaller valleys between with cattle; cotton is raised in great quantities in the center of the valley, but the bulk of the country is divided into small farms where all kinds of grain and vegetable crops are produced in rotation. The country abounds in rivers and streams, which are connected by innumerable canals, like the veins and arteries of the human body, and there are numbers of large reservoirs for storing superfluous water so that such a thing as a failure of crops is unknown, and the produce per acre is such as would astonish the most thorough-going scientific farmers of our own country. This result is owing not alone to the fact that heat and moisture are always supplied in sufficient quantities, but also to the elaborate system of returning waste products to the soil, which is provided for by a department of the government presided over by some of the ablest scientists of the country. The sewage of every city, town and village is carried underground to large reservoirs, and there quickly transformed into the most admirable fertilizers, which are sold to the farmers at very moderate rates, and the result is that the land is constantly growing richer, and the returns from it becoming greater with each decade.

The farms vary from forty to a hundred acres, and all the labor is done by the lessee himself, or in some cases by the farmer and his grown up son, who is very commonly his successor. For, although every farm pays rent to the government, the annual charge is very moderate, and the leases are made for a long period of years, and the same farms are sometimes held by the same family for centuries.

The farm houses are very substantial, and even elegant in character, and everyone has its flower and vegetable gardens, which are models of neatness and beauty. I noticed that all plowing, harrowing and reaping is done not by horse power, but by automatic machinery, electricity being, of course, the motive power.

"Where," I asked of Jason, "does all the electricity come from to accomplish such a great amount of work?"

"You will observe," said he, "that every farmer has a wind-mill, or in some cases two. These are going night and day during the most of the year, and they keep his water tank filled, do his plowing and reaping and supply all the power required to run every piece of machinery he can use."

"But I do not understand," said I, "how such great results can be accomplished by such an apparently inadequate cause."

"That is because you are not yet initiated into one of our greatest discoveries, which enables us to utilize the magnetism with which the earth is stored, and which requires only a small current of electricity to set it free and enable us to make use of it to an unlimited extent. Your scientists and economists have been calculating the extent of the coal stored beneath the earth's surface, and wondering what would become of your industries when it is exhausted, never dreaming that the great globe itself is a storehouse of force so infinite in extent that all that man can ever use of it is but like one grain of sand compared to the shores of the ocean. Your electricians are coming nearer to that grand discovery every year, and when it finally dawns upon them they will see that they have been like men groping about with bandaged eyes, while the sun has been pouring its floods of light upon the whole world around them. It will dwarf every mechanical invention and scientific discovery of past times, and will doubtless lead to the belief that a new era of prosperity is about to dawn upon the human race, but I question if it will be productive of any permanent benefit, and its immediate consequences will be disastrous to great numbers, for it will dislocate the whole industrial system, and bring starvation and ruin to coal miners and many others."

"Then you do not consider this as one of the fundamental secrets of the great advance your own people have made in civilization?"

"By no means. Science and mechanical improvements have multiplied our comforts, but they have played but a secondary part in raising the people to the high moral, intellectual and physical standard which they have attained. Their superiority in these respects is owing entirely to our beneficent laws, and especially to the four great laws of Timoleon, which I propose to explain to you in the course of these excursions, but in order that you may understand how they came to be enacted and how the memory of the great king, as we call him, is revered amongst us, I think it would be well for me first to give you a short outline of the history of Ionia, and especially of the life of Timoleon himself."

"That will give me more pleasure than anything else I could think of, and the pleasure will be less than the profit, for I came here mainly to know the secrets of your superiority to all other races and peoples, and I should be glad to have you commence the narration just as soon as you feel disposed."

"We must put it off till the commencing of our return trip, for we are now arriving at the forest, where we must disembark for a time and look around us."

This conversation occurred during the first of our excursions, when we traversed the whole valley of Ionia in a couple of hours, having the river directly underneath us nearly all the way, and passing many towns and villages, and especially the ancient capital, the city of Thalmon, whose handsome squares and gardens and magnificent buildings marked it as second only in beauty and grandeur to Iolkos itself. As we approached the head of the valley an opening in the hills appeared, covered with a dense growth of noble trees, and very soon I found that we were floating over a sea of foliage composed of many tints of green, rippling into silver as the wind passed over it. The sun poured a flood of warm light upon it, and birds of beautiful plumage were seen flitting about in great numbers; far away in front the purple mountains rose against a background of bright-blue sky, while the nearer hills were dark with pines nearly to their summits. It was a scene of unrivaled beauty, and the novelty of viewing a forest from above the tree tops lent to it a peculiar charm.

Presently an opening appeared, and we descended upon the roof of the Forest House, a handsome building of great extent, built in the form of a square, with the river flowing through the center. Descending to the interior court we found ourselves in a delightful garden and passed many groups of happy looking holiday makers, most of whom my friend saluted, without stopping to speak, for he wished me to see something of the forest itself. We entered it by one of several avenues leading from the palace and I was at once struck by the great size and perfect proportions of the trees. There were no saplings or misshapen, unhealthy specimens, but every tree was perfect in form and sound in every part. This, I was told, was the result of the labors of a corps of experienced foresters, maintained by the government to keep the extensive grounds in order, and they did their work well, for even in English parks I never saw such magnificent oaks, elms and beeches as abounded here. There were other varieties, including many which were new to me, but all seemed to be enjoying the right conditions for perfect development.

We walked along a beautiful avenue completely overarched by the foliage, catching sight now of a reach of the river with some merry company in barge or row-boat, and again of an open glade where young people were disporting themselves in athletic games on the turf. Five minutes' walk brought us to a lake in whose cool depths many swimmers were disporting themselves, and we remained for a time to watch their gambols. Then we passed still farther into the depths of the forest, where the silence was broken only by the music of the birds, which kept up a veritable concert among the trees. Farther on we saw a herd of deer which were so tame that they came quite close and allowed us to stroke their shaggy coats. Neither animal nor bird is molested in the forest, except such as are noxious and mischievous, so that it is a perfect paradise for them, and they exist in great numbers, and add much to the attractions of the place. Having walked about a couple of miles from the palace, we reached a boat-landing on the river, where we waited till one of the electric barges came by on its return trip. We boarded, and had a delightful run down past banks of ferns and wild flowers, with glimpses of mountain-tops beyond the trees, sunshine and shade swiftly alternating and a soft, sweet-scented breeze blowing in our faces all the way. A few minutes brought us to the Forest House, the interior of which we spent a little time in examining before we departed for Iolkos in our air-ship. We walked through the halls, which were of choice colored marble, those on every floor being different in design and material; we looked into the public rooms,—such as the dining-room, the parlors and reading-rooms, the concert hall and the gymnasium, and admired their fine proportions and decorations: the walls and ceilings were frescoed by masters in the art, and the furniture was rich, elegant and appropriate. Every room afforded entrancing views from the windows, and seemed designed for the use of persons of boundless wealth and taste, and yet they were intended for the plain people,— the mechanics, tradesmen, farmers and others, all of whom know how to appreciate and enjoy without abusing all these luxuries. The roof, which is flat, is mainly devoted to the landing of air-vessels, which are protected from the wind by high walls on each side, but all round the outside runs a parapet, furnished with innumerable seats, where the guests congregate to enjoy the cool evening air and the glorious sunsets for which the forest is celebrated.

Now, this is only one amongst a number of national parks where the people are privileged to spend their yearly vacations, which are taken by all as a matter of course. I visited most of them in company with Jason, and found them all equally attractive, and all designed and equipped with such exquisite taste and on a scale of such costly magnificence as showed that the government's sole care is for the comfort and well-being of the people at large. One of these parks is an island, situated in an arm of the lake, running up between high hills, a most romantic situation, and largely favored by those living inland, out of sight of Lake Malo. Another is in an upland valley, where there are miles and miles of beautiful springy turf, and where horses of a fine breed are kept for those who love to take exercise in the saddle. These are the only horses in the whole country, and for beauty, speed and sagacity they are not to be matched anywhere else in the world. Several of the parks are to be found scattered through the valley, and abound in pleasant groves and fountains, flower-gardens and green arbors, and are much favored by elderly people, who love to saunter in pleasant places and pass the time in conversation. One of the summer resorts (it can hardly be called a park) is amongst the perpetual snows of the high mountains, and here, in the midst of summer, all the winter delights are enjoyed,—skating, snow-shoeing and tobogganing on a grand scale down a mile of steep mountain side and across a valley two miles wide. The hotel at this place is built of double walls of aluminum, transported to the spot on air vessels, for there is no other way of reaching it. Another of these recreation grounds is among the hills on the north side of the great lake, where there are many fine trout streams, which unite to form a lovely sheet of water, stocked with many kinds of fish by the care of the fishing department of the state. There the lover of the gentle art may while away his time amid the loveliest scenery, and seldom fail to fill his basket. And there are many other such places by lake and mountain, so that the people have a great variety of choice for their summer vacations, and the certainty of facilities for all kinds of healthful recreation as well as comfortable quarters wherever they may go. In all of them, there is abundance of land and suitable buildings provided by the government, either in the form of grand palatial structures, as in the forest, or of a number of widely-scattered cottages situated conveniently to the sport, as is the case in the valley of the anglers. In the former class, the buildings are rented to a company or an individual, who performs the office of hotel-keeper, charging certain fixed and moderate rates, which are not in any case to be exceeded; in the latter, the cottages are rented to families or small parties who look after their own cuisine and keep the premises in order. Every family and every individual in the country is thus enabled to enjoy a change of air and scene on such terms as all can easily afford, and by varying their choice from year to year, the charm of novelty is added to all the other delights of their summer outing.

I visited all these splendid play-grounds with Jason in the air-ship, and by the end of October I had visited or passed over nearly every portion of the country. We devoted at least three days of each week to this pleasant work, and sometimes the lady Helen and sometimes her daughter accompanied us, and their presence always added to the enjoyment of the trip, but I never spent a dull hour in Jason's company, for his stores of information were unlimited, and his command of language such as I have never known in any other man.

He began his sketch of the history of the Ionians on our return trip the very first day, and continued it each time we went out alone. His narrative would be too long for repetition here, but a short abridgment of it will be necessary to show the circumstances under which this remarkable people entered upon their grand career of progress and development.

The Ionians are descended from a body of seven thousand Greeks, mostly Athenians, and natives of the Ionian cities, who were in the service of the Persian king at the time of the invasion of Alexander.

Being located in the southern part of the Persian empire, they found themselves isolated and cut off from all support at the time of its final overthrow. They scorned to place themselves under the banner of the Macedonian tyrant, and as a return to their own country was impossible, they struck out eastward to find a new home for themselves, and after many painful wanderings and some hard fighting, at last found repose in the valley now occupied by their descendants. The country was mostly desert at that time, and the inhabitants few, so the Greeks had no trouble in expelling them, retaining only such of the women as they wanted for wives. The Athenians knew something of the art of irrigation, and soon brought a considerable part of the land under cultivation. They lived in peace and prosperity for many centuries, unmolested by any intruders from the outside world. When the population became too numerous for the cultivated land to support, it became customary for bands of the young men to go out and serve as soldiers under the various Hindoo potentates, the survivors returning from time to time with their spoil and settling down to become husbandmen or mechanics and fathers of families. The government had been democratic for many centuries, but the captain of one of these bands of mercenaries made himself master of the country, and his descendants reigned as kings from the tenth down to the sixteenth century.

About the year 1575, one of the lieutenants of Akbar Khan, the great Mogul conqueror, penetrated the valley, overthrew the reigning monarch and brought the people into subjection. He caused every member of the royal family to be put to death except one, a boy of fourteen, named Timoleon, whom Aristarchus, a faithful minister of the crown, carried off, with a considerable amount of the royal treasure, and secreted in the mountains till an opportunity presented itself for their escape from the country. He caused it to be known amongst those who were faithful to the country's cause that the boy would return as soon as he became of age and attempt to regain his father's throne and drive the invaders out. There were still several bands of Ionian soldiers fighting in various parts of India, and some trusty patriots undertook to convey to them the secret of the young king's intended return, and the date of it, so that they should be ready at the appointed time to fight for freedom. Aristarchus, with his charge, made his way to the Dutch East Indies, and from thence to Europe. There they met the Prince of Orange, and also the young Henry of Navarre, and learned something of European soldiering in which the young prince distinguished himself on many occasions. They also visited Greece and Italy, and many other countries, and thus gained a much larger knowledge of the world than was possessed by most men then living. Aristarchus devoted himself to the education of his charge, and endeavored to instil into him such principles as would make him an able and wise ruler.

Returning at the appointed time by the way they came, they secreted themselves near the southern outlet of the pass which then led from Ionia to the outer world, and which was afterwards known as the Gates of Hades. Posting themselves so as to observe the approaches to the pass, it was not long before they saw some small bands of Ionian veterans returning in anticipation of the expected uprising, and through them they established communication with their friends inside. On a given day they entered, surprised and overcame the garrison at the head of the gorge, and sent word to all who could bear arms to assemble at that point. In this way they gathered together a force of several thousand men inured to fighting, and ready to die for their country rather than submit to the ascendancy of the hated Moslems. The mogul governor, finding himself trapped, assembled his troops and made a furious assault upon the Greeks, but Timoleon, who had assumed the command at once and showed himself to be a born leader, posted his men so skillfully and made such good use of the few small cannon he had found in the fort, that the Mohammedans were repulsed with great slaughter, and compelled to sue for peace. This was granted on condition that they should depart without arms or valuables, and carrying only a few days' provisions for each man. All the treasure they had accumulated and such of the Grecian women who had been compelled to live with them as chose to stay, were left behind. Timoleon, expecting their return at an early date with large reinforcements, set to work to form an army from amongst those of his people who had seen service in India, and drilled it in European fashion. He also strengthened the defences of the Gates of Hades and sent out spies to bring word of the approach of any invading force. Two years passed, and Akbar seemed to have forgotten them. He was busy elsewhere with larger schemes of conquest. Meantime, Timoleon occupied himself in improving the internal resources of the country. Roads and canals were built and repaired, and every encouragement was given to industry and trade. The fisheries on the lake were stimulated by the opening up of convenient markets, and many substantial boats were built and given to the fishermen on condition that they were to be used as a fleet of war in case of invasion. The approach to the valley from the head of the Gates of Hades was very long and narrow, winding for many miles between mountain and lake, and this Timoleon intended to use as a second line of defence, posting bodies of troops on precipices overhanging the lake, and thus, with the help of his fleet, take the enemy between two fires.

His little army was used as a police force, and the disorders which had arisen during the period of Moslem rule were speedily suppressed, and the country very soon began to wear the appearance of peace and prosperity. But Timoleon was far from satisfied with the condition of the people. There were no manufactures, and the system of irrigation was very crude and imperfect, so that not half the land was cultivated, and that only very poorly. Remembering the magnificent dikes and canals of Holland, he could not help wishing that he had a corps of Dutch engineers and artisans in his service to utilize to the full extent the unusual advantages of the country for irrigation and navigable waterways. Remembering also the situation of the people of the Netherlands at the time, and the apparent hopelessness of their struggle with the Spanish monarchy, he had little doubt that many of the choicest spirits and most capable artificers might be induced to leave their own distracted country for a quiet home beyond the seas.

With this end in view, he commissioned his old friend Aristarchus to make another visit to Holland, providing him with ample funds to charter a ship, and sending with him a chosen guard of veterans. That voyage was accomplished successfully in about two years' time, and resulted in the addition to the country's resources of fifty skilled artificers and engineers, including men who understood the manufacturing of cloth and of paper, printers, type-founders, masons, carpenters and other competent mechanics.

Hardly had the immigrants arrived when the long-expected attack was made by the mogul emperor. He sent some fifty thousand of his choicest troops to reduce Ionia to submission, but they never succeeded in entering it. Half way up the pass, where the river changed its course and was crossed by a wooden bridge, Timoleon had built a strong fortification, which commanded both bridge and road, so that the Moslems were unable to force their way through. On six successive days they advanced to the attack with great resolution, only to be mown down by the discharge of cannon at short range or picked off by the sharpshooters whom Timoleon had placed at every point of vantage amongst the rocks. Once they gained the center of the bridge, but the young king charged them so furiously at the head of fifty of his bravest soldiers that they were driven back with great slaughter, and not one of those who had set foot on the bridge returned alive. The next day the invaders disappeared, and the pass was left clear from end to end.

But Timoleon knew that Akbar was accustomed to conquer, and that this first attempt would of a surety be followed by another, and that so long as there was a road into the country he would never desist in his efforts to subdue it. The Ionian king therefore consulted with the most experienced of his Dutch engineers as to the feasibility of closing the pass altogether, and shutting the valley off from any practicable approach. It was found that there were many overhanging rocks near the bridge which could easily be dislodged by charges of gunpowder, thus creating a dam which would cause the water to back up and fill the whole space between the cliffs. This was accordingly done, and the second attack expected with grim determination. It took place within two months, and the second army was larger and better equipped than the first. They brought with them two heavy siege guns, which played upon Timoleon's fort with much destructive effect. The retreat was quickly sounded, and after firing the fuses connected with the mines, the Ionians retired to a considerable distance. The invaders followed up their seeming advantage, and crowded in great numbers over the bridge and into the fort, but their further advance was checked by the fire of a couple of small pieces which commanded the roadway. They kept crowding forward to the bridge, however, until it was covered by a solid mass of turbaned warriors, and then came a tremendous explosion, followed by others in quick succession. The fort, the bridge and all who were anywhere near them were crushed under great masses of falling rocks, and the water being effectually dammed up, accumulated rapidly, so that the Ionians had to retire farther and farther up the pass to save themselves from drowning. By ascending some of the crags higher up, they could see the host of the enemy gathered in the bed of the river at some distance below the scene of the explosion, evidently meditating another attack. The stoppage of the stream had left the river dry below, but it was only for a time. After several hours, the accumulated waters burst the dam and swept onward with irresistible force, and the Mohammedan army was caught in the current and destroyed to a man. The Ionians always supposed that Akbar was present with his army, and perished among the rest, but their descendants discovered, on renewing acquaintance with the outer world, that this was a mistake. History shows that the great mogul did not take the command of this expedition in person, but delegated it to one of his lieutenants. When it was found that the great explosion and resulting flood had made the gorge impenetrable to man or beast, Timoleon announced that no attempt would be made to reopen it for a number of years, as inaccessibility was their best security. He had probably no intention of making any attempt to reopen it while he lived, but thought it best to say as little about that as possible on account of his new subjects from the Netherlands. They, no doubt, pined sometimes for the cloudy skies and colder climate of their native country, and it was doubtless best to leave them with the faint hope of a possible return at some distant day, but as the years rolled on and new ties were formed, the desire doubtless died away, and there is no record of any dissatisfaction of the Dutch colony in their new home.

All fear of invasion being at an end, Timoleon settled down in earnest to the work of his life. A new system of irrigation was laid out and completed, rivers were straightened, deepened and made navigable, and the whole valley covered with profitable farms. Manufactories of every kind were established, the arts of printing, paper-making and type-founding introduced for the first time, and the whole valley ransacked for books in order that they might be preserved and multiplied. The new capital was laid out and built on a scale to suit many generations to come, and in the construction of sewers and the laying out of streets, such far-seeing wisdom was shown that very few changes have been necessary up to the present time. All the mountains round about were prospected for valuable minerals, and gold, silver, copper, tin and lead were found in abundance, but very little iron and absolutely no coal whatever. This was considered a great misfortune at the time, but has since proved a blessing in disguise in leading to the discovery of aluminum and electricity as substitutes for iron and steam. But the material well-being of his people was the smallest of the ends which the great king had in view. His supreme claim to the gratitude of posterity lies in the laws he promulgated, and the institutions he established to secure their moral and intellectual advancement. He founded schools and colleges in every part of the country, and made education compulsory. He endowed a school of science and mechanical art, and provided liberal rewards for useful inventions, so that without the institution of patent laws, the inventive genius of the country has ever been stimulated to the highest point of activity. He suppressed wrong-doing with a strong hand, and even before the close of his reign the criminal class had practically ceased to exist. Besides all this, he was superior to the weakness of leaving a race of descendants to enjoy the kingly power after him, knowing that while his own spirit was as pure and lofty as that of Marcus Aurelius, his son or his son's son might play the part of Commodus, and undo all the good he had accomplished. He therefore refrained from marrying so that, as he was the last of his line, there could be no claimants to his throne. He even relinquished the title of king, and allowed himself to be elected archon in order that the constitution he framed for the government of the country might be in good working order at the time of his death. The power he inherited was an absolute despotism, and no one ever questioned his right, not only to administer, but also to make the laws by which the country was governed, and to him alone belongs the credit of the legislation which lies at the foundation of all its prosperity and progress. During his reign, the people became educated and enlightened to such an extent that they were fit for self-government, and the constitution devised by Timoleon has been found amply sufficient for future generations, and has never been materially changed to this day.

X

TIMOLEON, THE LEGISLATOR

Having traced the history of the Ionian people down to the conclusion of the reign of Timoleon, Jason proceeded to enlighten me as to the character of the laws instituted by that monarch, the beneficial effects of which have exalted his name amongst them to the highest pitch of reverence and gratitude.

He began by saying:

"Our great king enacted many excellent laws, but amongst them all, four stand pre-eminent, as being the cause of all our great prosperity and social well-being. They are commonly known as, The Four Laws of Timoleon, and are, first, the Land Law; second, the Law of Inheritance; third, the General Criminal Law; and, fourth, the Marriage Law.

"The first makes the soil of the country the property of the people as a whole, and has prevented the formation of a landed aristocracy. The second provides that no person shall become possessed by inheritance of more than a certain limited amount of wealth, and has preserved us from the dangers of plutocracy. These two laws together secure a fairly equal division of the products of labor, and have saved us from the class distinctions which divide the people of all other countries according to the amount of their wealth.

"The criminal law exterminated the whole brood of evil-doers and relieved us from the necessity of keeping up jails, reformatories and a police establishment. It has reduced the legal profession almost to the vanishing point, and done away with the necessity of maintaining criminal courts, and thus effected an incalculable saving of expense to the community, besides providing absolute security to person and property. The marriage law, however, as it was the latest product of Timoleon's legislative wisdom, is the instrument by which, above all others, we have been raised in the scale of civilization. It provides that those who are unworthy to be the progenitors of succeeding generations shall be debarred from the privilege of parenthood, and thus secures an infallible advance from generation to generation in the physical, intellectual and moral character of the people."

"Before you go further," said I, "in explanation of the operation of each of these laws, I will ask you to give me an account of their origin, for it is difficult to understand how one man could arrive at so much wisdom as to originate laws so far in advance of his time, and calculated to produce such wonderful results."

"That I will, with all my heart," said Jason, "and, first of all, with regard to the character of Timoleon himself, I must remind you that great men often appear in groups in a way that is not easily accounted for; thus, in the golden age of Athens, Pericles, Phidias and the three greatest dramatists of Greece were all contemporary, or nearly so; and in the sixteenth century, Shakespeare, Elizabeth, William of Orange, and Henry of Navarre all lived at the same time as Timoleon, and it is just as difficult to account for the genius of the great poet of England as of the great legislator of Ionia. Moreover, he had the advantage of being schooled in adversity, and that of intercourse with some of the greatest men of his time, besides the benefits of extensive travel and of observing the manners and customs, the wrongs and sufferings of many different peoples, and the difference between nations which were free and self-governing, and those which were ruled by despots. In addition to all this, he was under the care of one of the wisest men of his time, who had been his guardian from childhood, and who devoted himself to educating and forming his mind during the years of their exile. Without Aristarchus' devoted care and training, the young king would never have survived, or, having survived, would certainly not have attained to the wisdom and philanthropy which distinguished his maturity.

"Having said so much to prove that Timoleon was partly what circumstances made him, I shall proceed to show you how his great genius enabled him to control the circumstances in which he was placed, so as to serve his great purpose of making his reign the starting-point of a new era of progress and prosperity for the people he was born to rule.

"When he had driven the moguls from the valley, it was found that the titles to all landed property were in the direst confusion. The heirs to many of the largest estates had disappeared, and their lands had been seized by strangers, or bought for trifling sums from the conquerors, while at the same time many citizens returning from foreign military service laid claim to these lands by right of kinship with the former owners. Much of the land, again, had been held by the conquerors and tilled for them by the old inhabitants as slaves, and the consequence of all this confusion was that the claimants to every farm were many and the difficulty of deciding among them so great that there was no possibility of making a settlement which should be satisfactory to all; and to investigate all the different claims would have been the labor of several years. Out of this dire chaos, Timoleon brought order and harmony by issuing a proclamation that all lands were to be considered as belonging to the crown, and that for the five years following his assumption of the governing power, the holders of them were to occupy the position of tenants and pay a yearly rent, which should take the place of all other taxes and furnish the whole revenue of the state. Before the five years were up, the amount of arable land had been doubled, and as the value of the new farms was produced solely by the extension of irrigation at the expense of the state, none but the state could claim any title to them. By that time, moreover, the principle of raising revenue by a rent for land had been proved to have many advantages, and the king had the wisdom to change a temporary expedient into the permanent law of the country.

"The Law of Inheritance, which I have set down as second of the great tetrad, was not enacted till about the twenty-fifth year of Timoleon's reign, and owed its origin, not to any series of accidental circumstances like the first, but simply to the far-seeing wisdom of the king. The prosperity which resulted from his beneficent rule, and especially from the operation of the land law, and the vast increase of tillable soil which was divided into numerous farms, instead of, as in most countries, into a comparatively small number of large estates, was enjoyed by the whole people, with a near approach to equality. But the increase of manufactures and the development of trade between the towns and provinces threatened the accumulation of wealth in the hands of a comparatively small number of the people to the loss and degradation of the majority. To avert this danger Timoleon promulgated the Law of Inheritance, of which the chief provisions are:

"First: That no person should be permitted to gain possession by inheritance of more than a certain fixed amount, which was equivalent to about a hundred thousand pounds of your money.

"Second: That heirship should be only in the direct line; that is to say, children should inherit from their parents only, and not from brothers, cousins, or other lateral relations. In the case of children dying before their parents, the latter might become the heirs.

"Third: That the power of bequest was limited to a fixed sum, which amounted to about fifty thousand pounds sterling, in favor of anyone person.

"Fourth: That all property over and above what the law permitted to be inherited or bequeathed should belong to the state.

"The next of the four great laws is that which relates to the treatment of criminals, and its operation has been so successful that for a hundred years and more it has become a deal letter, for the criminal class has ceased to exist.

"In order that you may understand the origin of this admirable statute, I must tell you that when Timoleon commenced his reign the country swarmed with non-descripts, who had come in the wake of the Mohammedans, and whom their lax administration permitted to live by pilfering and every kind of crime. Timoleon banished large numbers of them, but when the Gates of Hades were closed, there were still many of them left, and they increased like vermin in their holes, and became an intolerable nuisance to the industrious community.

"Believing that mercy shown to such miscreants meant injustice to the public at large, Timoleon ordained that every adult criminal convicted a second time should be punished capitally, and although this stern measure reduced their numbers to a certain extent, the jails were still crowded and the numbers of those who preyed on society seemed to increase rather than diminish, and the difficulty of dealing with them caused the king more anxiety and trouble than he had experienced with the Mohammedans themselves. Amongst his servants was a negro eunuch, who had been presented to him as a slave by an Egyptian grandee. This man had followed the king in all his wanderings, and was very much attached to him. Seeing his master sorely vexed and troubled by the scum of the community, he one day ventured to remark:

"'If they were all such as I am, they would not trouble your majesty forever.'

"The hint was sufficient, and Timoleon saw that the key to the difficulty was in his hands. He called a council of physicians, and the result of their deliberations was the embodiment of the law which put an end to crime in Ionia. It provided that all convicted criminals, male or female, young or old, should be subjected to a surgical operation which deprived them of the power of procreation. This served a double purpose: it put a stop to their increase, and made identification more easy in case of a second offence. Every opportunity was given to discharged prisoners to lead an honest life; the extensive public works furnished employment to all who were willing to work, but no mercy was shown to those who relapsed into crime. Their numbers from this time rapidly diminished, and before Timoleon had reigned for fifty years the criminal class had practically died out.

"It was, no doubt, the success of this important measure which suggested the last and most beneficial of the four great laws of which I am speaking. Timoleon's great ambition was that his reign should not only be known as a time of peace and prosperity, but that it should be the starting-point of a career of development and progress for the whole people which should be lasting as well as thorough. Having put an end to one class of evils by depriving of the rights of parentage those who were unfit to exercise them, he saw that there was practically no limit to the benefit which might be expected from the extension of the same principle in a milder form to all ranks of society. The subject was a difficult one, and although he had elaborated the idea in his own mind, he refrained from any attempt to carry it into practice while he remained on the throne. His power was absolute, and he could make such laws as he pleased, but in a matter of such transcendent importance, where the principle involved was so opposed to the usages of all nations, he preferred that the people should act for themselves through their representatives. At the same time, he was an old man, and had set his heart on this reform being inaugurated while he still lived, so he laid it before the senate at their very first session under the new constitution which he gave to the country.

"He prepared a very elaborate and earnest message, in which he set forth that the great prosperity which the people had enjoyed during his reign was owing in large measure to the fact that the population was limited in proportion to the size of the country, and although the land was still abundantly able to support all who were then living, in comparative comfort, the time might soon come when this would not be the case, and the people would relapse into that condition from which it had been his life-long endeavor to free them. They were doubling their numbers every twenty-five years, and at that rate of increase the great mass would soon be reduced to poverty, and would become, to all intents and purposes, the slaves of the few who, by financial ability and selfish greed, would be able to control the wealth of the country. Ignorance would go hand in hand with poverty, and the best school system which could be devised would fail to educate the children of parents who were unable to find bread for their families, for the children themselves would be compelled to labor to help support their parents. Early marriages and large families were the rule, especially amongst those who could least afford these luxuries, and the result in a few generations would be such as it was melancholy to think of.

"But it was the business of the state to look after the well-being of the people in the future as well as in the present, and he thought the state abundantly able to ward off the evil with which the community was too evidently threatened. The right of parentage should be limited to those who were able to show a reasonable prospect of supporting a family in comfort, and absolutely denied to all who were physically, mentally or morally unworthy to become fathers or mothers. In this way the too rapid increase of population would be checked and the character of the people steadily improved by preventing those who were depraved in mind or body from reproducing their kind. He had prepared for their consideration the draft of a bill embodying these principles, and while they might find it necessary to change some of its details, he trusted to see it in substance become the law of the land. He was now an old man, and could not live to see the benefits which would come in time from such a measure, but he felt sure that future generations would bless the first senate of Ionia for the establishment of such a law.

"And so he laid before them the law for the regulation of marriages substantially as we have it today, for the king was revered in his own day, just as he has ever been since, and his government had been so successful in everything pertaining to the happiness and well-being of the people, that they almost worshiped him, and were ready to assent to anything he desired. The senate passed the bill without change and without one dissenting vote, and steps were immediately taken to carry it into effect.

"Commissioners were appointed for every district, each having a staff of competent assistants of both sexes, with power to examine all candidates for marriage and issue licenses to such only as they found worthy according to rules framed for their guidance. The marriageable age was fixed at twenty-five years in the males, and twenty-two in the females. The former were bound to show that they were possessed of a certain minimum of property, and that they were masters of some trade or art which would ensure a reasonable prospect of ability to support a family. The commissioners were required to have the candidates examined as to physical development and health, mental capacity and character. They were also to enquire respecting the ancestors of the candidates, particularly in regard to hereditary diseases, and all forms of insanity. All extreme cases of dwarfed or stunted physique, personal deformity or ugliness,—particularly in the women,—lax morality or mental incapacity, and all drunkards, were to be peremptorily rejected, with a stern disregard to the social standing or wealth of the individuals aspiring to the wedded state. In ordinary cases, merit of one kind might be considered to offset deficiencies in others, but there were limitations which could not be set aside, and persons of feeble mind or loose character, or those having weak chests or any hereditary disease were absolutely debarred from becoming the parents of the future generation.

"To this law we attribute most of the advantages we enjoy as compared with all other civilized nations, and such a law, if properly administered in any country, will rapidly exalt its people to a much higher standard than any other nation can attain to under any other system.

"And now, friend Alexander, I have told you in few words the secrets of our success, and if you have any questions to ask in regard to the practical working of these laws I shall be glad to give you all the information at my command."

"I must confess," said I, "that these laws are admirably adapted to bring about the results which their founder had in view, but it seems to me that there are grave difficulties in the way of their adoption by any community I am acquainted with, and the first and most formidable of these is in regard to the marriage law. Any system limiting the rights of wedlock must inevitably lead to a great increase of the social evil. How did the great king contend with that difficulty?"

"By restricting and regulating the social evil so as to do away with its worst features. He regarded the women who sacrificed themselves to the community as public benefactors and gave them comfortable accommodation in quarters set apart for their use. His government protected instead of oppressing and harassing them, and provided an asylum and a maintenance for them in their old age."

"But," said I, "when you take away the pains and penalties of any particular form of vice, you inevitably increase the number of those who yield to its seductions."

"Undoubtedly," replied Jason, "but Timoleon did not consider that an objection to his system. His purpose was that the mothers of the nation should be chaste, not merely from the accident of circumstances, but by disposition and principle, and the weeding out from their members of those who were otherwise could not fail to result beneficially in the end. He regarded the social evil as a necessary, but temporary, one, and the results justified his wisdom, for it died out altogether in about a hundred years from his time."

"I fail to comprehend," said I, "how that came about. One can understand how, from pure mothers only pure daughters would be born; but surely it must have been otherwise with their sons."

"Perhaps you do not give sufficient credit to the mothers in this respect, for their influence over their children is almost unlimited. But other influences were at work as well. Amongst your people it is a common saying that a reformed rake makes the best husband, but with us it was different, for the rake never had a chance to show what kind of a husband he could make, and thus the morals of the men kept pace with those of the women, or nearly so."

"Then I am to understand that your people have learned how to keep the sexual passion under perfect control?"

"Yes, and all other passions as well. Our young people are taught as soon as they are old enough to understand it, that the essential difference between Greeks and barbarians (I trust you will excuse my using that word,—it is a very old expression with us, and no offence is meant by it) the source of all our advantages, lies in the fact that we have subdued and dominated our brute instincts, while they permit themselves to be controlled by them, and are thus a prey to innumerable ills from which we are free; and being blind to the results of their own folly, they blame their Creator for introducing them to such an evil world, or else make lame and paltry excuses for his supposed injustice."

"I should have thought that, in rising so far above the animal part of our nature, there would be some danger of the race tending to extinction. Do the facts relative to the fruitfulness of marriages amongst you lend any color to this supposition?"

"Not in the slightest degree. The marriages which are not blessed with offspring are very rare indeed. A rapid increase of the population is not considered desirable, and as the death rate is low, families of two or, at most, three children, are looked upon as the most desirable, and the latter number is very rarely exceeded. It would be considered cruelty to subject any woman to the hardship of bearing and bringing up any greater number. And you have seen the results for yourself: our women at sixty look as fresh and young as yours at forty, and their beauty never entirely forsakes them.

"But supposing that any signs of sterility should make their appearance, the remedy would not be far to seek. A premium would be put upon fertility just as in early days the opposite course was sometimes followed, and in a short time the balance would be restored."

"You think, then, that there is no evil which can afflict humanity for which the remedy cannot be found in your law of marriage?"

"That is my opinion, decidedly. By its means chiefly, aided by the other three of the great laws of Timoleon, we have banished crime, avarice, idleness, lust, intemperance, insanity, poverty and every form of distress and wickedness, while at the same time we have cultivated strength, beauty, industry, wealth, intellect and talent of every kind. The tendency is constantly towards what is higher and better,—physically, mentally and morally; and there is no limit to the progress that can be made. We are as far above the people inhabiting this valley before Timoleon's time as they were above the Fiji Islanders, and we have no manner of doubt that in three hundred years more our descendants will exhibit powers of mind and a mastery over nature's forces that will leave us relatively as far behind. And the advance will continue as long as the sun goes on to shed its rays of heat and light and life upon the globe."

"And after that?"

"After that is too far off for me to trouble myself about. Our posterity have millions of years of sunshine before them, and that is as much of eternity as my mind can grasp."

"One thing more I will ask you," said I. "How is it that with all your prosperity and the superabundance of blessings which are within the reach of all, your people retain such a capacity for enjoyment? Perhaps to you the question seems foolish, but it has often been remarked amongst us that those who have every luxury within reach soon lose their capacity for pleasure and that when they have everything that the human heart can desire they at once begin to discover imaginary troubles, as if they could not exist without something to grumble about. But with the Ionians it appears to be quite different: they do not take their pleasure sadly, as we English have been said to do, but, on the contrary, they engage in every kind of recreation with all the zest of children out for a holiday; pleasure never seems to pall upon them, and they seem to find enjoyment in the mere fact of living."

"Having spent so much of my time in Europe, I am well aware of the contrast which has struck you so forcibly. The difference is seen in the mere expression of the faces, and there are many reasons for it. One is, doubtless, that the cares and worries of life sit much more lightly upon our people than upon yours. The fear of want is something unknown to us, while with the majority of your people it is never wholly absent. Where that is not so, as in your own case, there is always the consciousness that misery, and disease, and every form of suffering are continually present amongst the mass of the people by whom you are surrounded, and that human life, as you know it, is, on the whole, rather a melancholy thing, and barely worth the living. With us it is altogether different: we know very little of suffering and nothing of the poorly requited toil which saps the foundation of vitality and makes life a mere endless struggle. We enjoy our work because it is always congenial, and because it is not too laborious. It does not exhaust our energies, but leaves us plenty of strength and inclination for intellectual pursuits and every form of recreation. Another reason is that we are taught to observe the rules of health, and look upon any indulgence prejudicial to them as both weak and wicked. Any person who enjoys perfect digestion and at the same time is free from worry and mental anxiety finds a natural enjoyment in every function of life. Where this is not so, there is something entirely wrong in the environment, and in some way or other the laws of nature are being violated.

"But our system provides against this as against every other evil or misfortune which can beset mankind. The commissioners of marriage have the means of learning thoroughly the character and disposition of all candidates. At the present day, the refusal of license is a rare exception, but this is simply because the operation of the law has eliminated all, or nearly all, unworthy traits from the persons forming the community. Yet they are, nevertheless, careful in making their investigation, and neither fear not favor stands in the way of the performance of their duties. In the first place, our books of public registration show the ancestry of every individual for many generations, and anything worthy of note is recorded either for or against each person who has lived and died in Ionia. In the second place, the school and college records are open to the inspection of the commissioners, and much can be learned from them. For example, all the boys at school are taught boxing, and although it is not carried to a brutal extent, their personal courage is sufficiently tested, and the commissioners take care that no coward shall ever be the father of children. The applicant is further required to give an account of himself after leaving school, and inquiry is made as to how he has comported himself as son, brother, and member of society in general. Now, if anyone should be found to have a morose and unpleasant disposition, it would take a great deal of merit in other directions to turn the scale in his favor and procure him the marriage license. Thus you see that there is no defect of character that our system fails to remedy, and everything that stands in the way of individual happiness or the good of society is sure to be eliminated in course of time."

"You are greatly to be envied," said I, "in having had the law established amongst you for so many generations and justified by the unspeakable benefits derived from its operation, but the difficulty of its adoption by any people brought up in liberty under a free constitution seems to me almost insuperable. It would be denounced as visionary and impracticable. It would be said that the proposal to place in the hands of anybody of magistrates the power to make a selection from amongst the strongest, handsomest and best of the people to breed from, while the rest were condemned to celibacy, would be treating them too much like cattle, and on all sides it would be denounced as an intolerable encroachment upon the natural rights of mankind."

"We recognize the greatness of the difficulty," replied Jason, "and are so far from undervaluing it that we have never made any attempt to grapple with it ourselves, and if you should recoil from the formidable task no one here will blame you, and you have the alternative of casting in your lot with us and enjoying all the blessings which fall to our lot. But your statement of the case is far from being correct, unless you mean it as the view which the average Englishman is likely to take of it. There never has been any such idea amongst us as making a selection of the best specimens to breed from, but simply a refusal of the right to reproduce their kind in the case of those who were clearly unworthy to do so, and as these have always been a small minority, there is very little hardship or self-denial required from the community as a whole."

"With regard to liberty and the natural rights of man you must admit that these phrases are very misleading, and calculated to undermine the very basis of society if insisted upon too strongly by the unreasoning, undisciplined masses, as, for instance, in the case of the French Revolution. The Western nations are given to making a fetish of liberty and worshiping it as a panacea for all political ills, whereas it is merely a negative quality after all, and means no more than the absence of despotism. Pure, unrestrained liberty is only possible to men in a purely savage state, and no advance in civilization is possible without some curtailment of it. The lowest savage enjoys the liberty of killing and eating his enemies, and his enemies comprise all other human beings on the earth except those of his own tribe or village. He has the liberty of killing his wives or his children if they displease him, and the number of his wives is limited only by his own individual strength. But as society becomes organized these natural rights and liberties are taken away from the individual, the number of his wives is reduced to a few, and finally to one, and the State steps between him and his family and denies his right to ill-treat them. Similarly with regard to property, the common saying is that 'a man can do what he will with his own,' but in civilized society that axiom is true only to a certain extent. The community requires that roads and bridges shall be built, that property shall be protected and the young people educated, and every man is made to contribute of his own to these and a thousand other necessary purposes. With us duty comes first and liberty afterwards, and as the good of the individual can only be obtained through the well-being of the whole community we insist that each member of it must sacrifice just so much of his liberty and his personal advantages as the present and future good of society requires. This principle is recognized by all nations with any pretense to civilization, and we merely carry it a little farther than you do. You say that a man can have but one wife, and we say that he cannot have the one if his enjoyment of that privilege will be harmful to future generations. Is there anything monstrous or unreasonable in that?"

"By no means."

"But yet you despair of being able to persuade your countrymen of the advantages of our system."

"I must say I have but slender hopes of being able to shake their deep-rooted prejudice against such an innovation."

"Well, it is not for me to blame you. On the contrary, I feel relieved to think that you are free to remain amongst us and become a citizen of Ionia. I have come to look upon you almost as a son, and should be sorry to think of your returning for good to the unhappy outer world."

"Your kindness to me almost makes me hesitate, and yet my duty demands that I should tear myself away from this earthly paradise."

"Why so?"

"While I despair of being able to induce the people of England to take steps in the right direction, yet I cannot forget that there are many lands and islands of the sea where people of our own blood are building up new communities untrammeled by the ancient customs and superstitions which bind us to the narrow ideas of our fore-fathers. To them my message must be addressed, and I must endeavor to rouse them to the conviction that human life need not always be a record of misery and failure, but that on-the contrary by adopting the simple and obvious means which your example has proved and sanctioned, any community may enter at once on a pathway of progress and bid defiance to almost every human ill."

"Perhaps you are right," said Jason. "In a new country you might be listened to, while in an old one your story would be treated with scorn and contempt. And if the experiment is once made in earnest a single generation will show such mighty results that the whole world will be compelled to follow suit. You are young yet and may live to see the beginning of the reformation of the world. But you have spoken so far of only one of our great laws, although that is by far the most important. Have you no question to ask concerning the other three?"

"It seems to me," said I, "that the law of marriage alone is sufficient for the renovation of society, if carried out fearlessly, honestly and intelligently, and yet the others would doubtless be of great help and benefit. The land law is not entirely novel to us in principle. The right of private property in land has been much discussed both in Europe and America, as you are doubtless well aware, and I have always felt that those who were opposed to it had the best of the argument, although the idea of making its reversal a panacea for all economical evils always seemed to me absurd. And yet without it anything like a fair distribution of wealth would be impossible. I am therefore prepared to advocate it as a measure which no progressive community can afford to overlook. Your method of dealing with criminals commands my hearty admiration, and it appears so simple and obviously effective that one cannot help wondering that it has not been generally adopted long ago. If I were to criticize it at all I should say that it leans too much to the side of mercy. A community which is resolved on making rapid moral progress has no use for deliberate criminals, and I do not quite see why felons who have arrived at the years of discretion should have two chances for their lives. But the law is excellent as it stands, and I would not seriously advocate changing it unless it were to include habitual drunkards in the scope of its preventive operation."

"An excellent idea," said my friend, "but drunkenness is a vice which pertains more particularly to Northern countries. Our people have never been much given to it, and hence stringent measures were unnecessary.

"What do you think of our law of inheritance?"

"I think it is entirely just and equitable. No man can fairly earn a million sterling during his lifetime, unless it might be the inventor who, like Watt or Stephenson, by new mechanical contrivances, enhances the efficiency of human labor to a manifold degree; but these are not the men who amass large fortunes, and no one grudges them such reward as they receive. The man who, by manipulating the markets either of stocks or goods, and by superior cunning amasses a colossal fortune, has simply filched from other men a part of the wealth they have produced, and has no more moral right to it than a pick-pocket or a house-breaker to what he steals. It is impossible to make laws to prevent men becoming rich by trade or speculation, but when he dies I think it is perfectly right for the state to step in and say: 'It is not for the good of the community that one individual should possess so much while others have none at all, and the greater portion of this wealth must revert to the people at large, from whom it has been taken without equivalent rendered.' But it appears to me that the men who have been able to outwit their competitors in the scramble for money will not fail to find a way to cheat the government in the end. What is to hinder such a man from dividing up his wealth before he dies, so that when his estate comes to be inventoried it will be found that the members of his family are already legally possessed of the great bulk of his fortune?"

"That indeed seems an easy way of evading the law, and our government found it necessary to supplement it by another law which made such transfers legal only when they took place twelve months before the death of the person bestowing the property, and by a thorough registration of all kinds of property it was made very difficult to evade this enactment. Then you must remember that those who are the most eager in the acquisition of wealth are precisely those who are the least willing to part with it, even to their own kith and kin, and as a man seldom knows the date of his death, it has very often happened that the subdivision of the estate of a millionaire has come too late to cheat the public out of what the law intended should revert to it.

"I speak of what happened in the early days of the republic, for we have had no trouble on this score for many generations."

"And is that simply because the people have become too honorable to endeavor to evade the spirit of the laws?"

"I think I may fairly say that such is the case nowadays, but it was not always so. There was a time when the law of inheritance seemed about to become a dead letter in regard to one section of the community, and then we had to fall back upon our marriage law, which is omnipotent in its scope and purpose. We had a small colony of Jews amongst us, who lived in obscurity in the ancient capital. How they came there no one knew, but as they are found in all quarters of the civilized world it is not perhaps to be wondered at that some of them found their way even into Ionia. The general prosperity inaugurated by the reign of Timoleon gave them opportunities of which their greed and their undoubted genius for business enabled them to make the utmost. They increased rapidly in wealth and numbers, and by the beginning of the Eighteenth century all the banking business of the country was in their hands, and it seemed as if in a short time they would be possessed of all the riches of the community. Their prosperity made them insolent, and they began to set the laws at defiance. Our young men became their servants and our young women their mistresses, and they adopted the style of a superior race, and behaved as if the Greeks were born merely to be the slaves of their luxury. The law of inheritance had no power over them, for every Jew that died was found to be without any considerable estate, and the vast wealth they had amassed passed from father to son without the smallest contribution to the state, and increased rapidly from generation to generation.

"The archon of that time was a man of the name of Theophilus, an able and fearless ruler. He saw plainly that the country was drifting to ruin if the power and wealth of the Jews could not be curtailed. To send them out of the country was impossible, as there was no way of exit, and as humanity forbade a wholesale massacre, he resolved to limit their numbers by the aid of the law of marriage. Calling the commissioners together he pointed out the danger which menaced the country, and persuaded them to refuse all license of marriage between a Jew and a Jewess. Either might be permitted to marry with persons of Grecian blood, but not with each other. The haughty Hebrews stormed and threatened, tried to bribe the commissioners, and did succeed in bribing a number of the poorer electors at the polls. But all was of no avail, and they saw that they were in danger of extinction as a separate race, and then they took the step which sealed their doom. The archon was assassinated. This roused the people to fury, and it was with difficulty that a wholesale slaughter of the hated race was prevented. A searching inquiry was made, several of the wealthiest of the Jews were found to be accessory to the crime, and they were executed without mercy. The senate passed a law that no person of Jewish blood should ever be allowed to marry in Ionia, and so the whole tribe died out and passed away forever."

"But what hindered them from marrying according to their own religious rites and having children just as much as ever?"

"That would be impossible in Ionia. I have not detailed all the provisions of the marriage law, but merely told you its main features. It provided for the case of natural children, and such all were considered whose parents were not publicly married. They were treated as orphans by the state and brought up at the public charge, inheriting neither name nor property. Their mothers were banished with them to a settlement amongst the hills, and never allowed to regain their liberty."

XI

THE SCHOOLS OF IOLKOS

Having explored the country pretty thoroughly, Jason proposed that we should spend sometime in visiting the schools and colleges of the capital, and we devoted several weeks to this undertaking.

It was evident to me at once that the national system of education is conducted on the most liberal scale, for the ample space and the splendor of the buildings devoted to it were far beyond anything to be seen in Europe. Each edifice is a master-piece of architectural art, and the adornment of the interiors by painting and sculpture is such that the taste of the scholars must be unconsciously educated by mere attendance at their classes. The ventilation and lighting are perfect, and care is taken to prevent over-crowding, so that there is abundance of space and pure air for every pupil.

The children commence their schooling at the age of seven, but for the first three years the curriculum is confined to physical training and such knowledge as can be imparted by object lessons. They are taught dancing and various forms of marching and drill, and such muscular exercises as will conduce to the health and vigor of their little bodies without any danger of over-straining. It was a pleasing sight to witness the motions of a hundred little girls, all as beautiful in face and form as so many fairies, going through what appeared to me very complicated manœuvers, stepping in time to music, and each little face filled with eager delight in the performance of the pleasant task. And when anyone made a false step or moved in the wrong direction the blush of confusion which clouded the little face showed that no severe discipline was necessary; the consciousness of doing wrong was a sufficient punishment, and the same mistake would seldom be made twice. The boys and girls are taught together in the dancing classes, and very quickly acquire the skill and ability to go through the most difficult and complicated figures with grace and ease. The children were always dressed with great taste, although plainly; in fact, I never saw a badly dressed person in the country, but these little ladies and gentlemen performed their parts and carried themselves with a dignity and elegance that would have made the courtiers of Louis the Great envious, and the perfect absence of self-consciousness which they attained would have been impossible in ill-fitting or poorly made garments. Yet these were not the children of a favored class, and it was impossible to distinguish by dress or demeanor the son or daughter of the artisan from those of the wealthiest merchant.

All these exercises take place in the open air when the weather is favorable, but when it rains or when the weather is cold, ample room is found for them indoors in right temperature. The gymnasiums are larger and more perfectly appointed than anything I ever saw in Europe, and from one to two hours are spent in them everyday by all students from the time they enter school till the day of final graduation. Both boys and girls enter into this part of their education with a zest which was exhilarating to witness, and the preceptors have more trouble in moderating their zeal than in teaching them how to learn the most difficult feats. Every muscle of the body is brought into play and exercised in moderation, under teachers who have learned all there is to be known of anatomy and physiology, and this has doubtless much to do with the perfect health enjoyed not only by the children but by all the inhabitants of the country as long as they live. The pupils are not taught the alphabet before they reach the age of ten, but their progress after that is so great that boys and girls of twelve and thirteen years know more than most of our undergraduates at Oxford or Cambridge, and I found that many of the youngest pupils at the university were further advanced in mathematics than our senior wranglers. All were able to speak and write one or more European languages, and their knowledge of their own tongue and its literature, ancient and modern, was such as could only be paralleled by a genius like Macaulay in respect to English. In botany, zoölogy, geology and astronomy they were equally proficient. I saw a class of high school boys at their astronomical lesson, and while I had not become sufficiently familiar with their language to understand all that was said, I could not help admiring their close attention and the quick replies that were given to the teacher's questions. When the lesson was over I asked Jason to explain to me the chart which the teacher had used during the lesson. It appeared to represent the solar system, but the planets seemed to me different in number and proportion from what I had always understood, and I was much puzzled over it. To my astonishment my friend replied:

"That was not the chart of our solar system, but represented the planetary system of Sirius."

"What," said I, "do you mean to tell me that these children know so much more of our stellar universe than all our Herschells and Proctors have ever dreamed of finding out?"

"Naturally they do know more in some respects, for their teachers have advanced much further. Our telescopes are far more powerful than any you have in Europe, and we have other instruments which your scientists have not yet invented. Surely you are not surprised at a little thing like that, since you were aware that our people were further advanced in all science and learning than any other nation?"

"Theoretically I knew it to be so, but this practical illustration bewilders me. I think we may as well stop here in our investigation of your educational system. I feel no more capable of appreciating it than a Hottentot would be of grasping the instruction given in our colleges at Oxford."

Jason laughed, and said:

"Your modesty makes you depreciate yourself altogether too much. There are many things you know more about than we do."

"What, for instance?"

"Modern European history and the condition of the various classes composing European society. If you should become one of our citizens and take up your residence here you will need some occupation like the rest of us, and I have no doubt but you will be offered a professor's chair in the university, which I am sure you could fill with great credit."

"I am afraid you are jesting with me in saying so, but whether you are or not, I assure you that if I should come here to stay the first thing I should do would be to ask permission to go to school and take my place amongst boys of fifteen or sixteen, and even then I fear I should be entirely out of the running."

"I assure you that you undervalue your powers and attainments altogether too much. But we need not discuss that question at present. You spoke of cutting short the investigation of our school and college system, but I beg of you not to entertain such an idea. You have seen comparatively little as yet, and there are many things that will interest you in the university."

"As you will have it so, we shall proceed, and I shall do my best with your help to understand what I see and hear."

So we went on from day to day, following the classes in ascending order, and as my friend had foretold, I found much to admire and interest me. The ground to be covered was very extensive, for the various buildings and enclosures connected with the university covered several square miles and included all the national art galleries and museums situated in the metropolis. These are open at all times to all the people, but are intended for the use of the students more especially, and everyday during school hours the professors can be seen with their classes studying the magnificent collections. These groups we frequently joined, and I had the pleasure of listening to the instructions given and was commonly introduced to the professor if occasion offered. I am afraid my attention was more occupied with the students than with the lesson in hand, for whether male or female, the charm of seeing so many handsome, intellectual faces eagerly absorbed in scientific problems or in the study of form and color possessed an irresistible attraction for me. They probably for the most part knew who I was, and, although none of them had ever seen a foreigner before, their excellent breeding forbade any scrutiny of my appearance, and I could observe them without being observed on my part.

The geological museum is more extensive and complete than anything I had seen elsewhere, and this surprised me not a little, for of course the specimens were gathered from many different countries, and I was not aware that the Ionians had been in the habit of sending out expeditions for such purposes. The same was true of the other scientific collections, which were all very complete and admirably arranged. Another thing that I noticed was that with very rare exceptions the specimens were not shut up in glass cases, but all displayed openly on shelves or tables, which rendered their examination much more easy and more satisfactory. This could only be done, of course, where the atmosphere is entirely free from dust, and where the utmost confidence is felt in the honesty of every member of the community.

The picture galleries are several miles in extent, and every painting is a master-piece which would be almost priceless in Europe. The hall of statuary is full of sculpture finer than anything else the world has produced since the days when Athens was in its ancient glory. I could have spent many days and even weeks in admiring these magnificent works, but Jason would not allow me to linger long amongst them at that time, for we had other work in hand. We spent a day in the botanical garden, which is a paradise of beauty, and contains living examples of almost every species of plant, flower and tree, from those of the tropics to the stunted specimens grown under the arctic circle. The extremes of climate are represented by different buildings heated or cooled to the requisite temperature, and the students are able to investigate the varied species of the vegetable kingdom growing under natural conditions within the grounds of the university.

The school of agriculture is one of the most important departments of the educational system, and has a large number of thoroughly trained scientists on its staff. Every young man aspiring to be a farmer must graduate from it, and that means that he must not only have a thorough knowledge of crops and soils, but also a very thorough grounding in botany and chemistry as applied to the conditions of agriculture in Ionia. Several thousand acres are utilized as an experimental farm by this department, with all the necessary buildings for lecture rooms, dormitories for professors and students, barns and houses for cattle and sheep, etc. This is located at a distance of some miles from the city, and we visited it upon several occasions, and found great pleasure in observing the beautiful order and cleanliness which prevailed in all its details, the fine development of the different breeds of stock and the attention given to making every foot of ground produce the largest possible yield of the most suitable varieties of grain, fruit and vegetables. The farmer students were young men of splendid physical proportions, and although this might be truly said of all the men of Ionia, yet I never felt myself quite such a pigmy as when following the professors and their classes through the fields or stock houses of the university farm. They were all men of six feet and over, with the chests and limbs of gladiators, and yet the most gentle mannered, scholarly, and refined set of young men it was possible to imagine. I made the acquaintance of quite a number of them, and received more invitations to visit them at the homes of their parents, who were mostly farmers in different parts of the country, than I could have accepted if my visit had been prolonged for several years.

Of the schools of electricity, of engineering, of mechanical and manufacturing arts, I shall not attempt any description, for it would require a volume to do them justice. They are conducted upon the soundest scientific methods, and provide the country with a body of thoroughly trained artificers and mechanics, masters of arts in the true sense of the word, whose skill is to be traced in every department of industry.

Adjoining the botanical gardens are the menagerie and the aquarium, both very extensive and well managed institutions. The aquarium contains only such fish as are found in the waters of Ionia, but of these not one species is lacking, and the numbers and variety are very great. Many of these have been brought from foreign countries and successfully introduced to the rivers and lakes of Ionia, and I recognized amongst them all the speckled and other beauties of our own island excepting, of course, the salmon, which could not thrive at such a distance from the salt water. The men who live by fishing on the shores of Lake Malo are all educated at the university of Iolkos, and that is perhaps one reason why the fisheries never fail on these waters. They are in close touch with the government, and make it their business to see that the supply is kept up by the government hatcheries, and that the young fish are not molested, and the close seasons carefully observed. They are a thriving community and own the stock in all the great institutions for curing and preserving the harvest of the lake, and thus providing a very important and palatable addition to the food of the people.

The menagerie surprised and delighted me by the completeness with which the animal kingdom was represented, and by the fine condition and thriving appearance of the specimens. The cages are of great size and arranged so that the animals live as nearly as possible in their natural state. The polar bears, for instance, have a building to themselves, enclosed by double walls, and kept at a temperature just a little above the freezing point, and containing an enormous tank in which they find abundant exercise, and they grow to a size which makes them seem gigantic in comparison with those to be seen at our London Zoo. The monkeys again live in a kind of crystal palace, which encloses a grove of well grown trees, and flourish as well as they possibly could in their native state. All the other animals are equally well taken care of, and have a sleek and comfortable appearance such as I have never before observed them to wear in captivity.

I inquired of Jason how they managed to transport so many wild animals from distant countries, seeing that they must be brought in airships, and those only of the smaller class, for the largest vessels are not allowed to leave the country.

"Most of the animals," said he, "are captured very young, and we have little difficulty in breeding them here, for we make their captivity, as you have observed, as pleasant as we can. But there are limits to our ability to secure examples of the different species. You may have noticed that we have no hippopotamus, and only three elephants, but with most of the other quadrupeds there is no difficulty. Our young men are very fond of going on hunting expeditions, and if you care to accompany one of these you will see that no opportunity is lost of securing desirable specimens of young tigers and other ferocious animals, as well as the milder species, to add to our collection."

"I should like very much to take part in one of these expeditions, and will embrace the first opportunity that offers. Are they generally successful in securing large game?"

"They very seldom fail," said Jason, "for they are always under the command of a hunter of great experience, and our method of driving the game is such as never fails to bring all the animals from a large section of the country within reach of the guns. It is very exciting sport, and I will see that you do not fail of an opportunity of witnessing or taking an active part in it."

Meantime we continued our round of investigation, and faithfully visited the classrooms as well as the great treasuries of art and science, which belong to the university, but long before we had reached the higher grades I found that the students had advanced much further than I had attained in my career at Oxford. We visited a junior class in astronomy, and enjoyed a rare, and to me quite unexpected, treat. We entered the hall before the hour for the lecture to begin, and seated ourselves behind the class so as to see all that passed without ourselves being conspicuous. Presently the professor arrived, and in a few sentences introduced the subject of the day's lesson, which was to be a general review of the fixed stars as they appear during all the various seasons of the year. While he spoke I was puzzling myself over the shape of the room, of which the walls and ceiling were shaped like the inside of a sphere, the floor occupying a space rather below its center. Suddenly the lights went out, and a most extraordinary transformation took place. We appeared to be magically transported to the open air, with the sky all around us, studded with all its stars and constellations. The illusion was so perfect that I could hardly believe at first that we were still in the same room till I had felt with hands and feet for the chair and the floor in my vicinity. The sphere which enclosed us had appeared a light, bright blue when illuminated from within, but now that all the light entered from without through the tiny holes representing the stars, it assumed the deep blue-black shade of the sky on a clear, starry night. Delighted as I was with this beautiful spectacle, I was still more surprised to find that the sphere was revolving, and that during the hour occupied by the lecture this miniature sky would mimic the changes of the whole year in the heavens, each month being represented by its movement during five minutes' time. Of course the smallest stars did not appear in this artificial sky, but all those down to the fifth magnitude were shown, and the milky way and the more prominent nebulæ were indicated with wonderful accuracy. The class faced the north pole of the sphere, and the professor dealt mostly with the stars of the Northern hemisphere, but now and again he would direct the students to look the other way while he pointed out the glories of the Southern constellations. The hour passed very quickly and pleasantly, and I felt sorry when the scene was changed again by the illumination of the interior lamps. I requested Jason to introduce me and thanked the professor for the great and unexpected pleasure I had enjoyed as well as for the instruction his lecture had afforded me.

In reply he invited me to renew my visit as often as I could find it convenient, and explained that the course covered a very thorough study of the fixed stars, and also of the motions of the different bodies of the solar system amongst the constellations, the sun and moon being represented by discs only faintly illuminated, so as not to hide the light of the stars.

I promised to avail myself of the invitation as frequently as I could, and did so upon more than one occasion with never failing enjoyment, and much benefit to my rather scanty astronomical education.

Upon another occasion we visited a class of young ladies engaged in the study of English literature. The lesson was already well advanced when we entered, but the professor, observing us, interrupted the examination by saying that he hoped to give the students the rare opportunity of hearing the language which formed the basis of their studies spoken by a gentleman from England, and stepping down from the platform he saluted Jason as an old friend, and requested an introduction to their distinguished visitor, as he was pleased to call me. Then, in very polite and flattering terms, he requested me to address a few remarks to the class, who would esteem it a very high and unexampled privilege. My first impulse was to refuse at once, for I am no orator, and although I had sometimes overcome my natural diffidence so far as to speak occasionally amongst my fellow-students at Oxford, it was always a great effort to me, and I had seldom attempted it without some preparation in advance. But this was a much more formidable undertaking. I had to face a company of sixty or seventy young girls from seventeen to twenty years of age, everyone of whom was radiantly beautiful, which of itself was enough to drive all the ideas out of the head of a young man; but in addition to this I knew that these girls were addressed daily by the most eloquent teachers, and that everyone of them was vastly my superior in natural powers and intellectual attainments. But while my heart beat as if it would choke me, and I felt myself blush to the roots of my hair, I remembered that I represented England there, and that Britons were not in the habit of acknowledging themselves beaten, and, somewhat to my own surprise, I accepted the invitation. To give me a little time to collect my thoughts, however, I asked if Jason might say a few words by way of introduction, and we all three ascended the platform together. My friend paved the way for me with a few eloquent sentences, which I wished he would extend to an oration, but he came to an end very quickly, and the ordeal was before me. I spoke very slowly at first, and in a very low voice, not daring to look up and face so many beautiful eyes. I told them that I felt myself in quite a false position on that platform, for so far from coming to Ionia as a teacher, I was there in the position of a very humble and modest learner. I spoke of their magnificent university, and made some comparison between it and my Alma Mater, and went into some detail in regard to the difficulties in the way of women who desired to attain a university education in my own country. Speaking of the prejudices of some of our most eminent professors on this subject, I quoted the remark of some crusty old don about the duty of women being to attend to their babies and their husbands' dinners. A ripple of laughter from the class at the absurdity of the speech caused me to look up, and perceiving that the young ladies were all really interested and sympathetic, my nervousness left me all at once, and I was able to make an address of some twenty minutes' duration, and sat down with the feeling that I had not altogether disgraced myself.

The professor thanked me in very pleasant terms, and congratulated the students on the lesson they had that day received in English pronunciation, and time being up, dismissed the class. He then said some flattering things to me of the satisfaction he felt and had already expressed in hearing me speak, and went so far as to say that if I could be prevailed on to stay in Ionia my services would be greatly valued as a teacher in connection with the study of foreign languages and literature.

Jason seconded him in this, and they almost succeeded in persuading me that I could be of some use in a country where all were my superiors in nearly every respect, but I could not help thinking that they were influenced in this by their natural desire to make things pleasant to me, and assured them that I should not think of undertaking to teach without a long course of study, and that for the present, at least, my duty required me to relinquish so pleasing a prospect.

I felt thankful that I had come through the ordeal of addressing the students so satisfactorily, but admonished Jason on the subject, and adjured him not to allow me to be caught in such a position again.

We continued our course of investigation, however, and before we had finished I obtained a pretty good idea of the work accomplished in the university, and the high standard of attainments required from the students. There is no school of law in the university, and none of divinity. Neither is there any school of medicine, but the department of health is a very important one, embracing an exhaustive course of study in physiology, anatomy and hygiene for all the students, but more especially for the ladies, who, in having the care of the children as part of their future work, are expected to lay the foundations of robust and healthy living for all. There are few physicians in the country, for there is but little need for them, but those who do resolve to adopt that profession have to study for five years beyond the usual course, and must become not only doctors of health, but also masters of surgery, and the curriculum is so severe that none but the few who are specially gifted in that direction ever undertake it.

The study of music fills a large part of the educational course of the young people, and its practice and enjoyment provide much more of the entertainment of their after lives than is the case with any other nation. I never found any of them deficient in musical appreciation, and the great majority of them would be considered as gifted performers amongst us. All the children are trained in singing, and almost without exception take great delight in it. In the university, music is not compulsory, although the great majority of the students devote a portion of their time to it, but its higher departments are open only to those having special ability. As there are several thousand students embraced in the various classes there is material amongst them for the formation of the finest choruses and orchestras, and the pleasure of hearing their rehearsals was vastly greater than anything I had ever experienced in Europe.

I may mention here a custom which is without parallel in any other part of the world, so far as I know, and which provides a means for the diffusion of knowledge in the higher walks of science and art, and shows how much the Ionians appreciate purely intellectual pleasures. During the college season, which extends through nine months of the year, the chief professors hold receptions in the halls of the university, each one having his special evening during the week. More than one are given on the same evening, and in one building the professor of botany entertains, in another the professor of music or of architecture; the next evening the professors of geology, of electricity or of painting, take the places of the first, so that during the week every branch of learning has its turn. These receptions are open to all the people, and are very well attended, the visitors forming groups and discussing such subjects as they please, but as each particular branch of learning has its votaries, there is generally a large number assembled who are capable of taking part in the most interesting discussions in regard to the science or art of which the host of the evening is the public representative, and the result is that the latest views and discoveries in each are thoroughly digested at these assemblies, and in this way the people keep abreast of the steady march of learning.

I once listened to a most interesting controversy on the duration of the last glacial epoch, in which the principal speakers were the professor of geology and a young gentleman of thirty who seemed to have made a most thorough study of the subject, and upheld his side of the argument with great ability and eloquence, although deferring with much tact and modesty to the professor's high reputation and learning. I afterwards inquired of Jason who the young man was, and he told me he was a working ship-builder in the employ of our friend Leonidas Van Tromp, and that he was as good a workman as he had proved himself a student of science. Such cases are not exceptional, but occur at everyone of these assemblies, and no one is surprised to find in a mechanic a consummate art critic or a profound scholar.

During all these receptions the splendid music hall of the university is open and choral and instrumental music of the highest order is rendered by the students, each chorus and orchestra furnishing the entertainment for one evening, and providing the most superb soloists from amongst their number. The performers occupy a high gallery at one end of the hall, and are not individually visible. The attendance is always large, and the audience listen in respectful silence. Neither talking nor encoring are indulged in, and even applause, although sometimes irrepressible, is never encouraged nor allowed to delay the programme of the evening.

In connection with the school of health we visited the dissecting rooms, where a number of young men were busy at their examination of various portions of the human anatomy. I asked Jason where they obtained their subjects in a country where there were neither criminals nor paupers, and he said, in reply:

"We do not care what becomes of our bodies after we are done with them. Sanitary law requires that they should be reduced to their original elements as soon as possible, and cremation is the almost universal rule, but if a man (or a woman, either, for that matter,) can be of any service after he is dead, what can be more natural than that he should bequeath his body to the cause of science. When a man is married his wife or children would not like to have his remains so treated, but where there are no such near relations, there can be no objection; nevertheless, except where the subject has expressly donated his body before death, it is always cremated, and yet the students never lack for subjects."

"If anybody should make such a disposition of his remains in England," said I, "he would be considered little better than a monster in human form."

"The feeling is natural," replied Jason, "and yet it is only a superstition after all, and the desire to help the cause of science, even after one is dead, is altogether rational and laudable."

The last of the institutions connected with the university to be visited was the hospital. This is situated on a hill some miles below the city, rising steeply from the lake, and with quite a deep valley between it and the higher mountains, a situation which procures it the freshest ozone-laden breezes from all sides. Like all the other public institutions of the country, it is palatial in structure, and of very great extent. There are two separate buildings, one of three hundred by a hundred and fifty feet, and the other two hundred feet long by a hundred and fifty feet wide. Both are surrounded by pretty flower gardens, and a handsome colonnade surrounds each on all the four sides, so that the convalescent patients have ample opportunity for walking or resting in the sun or the shade, according to the season and the strength to which they may have attained. Each building is four stories high; wide halls occupy the center of each floor; every room is an outside one, with spacious views of mountain or lake from every window. The larger building is devoted to cases of child-birth, and the smaller to those of a general character, and while the former is generally pretty well occupied, the latter is seldom more than half filled. No payment is accepted from any patient whatsoever, so that no one need ever feel any compunction in accepting the benefits of the hospital, and although a majority of the inmates belong to the least wealthy class, it is not at all uncommon for well-to-do people to take advantage of the magnificent accommodation which the hospital affords. Visitors are not allowed in the ladies' hospital unless they are members of the family of the patient, or very intimate friends, so our inspection was confined to the other building. With one of the doctors for a guide we visited many of the rooms, which were all large and airy, having walls and ceiling painted in light, creamy tints, with tasteful ornamentation, devoid of all glaring or violent effects; the windows beautifully draped with flowers and delicate creeping plants, made to grow on pretty movable frames surrounding them; double shades which could be arranged to admit the exact quality and amount of light desired; handsome beds of bright aluminum; comfortable easy chairs and lounges; luxurious rugs on highly polished floors; such were the furnishings of all the rooms, and they seemed fit for the accommodation of princes.

But what made the lot of the patients appear truly enviable was that each was waited on by a beautiful young nurse, arrayed in a becoming dress of soft pearl-gray, moving about with light, noiseless step, and with deft hands arranging pillows and ministering to every want before it could be realized. These are the young ladies of the university, who have to serve for three months as hospital nurses to finish the university course. There are enough of them to provide four nurses to each patient, the day and night being divided into as many equal parts, so that each has a spell of six hours duty, with eighteen for rest and recreation. In addition to the student nurses, there are a number of matrons attached to the hospital, whose business it is to instruct the young ladies in their duties and give special assistance in difficult cases. But I saw no symptoms of awkwardness or inattention on the part of the young nurses, nor, judging by the expression of their faces, did the work seem distasteful to them: a divine pity for the suffering of their patients seemed to possess them all, and the grace and beauty which characterized each one gave them the appearance of ministering angels.

The doctor knocked quietly at each door which he proposed to have us enter, unless where it happened to be open, and a soft-spoken colloquy passed between him and the nurse before we were admitted. Sometimes the patients were well enough to converse with us, and they all appeared highly pleased with our visit. Each spoke enthusiastically of the hospital and the treatment they had received in it, and some of them even seemed to be sorry they were getting well and would have to leave it soon.

Our guide tapped at the door of one room whose occupant was a young man who had sustained a serious injury in making some chemical experiments. In a moment it was noiselessly opened, and as the nurse whispered to the doctor that her patient had just fallen into a quiet sleep, we refrained from entering, and passed on. I had just caught a glimpse of the face of the sleeper, which was very pale and emaciated, and a few inches over his head hung, suspended from a rubber tube, a cone of metal, the use of which I was somewhat puzzled over. I asked the doctor what it was for, and he said he would explain it to me as soon as we came to an unoccupied room. This was not far to seek, and I was told to take the place of a patient in the bed.

"Now," said the doctor, "I place this cup over your head. What do you feel?"

"Nothing at all."

"Well, suppose you feel hot and tired and restless, and wish to sleep but cannot; I turn this little stop, and what is the result?"

"A most delicious zephyr gently fans my face and head, bearing in its cool breath the scent of a thousand flowers. One could go to sleep under its influence and dream of heaven."

"And now," said the doctor, "suppose your head aches and your temples throb with pain and fever; I make a little adjustment, and what do you find?"

"A cool stream of air flowing past my temples, which I am sure would cure any headache ever I experienced."

"That is about all that this little apparatus can do," said the doctor.

"And that is a great deal," said I. "But tell me by what miracle of chemistry you manage to infuse the scents and the balmy freshness of the woods and the hills through this rubber tube?"

"By no miracle of chemistry, but by a very simple mechanical device. Not more than seven miles from here, as the crow flies, is a little valley noted for the multitude and the fragrance of its wild flowers and surrounded on all sides by pine woods, so that its atmosphere is laden with sweetness and health. The managers of the hospital have built a little house there with fine wire screens on all sides, in place of windows, to prevent the ingress of insects, and from its interior the air is pumped through aluminum tubes to this place. It is received in a reservoir built on the roof, where the temperature is regulated, and from there it is conveyed to every room in the house. The flow is constant day and night, and the patients breathe it constantly, but as you have seen, it is a very simple matter to make local application of it when desirable."

The doctor now invited me to inspect the rooms in the upper story, which were reached by a commodious elevator in the center of the building. We found there a spacious, airy and handsomely furnished room, where convalescents lounged and talked and read, or admired the glorious views of mountain and lake, which could be seen from the windows. There was also a fine billiard room, and another devoted to cards and chess, in all of which we found the patients cheery, chatty and full of the enjoyment of returning health. Last of all we examined the kitchen, which was also on the highest floor. A perfect palace of a kitchen,—marble floors, snowy tables, brightly burnished stoves, heated by electricity, at which a number of handsome women in dresses of spotless white were preparing all kinds of delicate dishes to tempt feeble appetites. It was near dinner time, and there was a great deal of bustle and activity, but without noise or confusion; order and cleanliness prevailed, and, judging by the savory odors of soups and other dishes which were being prepared for serving, there needed no male chef to teach these deft-fingered ladies their trade. The doctor invited us to dine with him, and we partook of a banquet of which the dishes were fit to be served up to the gods. We were not wearied with infinite variety, but everything was exquisite in quality and exquisitely cooked. I had been struck with the excellence of the cuisine at the table of my host, but I found that here and everywhere else in Ionia the science of cookery was carried to the highest point of perfection.

XII

A Modern Crœsus

The marriage of Leda Delphion to Leonidas Van Tromp was a very brilliant affair. The archon himself officiated, which of itself gave much éclat to the ceremony, especially as he has only twice before honored bride and groom in the same way. Any magistrate in the country can perform the marriage ceremony and no publicity necessarily attaches to it, for it can be done at any place and time. The important thing is to get the license, and when that is obtained the rest is mere matter of form. The temple of music, however, is generally chosen for marriages, and, just as with us, music and flowers are employed to lend their aid to the rejoicing natural to such occasions.

The temple was nearly filled with a gaily-dressed crowd when Leda arrived, surrounded by the members of her family; the great organ filled the hall with joyous music as we walked down to the farther end,—the bride first, on her father's arm, followed by the lady Helen and myself, with Dion and Eurydice bringing up the rear. On a platform slightly raised sat the venerable archon in his purple robes, the space around him having been converted into a veritable bower of roses.

The bride and the members of her family seated themselves on the front row of seats on the archon's right, bridegroom and his father and mother and the beautiful Daphne occupying the corresponding places on the left. Immediately behind were the young unmarried friends of each,—the ladies behind the bride, and the gentlemen opposite. After a short pause, the organ commenced a choral symphony, in which first the girls sang alone and afterwards the men, then both together in delightful concord. I thought it the finest piece of choral music I had yet heard. It was composed by the master, Theseus, expressly for this occasion. The words were not new, but full of poetry and beautifully expressive of the felicitous wishes natural to the circumstances. I felt that even so modest a man as Leonidas ought to be able to cast off his natural shyness under the influence of such poetry and such music.

The ceremony was very similar to our English marriage service. The archon rose as soon as the singing was over, and in a clear, distinct voice, stated that they were assembled to celebrate the marriage of his dear young friends—Leda Delphion and Leonidas Van Tromp—whom he requested to approach and stand before him. When they had taken their places side by side, he read from a book certain passages appointed by the government for the ceremony, setting forth the great responsibility of the parties to a marriage contract in view of their probable relation to future generations, but comforting them with the assurance that the State itself had weighed them in the balance of its judgment and declared them worthy of the great trust which they were about to accept. The reading did not occupy more than five minutes, but the effect was most solemn and impressive. Closing the book, Minos said that he had known the bride and groom all their lives, and their families for the best part of a century, and that he was glad to unite so worthy a couple in marriage. Then, addressing each by name, he intimated that if they loved each other with their whole hearts and wished to take each other for husband and wife as long as life lasted, they should join hands before him, and when they had done so, he pronounced them man and wife. Then stepping down, he shook hands with both and congratulated them, kissing the bride's forehead. The organ broke forth in a glorious wedding march, and the bridal party proceeded by a side door to an elevator, which took us all to the roof of the building, where an air-ship stood waiting. It was very handsome outside, having been built for the occasion, but the glimpse I caught of its interior showed that it was splendidly upholstered in pale rose-silk, and the friends had almost filled it with beautiful flowers. The young couple having made their adieux, stepped inside and flew off through the air to enjoy their honeymoon. A delightful dinner party at the Delphions wound up the day very pleasantly, and prevented the beautiful mother from realizing that she had lost her still more beautiful daughter, for the time being, at least.

Invitations to dinner and receptions came thick and fast to the Delphion mansion at this time, and as my name was always included, my host affirmed that the motive in most cases was simply to see what an Englishman was like. I contended that, as he had retired permanently from his labors in foreign fields, it was natural that his numerous friends should desire to renew their old acquaintance with him, and I was included only out of natural politeness, but I suspect that curiosity in regard to the appearance and manners of an English barbarian had a good deal to do with the invitations, for they were so numerous that it was quite impossible to accept more than a small proportion of the hundreds that were received. We spent a great many evenings out, however, both in town and country, for the speed of aerial traveling made a journey of thirty or forty or even fifty miles a very slight difficulty. I never failed to enjoy the society of the Ionians, and as I had made considerable progress in their language, was able to take a part in all the conversation that was going on, and would have had to take the lion's share in it against my own will if I had not had friend Jason to help me out in answering questions in regard to foreign countries and peoples. He was such a wonderful conversationalist and had such vast stores of information about everything under the sun that it was always easy to get him to talk by referring some question to him, or asking him to corroborate my opinion on any point under discussion, and once under the spell of his eloquence our friends would forget to question the little barbarian.

We visited many beautiful houses, sumptuously furnished and adorned with masterpieces of painting and sculpture, but few of them built on so extensive a scale as the country houses of our English nobility. There was one, however, which surpassed them all in magnificence, and that was the house of a wealthy merchant of Iolkos, named Theophilus Myron. He was about to give a children's party on the occasion of his daughter's twelfth birthday, and wrote to the Delphions asking them to come and bear him company along with one or two other old friends. Jason told me that, as a rule, it was difficult for people who were very wealthy to induce visitors to come to their houses, for anything like ostentation was looked upon as vulgar, but that this gentleman's place was so well worth seeing that on my account he was in favor of accepting this invitation, especially as Theophilus was really a very genial and intellectual man, and far too sensible to assume any airs on account of his superior wealth. So it was arranged that we should all go to the dinner, except Eurydice, who positively declined, and said she would take the opportunity of visiting her parents on that day, as she had not seen them for sometime.

On the day appointed, which happened to be Sunday, we set out in the same air-ship which brought me into the country,—Jason, and the lady Helen and myself, with Dion as engineer and conductor.

Our way took us down over the lake: it was a bright December day, and we started about noon with a favoring breeze and a bright sun, although there were some heavy clouds in the sky. We had pursued our flight for but a few minutes when suddenly we rushed into the midst of a most terrific storm: first a blast of wind struck the vessel, and made it roll like a ship at sea; then a shower of hail fell upon it with a noise like the fire of musketry at close quarters; then came rain, which fell in sheets and streamed over the windows as if we were submerged in some river; blinding flashes of lightning followed in quick succession, and thunder roared all around us without a moment's intermission. I thought our time had surely come, and tried to resign myself to what appeared inevitable destruction, and yet the faces of my companions, seen by the lightning flashes which relieved the gloom of the storm, showed no signs of alarm. Even the lady seemed to feel no fear, but sat calmly back in her chair, apparently in serene enjoyment of the elemental war going on around us. It was all over in a few minutes; perhaps it was only a few seconds, but they were the longest I have ever known. The light began to break upon us from above, the rain ceased, and soon we were floating in brilliant sunshine, while the storm roared on below. Dion had turned on the elevator and tilted the sails upward to their utmost extent, so that in spite of the heavy downpour of rain, we had shot upward through the storm-cloud and sailed into a region of calm and sunshine. At Jason's suggestion, I went forward to the bow and looked down upon the scene from which we had just emerged, and instead of the black cloud which had overshadowed us, I saw a sea of opal with rolling billows of gorgeous and ever-changing hues bursting here and there into flame as the lightning bolts shot downward to the lake. The thunder still rolled on, but it sounded distant and harmless, and presently the storm swept northward to the hills and the blue water came into view a long, long way beneath, while our ship swept on its course with the swiftness of an eagle's flight.

The residence of Theophilus more than justified all that I had heard in its praise. It occupies the level summit of a hill whose precipitous slopes are washed on three sides by the waters of the lake, and affords from every point the most beautiful views imaginable. The house itself is built of pure white marble, forming three sides of a square, the enclosed space beautifully laid out as a flower-garden, with a splendid fountain in the center. Surrounding it on every side is a park something like half a mile in area, with the noblest of the forest trees left standing. Towards the south the trees gradually become thicker and merge into the original forest, which covers the hills for many miles. A smoothly-paved road, fifty feet wide, leads into the heart of the forest, and connects with a stairway leading to a little harbor at the neck of the peninsula, where several yachts are generally lying at anchor. There is no other road connected with the place, all communication being by air-ship or water craft. The magnificence of the palace itself and the beauty of its situation proved that Theophilus was a man of taste as well as wealth. He received us very graciously, but had the air of a man born to command: he was tall, even for an Ionian, but rather portly in build; a wide forehead, piercing gray eyes, firm mouth and strongly molded jaws were the most striking features of his smooth-shaven face. He was about fifty-five years old, but looked to be about the same age as Jason Delphion. His wife was a year or two younger than himself, and looked rather thin and careworn. She had been very beautiful, but showed the wear and tear of time vastly more than the lady Helen, and I could not help thinking that if the burden of riches produced such results it would be much better to be free from it. We found the other guests assembled, to the number of six, amongst whom were Daphne Van Tromp, and her father and mother, a handsome couple, whom I should have mistaken for her elder brother and sister, so young-looking they were. As soon as we were all introduced, Theophilus invited us to the theater, where the young folks were already assembled, so we followed him round to the eastern wing, where the pretty little theater is situated. The auditorium, luxuriously seated for two hundred and fifty people, is enclosed by semi-circular walls of pale rose-colored marble, of which the lower portion is handsomely carved and graced with many statues in bronze, while the upper part is formed by arches which unite in the center, beautifully painted in the intervening spaces.

A cluster of powerful electric lamps hanging in the center shed all their rays upon the walls and ceiling, illuminating them brightly and adding to their beauty by making them appear self-luminous.

The stage was framed by a handsome arch of bronze, and the drop-scene presented a view of the palace itself, with its splendid background of forest and mountain.

The young folks were already assembled in the theater, and occupied all the front seats, and we elders took the places left vacant behind. A very efficient orchestra was playing when we entered, and in a few moments they had finished and the curtain rose. The play was a comedy founded on the mummeries of a petty German court, and full of amusing situations. It kept the little folks in the audience heartily entertained, and the big folks enjoyed it almost as much. The dialogue was bright and witty, the dressing correct in every particular, and the talent displayed by the actors and actresses extraordinary, considering that they were all amateurs and none of them over fifteen years of age. There was no hitch from beginning to end, and no tedious waits between the scenes, and the whole performance passed off with a sparkle and vim that I had never seen equaled anywhere. The play over, the whole party were escorted to the dining-hall, situated in the top story of the palace, and extending from side to side of the eastern wing at its northern face.

We were conveyed in commodious elevators, of which there are no less than a dozen in different parts of the building, and in a few minutes the whole company were seated round one long table, the elders at one end, with the young people filling all the other places,— boy and girl alternately,—all as beautiful as angels, handsomely dressed and behaving like the well-bred little ladies and gentlemen they were. The table was dressed with flowers in lavish profusion and excellent taste; the windows on the three sides looked out on distant lake and mountain, which took on the loveliest tints of purple and rose as the sun declined. The wall on the fourth side was divided by Corinthian columns of alabaster into three spaces, on which were painted splendid battle scenes, representing Marathon, Salamis and Platæa. From somewhere out of sight came soft strains of music, and the murmur of the sweet Greek voices was like music itself. I would fain have remained silent, enjoying in a delicious reverie the pleasant sounds and the beautiful forms within and without, but our host seemed to think he owed me particular attention, and addressed his conversation in an especial manner to me. I complimented him on the beauty of his residence and its magnificent situation, and he answered:

"I am delighted with your approbation. I suppose you have seen many of our people's playing-grounds. Do you think this will make a worthy addition to the rest?"

"Did you plan and build it with that end in view?" I asked.

"Not exactly so," said Theophilus; "it was partly to gratify myself and partly to use up some of the wealth that I cannot help accumulating. But of course I knew that it would be owned by the people after me, for it is of more value than the law will allow me to leave to my son. I have a choice in the matter only so far as this: I can make a gift of it to the nation while I live, or I can die and leave them to take it in spite of me. In the former case, the government would cause a tablet to be inserted in some prominent part of the building, stating that in such a year the merchant Theophilus presented this palace to the people, to be enjoyed by them forever as a holiday house, whereas if it goes by default, they will probably erase my monogram from the principal entrances and my name will be promptly forgotten. In the one case, it would be a monument to my liberality, and in the other a monument to myselfishness."

"And which course do you intend to follow?"

"If I live till my daughter marries, I shall probably build her a house somewhere else, not so large or costly as this, but large enough for me to have a corner in it for myself, and assume the part of a generous patriot. If death claims me before then, I cannot help it, and I am sure I shall not distress myself over it."

"In any other part of the world," said I, "a man who had acquired a large fortune would esteem it a hardship not to be allowed to pass it on to his family, and thus become the founder of a house which should be powerful and respected in the state for generations. Do you not share that feeling?"

"By no means. I have not the wish anymore than I have the power to place my son above the necessity of labor. It is a mean spirit which would seek to enjoy what others have produced without rendering any equivalent. All children in this country have the benefit of the best education, and to do much more than that for them would be to sap the foundation of their energies and render them unfit to be citizens, self-respecting and self-supporting. Furthermore, we look upon ourselves all as one family. Our national registration offices show that each of us can claim several thousand ancestors in the time of the great king, in three hundred years more the number of my descendants may be as great, and thus as an ancestor I have a large interest in the general welfare, and desire that comfort and prosperity should fall to the lot of all, which would be impossible if the gifts of fortune were to be reserved for a favored few."

"That sounds like true patriotism," said I, "and when I hear such sentiments from one who is placed in your position, I cannot wonder at the great advances your people have made in all that tends to ennoble humanity; but one thing still puzzles me, and that is,—how amongst such a people you manage to find servants to do the work of such a palace as this?"

"Softly," said our host. "I would not have one of my lady friends who are waiting on us at this moment hear you speak of them in that way."

"I beg your pardon," said I; "the word slipped out inadvertently. I ought not to have used it."

"No offense in the world," said Theophilus. "I am sure it was not overheard; and you have touched upon one of the greatest difficulties we have to contend with. The ladies of my household are all capable of filling much higher positions, and it is only by great favor that I persuade them to come and live here at salaries which would astonish you if I should name them. The work is very light, for everything is done by machinery,—scrubbing, sweeping, washing, dusting, and all labor that might be termed menial, are done by machines, and the ladies have only to superintend them and see that they do their work properly. Then I have to provide a library, a music-room, and the most splendid accommodation for my lady helps; the whole of the other wing belongs to them, and they have as much enjoyment from the comforts of the house as the members of my family."

Jason, who had been an amused listener to these remarks, here observed:

"I know of few men, Theophilus, who would have the courage to undertake the task of carrying on a huge establishment like this, and if it were not that you are gifted with a quite extraordinary genius for organization, you would have given it up in despair long ago."

"And after all," said Theophilus, "the brunt of the task falls to my wife, whose talent for management is far superior to mine."

The lady thus complimented replied:

"For my part, I am ready to give it up at anytime. I do the best under my husband's directions to keep everything running as smoothly as possible, but although we have a very efficient and capable household staff and I look upon all our helpers as dear friends, I often sigh for the quiet and repose of a smaller household. But I see that our young friends are getting tired of sitting still so long; it is time to give them the opportunity to take a little exercise."

The remainder of the evening up till nine o'clock, at which sensible hour the party dispersed, was spent in a large hall occupying two stories of the main building on the ground floor. Here the young people danced, while the elders of the party looked on from comfortable chairs on a dais at one end. This was a very large room, some three hundred feet long by half that in width. It was provided with a double ceiling, the lower one being of stained glass, supported by numerous columns of bronze, which stood in parallel rows about three feet from the walls.

The prevailing tint of the false ceiling was a rich cream, with a series of pretty scenes depicting the dances of all climes and ages worked in varying shades of rose-color. The spaces between the rows of pillars and the walls were filled with all kinds of rare and beautiful plants, growing in handsome pots and boxes of aluminum. The room was flooded with light, but all of it came either through the tinted ceiling or from the mass of greenery at the sides, upon which numerous electric lamps poured their light, while they were themselves concealed. The effect was delightful in the extreme, and with the soft music which came from the farther end and the beautiful forms and graceful motions of the little folks on the floor, made up an ensemble which might well pass for fairyland.

"I think," said I to the lovely Daphne, who sat next to me, "we can well find it in our hearts to forgive our friends their enormous wealth for providing us with such an enchanting scene as this."

"Indeed," said Daphne, "it is perfectly enchanting. But you must not suppose that anyone grudges Theophilus his great fortune, for he is the most generous of men. While his genius enables him to prosper in all his undertakings, he takes care that all who are associated with him share in his profits, down to the humblest clerk. And although there is no need for charity in our country, yet he finds means to spend money lavishly for the good of the people, and has presented libraries and gymnasiums to at least a score of the smaller towns and villages throughout the country. He can well afford to jest about being held up to posterity as a sordid or selfish man, for he is known throughout the country for his liberality and open-handed generosity, and will be long remembered for his munificence."

"I am greatly delighted to hear it," said I, "and yet I am not surprised after the sentiments he expressed at the dinner-table. But look at those pretty children below us; what beautiful figures they are dancing, and how well and gracefully they all go through their parts. That is truly the poetry of motion. Why is it that none of the grown people dance?"

"We look upon dancing as suitable only for children. They enter into it with all their heart and soul, and it is a charming sight; but for men and women to be cutting capers in that way would be merely to make themselves ridiculous. Besides, it tends to a kind of familiarity which, while perfectly harmless in children, could not but be offensive when the years of discretion are attained. I understand that people of all ages dance in other countries, but it would not seem right to us."

"Well, doubtless you know best, but there is another thing I would ask, and that is—why is it that I have never seen a theater or an opera-house since I came to the country? I had never thought of it before, but that little jewel of a play-house we passed the afternoon in brought the matter to my mind."

"That," said Daphne, "is another form of amusement which we have outgrown, and leave to the children. You could not get women to exhibit themselves on a stage in Ionia upon any consideration, and even men would be held to demean themselves by playing imaginary parts in public. To the children it is all very real, and furnishes great amusement, both for actors and spectators, but if the performers were adults it would savor too much of sham and folly. Dramatic performances are suitable for childhood, either of the individual or of the race. The adult mind refuses acceptance of the illusions of the stage, and is therefore unable to interest itself in plays and players."

"And have you not devised anything to take the place of these two forms of amusement?"

"I cannot say that we have," said Daphne; "but that is merely because we do not feel any need to be amused. Do you think we seem a melancholy people?"

Daphne smiled as she said this, and looked as if she thought the idea of requiring to be amused was the drollest thing she had ever heard of for a long time, so I laughed with her and said:

"On the contrary, you appear all as happy as children, to whom life is one long holiday."

"And why should we not be as happy? It is a beautiful world, providing full satisfaction for every want and desire of our nature. And we have books and pictures and music and friends. It is very, very pleasant to live. Stay with us, Alexander, and perhaps you may be able to become a happy child like the rest of us, and get rid of the atmosphere of sad gravity which envelops an Englishman."

It was a very tempting invitation, and one which it would have been impossible to resist if one could have flattered himself that any interest warmer than mere humanity inspired the adorable woman who uttered it.

XIII

LAST DAYS IN IONIA

I have now to relate the history of a pleasant little excursion beyond the mountains of Ionia. I was invited to accompany Leonidas and Dion, with a few others, on a shooting trip in which large game were expected, the locality chosen for the hunt being a very inaccessible portion of Southern Thibet, where tigers and leopards were plentiful.

We started about an hour after sunset in five air-vessels, each carrying from two to four men. The hunting ground was a long way off, and it took the whole night to accomplish the journey. I traveled with Dion and another young man of the name of Cleon, who was nearly as skillful an aerial navigator as Dion himself. Each took charge of the vessel for half the night, so that each had a chance to obtain some sleep and arrive at the scene of operations in good condition. The vessels kept in the same order all the way, that of the master of the hunt going first, followed by the others, two and two, each keeping his neighbors in front and to the right or left at a certain distance, and always clearly in sight.

For my part, as I had nothing to attend to in the way of duties, I slept very soundly all night, the smooth motion of the vessel and the hum of the propeller contributing very much to drowsiness. I awoke just as the light of day began to break on a range of mountains far away before us: the stars were fading from the scene, but one splendid orb disputed with the coming sun the supremacy of the eastern sky. Between us and the mountains a great river rolled majestically, reflecting from its broad bosom the azure-light of the dawn, and a giant palm tree on the nearest shore stood boldly outlined by the silvery sheen. Not a breath of wind was stirring, and yet it seemed to me I heard some sound besides the drone of our ship's revolving fan. It was a strain of soft harmony like the sound of manly voices, beautifully blended and softened by distance to exquisite sweetness. Heard there in the dawn, so far above the earth and with the sky seemingly so near, it suggested a chorus of archangels, and I held my breath and listened, but alas, it stopped too soon. But again a single voice took up the melody,—a clear, mellow voice,—and it came nearer and became more and more distinct, a beautiful song indeed, and beautifully sung. Again the other voices joined; this time much louder than before, but finely blended, and I fancied I could make out the grand rolling thunder of Leonidas' bass. Solo and chorus were repeated several times, and only ceased when the stars had disappeared, and the sun came up from behind the hills and flooded the whole world below us with golden light.

"What was that music?" I asked of Cleon, who was in charge of the ship while Dion calmly slept.

"That was the song of the morning star, sung by Leonidas and his friends on our right hand."

"And how was it that it was so faint at first and afterwards so loud and clear?"

"I saw that you were listening, and I steered our vessel closer to theirs, so that I might give you the chance to hear it better. It is a beautiful song, and they have all good voices."

"I thank you very much. I would not have missed it for a great deal."

We soon reached the hill country, which was destitute of all signs of cultivation. All the vessels landed in a secluded valley, beside a clear running stream. In a wonderfully short time an excellent breakfast was prepared, and these young men showed that in the absence of their sisters and wives they could play the part of cook with much skill. But there was a great deal to be done that day, and the meal was disposed of in short order; then to the vessels again, and we went skimming over the wild mountain country in the wake of Philenor, the master of the hunt. We landed at the foot of a long ravine filled with a dense growth of trees and underbrush, through which a slender stream of water trickled on its way to the plain below. Two precipitous walls of rock approached each other at the lower end to within a distance of fifty feet, and the pebbles and boulders filling the intervening space showed that in the rainy season this streamlet must be a roaring torrent, but at this time the water seemed to lose itself among the stones which formed a rough but perfectly secure road for beasts of prey. Above this narrow gorge was a clear space of level sod about an acre in extent, and there it was we landed, taking up a position on one side so that whatever might pass from the upper part of the ravine should come within reach of the guns. And now the party divided, and while some prepared for the shooting, the rest undertook the part of beaters. One of the vessels was moored against the steep side of the ravine in such a way as to screen the hunters from the sight of approaching animals, while the others took to the air again—two men in each vessel, one to navigate it and the other to drive the animals in our direction.

In a few minutes they were out of sight, beyond the tree-tops, and absolute silence reigned in the valley. Not a word was spoken, each man stood with a gun resting on his hip, and two more at his feet ready to be used without the loss of time. Presently a distant crackling fire was heard, like musketry file firing, and it crept nearer and gradually became louder, until I could distinguish the vessels coming down the ravine, crossing it in zig-zag fashion from side to side as they advanced. The sounds came from the dropping of small explosive balls from the vessels, which made a loud explosive noise when they reached the ground, but without causing any combustion. The effect of this was to frighten whatever animals the woods might shelter, and cause them to fly before the approaching fusillade. At first it seemed as if the cover must be destitute of game, for not a living creature appeared, but when the vessels had arrived within half a mile of us a great boar with tremendous tusks rushed past us and plunged through the stones of the gorge out of sight. No one fired; evidently this was not the kind of game they were after. I waited in breathless expectation to see what would come next. Philenor named one of the hunters, which was equivalent to an order to shoot; the young man quickly raised his piece and fired, and a beautiful striped panther sprang up into the air on the other side of the glade and fell back dead. Then came a great serpent gliding along by the water, and concealing itself amongst the grass, so that only a small portion of its body was visible at one time. A shot through the head ended its career of wickedness. Next came a large tigress, with two cubs running by her side. A shot from the rifle of Leonidas found a vital spot, and stretched her dead on the grass. At first the cubs stayed by the body of their mother whining and licking her side, but the near approach of the dropping fire from the vessels frightened them, and they ran off and would have made their escape, but Philenor, believing that the valley must now be empty of all large game, gave the word, and Leonidas and Dion each ran out armed with the instrument used for capturing young animals of this sort, which consisted of a net made of fine wire attached to a stout pole about six feet long. Leonidas was two or three feet ahead of his friend, and had just succeeded in netting one of the cubs when a large male tiger rushed with the speed of a whirlwind from under the trees, and uttering a terrific roar, sprang at him. Leonidas turned his head only in time to see the tiger in the air just a few feet behind him. He sprang nimbly to one side, but quick as he was the tiger would have descended upon him had not Dion, with rare presence of mind, caught the beast's head in his net, and with a powerful jerk brought it to the ground so that the tiger rolled head over heels on the grass, the impetus of his spring carrying him quite a distance. I expected that the two young men would now spring back, out of the line of fire, and allow the other hunters a chance to shoot; but, to my surprise and horror, I saw that they were bent on fighting it out with the poor weapons they happened to have in their hands. The tiger was quick in recovering itself, but Leonidas, the trained athlete, was quicker. He had disengaged the net from his pole in order to use it as a club, and, rushing after the great beast, dealt it a terrific blow on the head as it was turning to attack them again. The tiger had never met such a doughty antagonist before; it fell to the ground stunned and blinded, beating the air with its paws. The stout ashen pole was shivered to splinters, leaving but a fragment in the hand of Leonidas, but Dion had rushed to his friend's side and was about to follow up the attack when Philenor sternly ordered them both out of the way. Being used to discipline, they at once leapt nimbly aside, and the master huntsman himself finished the tiger with a shot through the head.

The cubs were now secured, and placed safely in a chest in one of the air vessels. The other animals were skinned, and the furs awarded to the huntsmen who brought them down, a point which, in case of doubt, the master of the hunt invariably decided, and from his decision there was no appeal. Philenor awarded the skin of the large tiger to Dion, since, though he had not killed him, he had foiled his attack on Leonidas, whose life he had doubtless saved, but Dion demurred to accepting the trophy in this irregular way, and proposed that if Philenor would not accept it, as he had every right to do, it should be given to me. This seemed to please all parties, and I accepted it with gratitude as a souvenir of one of the most exciting episodes of my life. I brought it back to England, and it is allowed to be one of the largest and finest skins ever taken from the body of a tiger.

The day's work was only begun, however, and in a few minutes we were miles away looking for another favorable spot for large game. This was soon found, and the same plan of operations followed with good results, only this time the hunters and beaters changed places, those who had manned the vessels the first time doing the shooting the second, and thus before the day was over each member of the party had the chance of bringing down a tiger or a leopard or a deer, and there were very few misses, so that all went home satisfied. In the course of the day we passed over at least a hundred square miles of territory, and cleared that district of some very formidable pests. Even I, although I had never handled a gun before, managed to bring down a good-sized leopard. It was an easy shot, and that was why Philenor reserved it for me. The animal, skulking away from the terrifying fusillade of the vessels, had taken refuge in a tree on the verge of a forest near where we were stationed; it had not seen us, as its attention was taken up by the approach of the vessels. It was a long time before Philenor could make me see it, as its head only was visible, but it was perfectly still, and not more than forty feet away, so I took a steady aim and pulled the trigger, and, to my great surprise and delight, the leopard dropped from the tree stone dead.

A most jovial al fresco supper concluded the pleasures of a rare day's sport, and we started on the return journey as the sun was setting, and I slept so soundly all the way home that I was surprised to wake up and find that we were once more in Iolkos.

Early in the year invitations were received by myself and most of my friends to spend a week or two at Laureion, the mining city at the foot of Mount Olympus. I had heard much of the delights of this city in the mountains, but the reality far surpassed my expectations. The public buildings are very little behind those of Iolkos in grandeur and beauty, and the private residences are without exception perfect models of taste and comfort. The inhabitants are all wealthy, the head of every family being part owner of the mines which draw from the surrounding mountains vast stores of gold, silver, copper and every other metal except iron. The production is so great that it is necessary to shut down the mines for a month or two every year, and the winter is chosen as the season of rest and recreation, because mining is more difficult then on account of the cold, and because of the great enjoyment the citizens derive from winter sports. Skating, tobogganing, snow-shoeing, and every form of exercise to which a cold climate lends itself are practiced on a great scale, and with wonderful skill and grace, and the hospitality of the people is such that the population of the city is often nearly doubled by the guests invited from all parts of the country at this time.

The city itself is a wonderfully attractive picture, the splendor of its streets and buildings contrasting strangely with the savage, snow-clad mountains by which it is surrounded on every side. The level land is thoroughly cultivated, but its extent is only a few square miles, and the high mountains make it appear less than it is, so that this splendid city of granite and limestone, with streets of aluminum paving as bright as silver, seems like the work of some magician in the savage wilderness. Snow falls to a great depth in this little valley sometimes, but the people do not mind it; the streets are cleared by powerful sweeping and shoveling machines, and there are numerous large buildings whose floors are covered everyday with a fresh coating of ice, and the games go on in defiance of the wildest weather. The snow had not yet begun to fall on the lower ground when we were there, and one bright afternoon Dion and myself, with Daphne Van Tromp, set out for a long skate up the river, which runs into the valley from a wild and romantic glen on the north. The air was keen and fresh, the sun shone bright on the hills and woods, and we sped merrily on past dark precipices and copses of evergreens, with great mountain peaks showing high above us through the trees. In a very short time we reached the limit of our excursion, which was a beautiful waterfall a hundred and fifty feet high, framed in the most beautiful frost work imaginable. Here we sat on a fallen tree to rest and admire the beauty of the scene. The noise of the fall made talking impossible, so after a few minutes of repose we commenced our return journey. We had but seven miles to go, and plenty of daylight to do it in, so we went very leisurely, and stopped now and again to admire the lovely vistas of mountain scenery which presented themselves at intervals on either side. About a mile below the falls a cluster of distant peaks seen through a narrow valley arrested our attention, and we stood stock still to enjoy the splendor of the view. The silence was absolute, and the majesty of nature's grand architecture awed us so that we spoke only in whispers, when suddenly a long-drawn howl of some animal, apparently not far off, arrested our attention.

"What was that?" I asked.

"Wolves," said Dion, "and we must make haste and get away from here."

So we started off with what speed we could, but I soon felt that I was a drag upon my companions, and begged them to leave me and seek their own safety. I could climb some tree and wait till help came.

"If you could leave us both," said Daphne, "in some safe place, you could easily distance the wolves and return and rescue us."

I will not leave you unless it is your wish," said Dion; but there is a large rock standing against the precipice just beyond the next turning. There you would both be safe, and I should soon return with all the help necessary."

Meantime the howling increased, and it was evident that the pack was in chase of us and gaining every minute.

"Yonder is the rock," said Dion; "it is twelve feet high; you will be quite safe, and have plenty of room on the top. Is that to be our plan?"

"By all means," said Daphne, "let us make haste."

So we stopped below the rock, but for my part I could not see how we were to scale it ourselves. Dion soon solved the difficulty; he said to Daphne:

"Put your foot on my hand as I kneel, rest your hand on my head, and spring when I say 'Now.'"

This was no sooner said than done, and the lady sprang like a bird to the top of the rock. My turn came next, and although I made a much more awkward job of it, I managed by Daphne's help to scramble up beside her. Dion then took off his cloak and threw it up to us to use as a cushion to sit upon, and he was off like the wind, and out of sight in a moment.

"Now," said Daphne, "we must stop the wolves here. They could never overtake Dion or come within sight of him, but an accident might happen—he might trip on a fallen branch and fall stunned on the ice. It is not likely, for he will be careful as well as swift, but we must not expose him to the chance of so awful a fate as to be devoured by the wolves, so we must both shout our loudest when the leaders come near. And if we had some stones,—see there are some good sized ones in that rift behind us. Can you throw well?"

"I used to be able to throw a cricket ball pretty straight."

"Well, take two or three on your left arm and try to hit one of them. That will stop them if our shouting not. Stand well back lest you overbalance yourself, and I shall grasp your left sleeve as an additional precaution."

The wolves were now very near, and they were not few in number as we could tell by their continuous howling. At length the leader dashed round the rocks which marked the bend of the river. He was a ferocious looking beast, as large as a great Dane, with a gray, shaggy coat, fierce, blood-shot eyes, and jaws dripping with foam. Close after him came the pack, not less than thirty in number, howling and snapping at each other, ferocious looking brutes, with dreadful fangs. It was a sight to make a brave man tremble, but the beautiful girl beside me remained as cool as if she were in the safest corner of Laureion.

Now they were abreast of us, and would have passed, but we both raised our voices and shouted in unison. At the same time I took good aim at the leader and bowled him over on the ice. He was not much hurt, however, and seeing us, made a dash at the rock on which we stood, as if he thought he could reach us with a leap. He failed, of course, and fell back with a yell of disappointed rage. The others also turned aside and sprang at the rock with such a chorus of howls as almost made my blood curdle. I threw all the stones I had on my arm, and with so good an aim that one of them was struck down senseless and the others turned upon him and devoured him alive before our eyes.

I turned to pick out some more stones from the crevice, but Daphne stopped me, saying, "Don't throw anymore, if you please, Alexander. I could not bear to see anymore of them torn to pieces in that way. It is too horrible. Let us sit down with our backs to the precipice. Now we shall be quite comfortable, and we shall not wait very long for rescue."

And the fearless girl took a sketch-book from her pocket and began rapidly sketching the ferocious animals below us. Some of them kept springing vainly at the rock on which we sat, but most of them sat on their haunches in a semi-circle, alternately howling and licking their chops in anticipation of the meal they expected to make of us before long.

Meantime Daphne sketched away rapidly, filling page after page with vigorous outlines of the wolves in all the various positions they assumed in their frantic rage.

I was lost in admiration of her coolness and nerve, and when the noise of the angry beasts had somewhat diminished I said:

"Daphne, do you know anything of the emotion of fear?"

She turned her beautiful eyes on me with a look of astonishment, and said:

"Surely, Alexander, you do not think Dion would have left us if we had been in any danger?"

"Certainly not," I said; "but at the same time the sight of these ferocious animals and the dreadful clamor they make would unnerve the boldest spirit that ever wore a gown in my country."

Daphne laughed, and said, with a blush:

"Then I am afraid you will think me very unwomanly, for to tell you the truth, I cannot remember ever being afraid of anything. Indeed I have never seen anything to be afraid of anymore than I do at this moment."

Just then, as if to test the undaunted Daphne's courage to the utmost, the wolves, tired of waiting for their prey, rushed at the rock of refuge in a body, snarling and yelling like fiends, and the great gray wolf which we had distinguished as the leader, ran to the middle of the ice and rushed frantically towards our position, and, leaping upon the backs of the others, actually succeeded in touching the edge of the rock with his paws. He slipped back again, but only to make another determined attempt to reach us.

Daphne tucked her dress under her, and folded in the edge of the cloak on which we sat, and then coolly remarked:

"His wolfship is presuming too much on our acquaintance. If he repeats that experiment I shall offer no objection to your crippling him with one of these stones."

The wolf lost no time in making another rush, and for a moment it seemed as if he would make his footing secure, but I had a large stone ready, and brought it down with all my force on his right paw, which made him drop back with a howl of anguish, and the attempt was not again repeated. Daphne calmly resumed her sketching, and while admiring her rapid, vigorous work, I replied to her last remark.

"The more I see of the women, as well as the men of Ionia, the greater I feel to be the immeasurable superiority of your race. It seems to me as if I had been sojourning amongst the gods, and, although you have all had the unspeakable kindness to treat me as an equal, I cannot help thinking that when I am gone you will utterly forget me, or at the best think of me as a poor little barbarian, whom you petted while here as a kind of foreign curiosity."

"There you wrong us, Alexander, for indeed we look upon you as a friend, and while sympathizing with the task you have undertaken, we shall hope and expect to see you back amongst us, and the warmest welcome awaits you when you return. And I am at this moment preparing something which may serve to keep us in your remembrance. You know that I paint a little, and I propose to make a picture of this very scene, which you shall take as a present from me to your mother, of whom we have heard such great and noble things. The point of view will be down there on the other side of the river, with the wolves in the foreground, a young man and a maiden on a rock in the middle distance, with this great precipice behind, and perhaps there may be a mountain peak somewhere far away above us, and the red sun setting on the right. Don't you think it will be an excellent subject? I must come again to make a sketch of the whole scene—tomorrow, perhaps, if you and Dion can come with me—what do you say?"

"I say that you will give my mother a great deal of happiness, not unmixed, perhaps, with terror at the supposed danger of her son and the brave young lady beside him. But if you would make her happiness complete, you might add a portrait of the artist as well."

"I do not promise that, but you shall have something else to remind you of this little adventure."

"And what will that be?"

"You see that great wolf limping about and licking the paw which you so cruelly maltreated—you shall have his skin for a rug, and a fine one it will make."

"Now you are jesting, Daphne. How can you promise that?"

"Because Dion will be here in a few minutes with a number of the young men of Laureion, and they will not let one of those wolves escape. It is years since the creatures ventured so near any part of our country, and they will be sure to kill them all, and I know that they will offer the choicest skins to you and me."

"And will they shoot them all here before our eyes?"

"No, I am sure they will not do that, for they know that such a butchery would be very painful both to you and to me. How they will entice them away I do not know, but they will find a way. You see the poor wolves are in a trap between these two great precipices; we are the bait, but the bait will come off safe and sound, and the wolves will be the victims."

Just at that moment an air-ship flew by overhead, and a voice called out:

"All safe, Daphne?"

"All safe, Dion."

The response rang out clear in Daphne's musical tones, and must have removed any doubt in Dion's mind as to the wisdom of leaving us where we were.

Another air-ship flew by, and another, and another, till in the space of two minutes a dozen must have passed by, and still they kept coming.

The sun was near its setting, but there was light enough for the work to be done. After a short interval we heard a shot from beyond the turn of the river above us, answered by a shot from below. Then we saw Dion on foot on the ice. He threw two large stones, which came skimming along like cannon balls amongst the wolves, while at the same time he shouted his loudest to attract their attention. In a moment the whole pack made for him with frantic yells. Dion disappeared behind the rocks, and, as it seemed to us, the wolves were out of sight almost at the same moment. Then came a sharp fusillade of fire-arms which was kept up for two or three minutes. Then there was silence, and our deliverers came and helped us down from our perch. Every last wolf was dead, and we returned in Dion's vessel to Laureion, escorted by some hundreds of airships. They kept streaming out of the city as we approached, and turning as they met us, swelled the procession to such an extent that we seemed to be returning in triumph from a great victory.

The few remaining weeks of my stay in Ionia sped by with amazing swiftness, and when it came to the end I was perfectly overwhelmed with the kindness of those who had been strangers to me but a short time before, but whom I now regard as the dearest of friends. Everyone insisted on my promising to come again, and they loaded me with presents of great beauty and intrinsic value. Not the least prized of these is the painting by Daphne of our siege by the wolves, which now hangs in our dining room at the Grange. It is much admired by connoisseurs, who find it difficult to believe that it is the work of a young lady of twenty summers, for they declare it to be a master-piece which is scarcely equaled in the finest galleries of Europe. My mother is very proud of it, but protests that she can never look at it without fear and trembling.

On the last day of my stay I had a parting interview with the venerable archon. Jason went with me to the Acropolis, and Minos spoke with great kindness and feeling, saying that he regretted losing me as a citizen, although he could not but commend my choice of return to the outer world.

"I can easily find it in my heart," he continued, "to envy the part you propose to play, for you are young and have, I trust, a long life before you. You are free to undertake the cure of a world sick with innumerable maladies, and you know of a regime which will infallibly cure them all, if you can but succeed in getting it adopted. You might well say with Hamlet that the world is out of joint, but you need not regret like him that you were born to set it right. On the contrary, you must feel it a great privilege to make the attempt, and it requires no gift of prophecy to predict that you will succeed."

"I am glad to hear you say so," I replied, "but there is a vast mass of prejudice to be overcome, and I feel that it will be a work of time and difficulty."

"Undoubtedly," said Minos, "but you must not allow that to discourage you. I do not say that the story of what you have seen here will be believed at once, or that the system which has done so much for us will be considered applicable to other conditions of society, but sober reason and sound sense will ultimately prevail. You must be prepared for opposition from every class of society; from the conservatives, because they are opposed to all innovations; from liberals and reformers because they have their own pet schemes for ameliorating the condition of the people, and are unable to see any virtue in other methods; from the privileged classes because they believe that their advantage consists in the maintenance of the prevailing injustice and inequality; from the very religious because they consider sin and suffering indispensable to human life on earth, and would look upon any proposition to do away with them entirely as little short of impious. You must be prepared to find yourself held up to universal scorn and execration as one who presumes to interfere with the most sacred of human rights. But you must never allow yourself to be discouraged under any circumstances. If the people of England will not listen to you, those of America may; and if not, there is Australia, there is New Zealand, there are people of your race scattered all over the globe, and the smaller the community the greater the chances of success for an experiment with our Ionian laws. But I believe that you will meet with a certain amount of sympathy and encouragement wherever you go. There are reasonable people in all parts of the world who are dissatisfied with the existing state of society, people who lament the miserable terms upon which the majority of their fellow-creatures are compelled to accept existence, and who will gladly listen to any proposition which offers a just hope of radical improvement. In any case you must not forget that you have warm friends here whose best wishes go with you, and if at anytime you should feel despondent or disposed to believe that after all the whole world may be right and yourself wrong, just come back to Ionia for a season, and I am sure that you will find such sympathy and encouragement here as will enable you to renew the fight with unabated vigor and determination to conquer."

"I thank you, Minos," said I, "for all your kindness, and, although I may be very glad to accept your invitation and come back for a time to renew my acquaintance with the noble people of Ionia, I can never despair of final success after what I have already seen of their great achievements. Through you I would express my gratitude to them all, and now I must say farewell."

"Goodbye, Alexander. I am an old man, but I do not despair of seeing you again. I shall hear of you in any case, and you take my best wishes for success, and an old man's blessing."

That same evening I sailed away over the lake from Iolkos as the sun was setting, and as the beautiful city faded from my sight I felt like a lost soul shut out of paradise, and if Jason had not accompanied me I should have given way to the utmost dejection; but he allowed me little time to think of all the dear friends and pleasant scenes I was leaving behind, talking cheerily of future visits and of all the great things he expected me to accomplish. He accompanied me for several days, and did not leave me till I was on board ship at Bombay. He even seemed sorry to let me go then, and, as we stood at the ship's side, insisted on my promising to return at no distant date.

"For you know," said he, "that I look upon you as one of my family, and I have some qualms of conscience in allowing you to undertake this great mission alone. Ever since I commenced to mingle with the people of Europe I have felt that we were in some manner called upon to open their eyes to the folly of continuing from generation to generation to cultivate ignorance and disease and crime, knowing as we did that all these evils can be eradicated by the simplest means. The convictions of our ruling men, however, were not to be disregarded, and I could only look for another to take up the task I was not in a position to assume. I found in you the man I wanted, but my feeling for you has become like that of father to son, and I almost feel ashamed to devolve upon your young shoulders the duty which at times I have felt should be mine."

"Your kindness is too great, Jason, but as I never knew my father, I shall be glad always to think of you in that relation. And if anything should encourage me to assume with confidence the great work before me it is that you have thought me worthy of it."

"I am sure of it, Alexander, and there is much in what Minos said: it is a great privilege as well as a great responsibility. Goodbye, my son. Remember that Ionia expects great things from you."

XIV

Conclusion

London seemed to me to be very much changed for the worse when I got back from the East. The smoke which filled the air obscuring the light, and rendering breathing difficult; the accumulated grime of years streaking the public buildings with sooty black; the mud and filth of many of the streets; the employment of animals for the movement of vehicles, animals with iron-shod feet, calculated to destroy the best pavements in the shortest time; the poverty of design and material in most of the buildings, and the utter absence of harmony or congruity of architecture in the structures of each street or block; all these combined impressed me with the crudeness of our so-called civilization.

But what I saw of the people themselves affected me still more unpleasantly. It was a raw March day, with a chill east wind, and I saw with sorrow and shame poor little children and wretched-looking old men and women dressed in scanty, thread-bare garments, shivering with cold. A blind old man begging for public charity; a blaspheming, drunken wretch with his coat in rags staggering down an alley, followed by a troop of boys who pelted him with mud and stones, yelling after him in fiendish glee; an unhappy urchin, discovered in some petty crime, and dragged off to jail by a policeman, the sulky scowl of ignorance distorting his features; such things as these seen from a cab as I passed from station to station, things which formerly I should have taken as a matter of course, now affected me very painfully. Knowing that my mother awaited me anxiously, I meant to take the very first train for Chingford, but as I passed through the city, I felt as if I could not bring myself to endure its obnoxious sights and sounds for many a day to come. The people all seemed to me to be dwarfed in stature, homely in feature, and clumsy in figure, and very badly dressed. Care and trouble seemed to cloud every brow except the very youngest, and to have left its traces in lines and wrinkles which never could be smoothed away. I had been sojourning amongst the gods, and the faces of ordinary mortals seemed mean and abject by comparison. When I got down at the station I paid the cabman double or triple fare, and he bowed and touched his hat with fawning servility. This made me feel like kicking him, and I blushed for shame to think that Englishmen could be such slaves.

Fortunately, I had not long to wait for a train, and when I reached home my mother's loving welcome made me forget the unpleasantness of my drive through London.

After dinner we sat and talked as we had so often done together when I was a boy. Mother said:

"You have no idea, my son, how long your absence has appeared to me. It seemed as if these six months would never come to an end, and at times I felt as if I never should live through it. But I knew from your letters that you were enjoying your visit more than you could tell in words, and I tried to make you believe that the time passed tolerably well with me."

"Mother, I shall never leave you so long alone again."

"What, after tasting the joys of this earthly paradise, do you think you will ever be content away from it?"

"My duty requires it. But I am free to visit Ionia again, and have the most pressing invitation to return when I please, and to take you with me if you will consent to go, which I sincerely hope you will."

"What, you want your old mother to take a flying trip through the air like a witch on a broom-stick? I am surprised to hear you suggest it."

"My dear mother, I protest against such language, for in the first place you are not old, and in the second place you could make the trip without the slightest sacrifice either of dignity or safety. You take your seat in a most comfortable car just as you would in a railway carriage, and electricity does all the rest."

"But I should die of fright. I do not think you will ever be able to persuade me to go, but of course that need not prevent your going by yourself sometime or other, but not for a good long while. Now, I wish to ask you one thing: Did you lose your heart in Ionia? Did you fall in love with any of the beautiful young women you described in terms of such unbounded admiration?"

"I think not, mother. Indeed I took special pains to guard against any such catastrophe. It would have been the sheerest presumption in me to pay my addresses to any of these adorable women, for in the first place, they are all too good for me, and in the second place I could not ask one of them to live with me in this unhappy outside world anymore than I could ask to drag an angel down from heaven."

My mother looked grave at this, and said:

"I think you humiliate yourself too much. At least you must allow me to differ from you to this extent, that I think no woman on earth can be too good for my boy."

"Ah, but mother, you have not seen these Ionians, and until you have seen them, you will never know how perfect in form and feature they are, nor how to all the personal graces they unite those of the mind and heart. You cannot understand how different our own people look to me since. All the faces I saw in London looked to me like caricatures; those of the men as well as the women. Faces that I should formerly have thought handsome strike me now as remarkable only for the lack of something necessary to make them really attractive. Whether in form, complexion or expression, all appeared to have some conspicuous defect."

"Now, if you say much more I shall begin to hate your Ionian friends. Even your poor mother, I suppose, seems to you a very inferior sort of person, now that you have come back to your own poor country."

"No, no, you must not entertain that idea for a single moment. You know that I have always thought you the best woman on earth, and I think so still. Without the advantage of being born in Ionia, you have all the grace and all the sweetness of perfect womanhood, and therefore I honor you more than all of them. You are enshrined in my inmost heart, and shall be so while I live."

"I fear you are flattering me, my boy, and yet I could not bear to imagine you thought any less of me than you have always done, so I will try not to be jealous of Leda and Daphne, and the rest of them. And now that I have you safe home again, I trust you will stay with me for sometime, but I suppose you will be running off to London to see how things are going on in that dreary east end parish."

"No, mother, I am not going to leave you. The work in London is in good hands, and does not need my supervision. I should like to hear what is going on, but instead of running up there myself, I propose to invite Mr. Calderwood and one of the young men down here for a day or two. The rest will do them good, and they can tell me all I need to know. Besides, I should like to talk with them about all I have seen and learned while I have been away, and get their advice as to the work which lies before me."

"I see your old enthusiasm is not dead, but seeks a wider field. You were once ambitious to save the London poor, and now you dream of raising the whole human race to the standard of Ionia."

"My past experience teaches me to expect failure rather than success, but I must do what I can for my poor fellow-creatures."

"And if a mother's prayers will help you, success will surely crown your efforts."

Within a week the rector of St. Oswald's came to the Grange, and with him my agent, Mr. Manson. They enjoyed a few days of rest and change, and gave me all the news of our London enterprise, and I related to them my wonderful experiences in the East, substantially as I have done in the foregoing pages. They listened with wonder and admiration to all the strange things I had to tell them, but seemed somewhat bewildered by the new light thrown upon the old question of helping downtrodden humanity, which both had grappled with like earnest, single-hearted men as they are. I let them think it over without asking for their opinions till the last evening of their stay, when I had my grandfather, Dr. Wolverton, over from the rectory to dinner, after which we all repaired to the library and seated ourselves round a glowing fire of logs, the cheering comfort of which was intensified by the wind and rain beating spitefully upon the windows. The old doctor occupied a great arm-chair on one side of the fire, with Mr. Calderwood next to him; my mother sat opposite, and I by her side, while the young curate sat in the center, and completed the semi-circle.

The two rectors had talked all through the dinner about the days of their youth, and the changes that had taken place in church and state since then, and would have kept on with their reminiscences till morning, but when we were fairly seated in the library, I told them that I wished to hear what they had to say about the use I ought to make of the great privileges which had been accorded to me in becoming acquainted with the people of Ionia and learning their remarkable history.

"You have heard my story," said I. "You know how, in an obscure corner of the earth, a race of husbandmen and soldiers has grappled with the problems which have baffled the greatest nations of the earth, and solved them with such triumphant success that they are now a thousand years ahead of the rest of the world in all that concerns the grandeur and the happiness of mankind. The means by which they have arrived at such an enviable result, appear to me so simple and so sure, that no people or state which has the wisdom to adopt them can fail of accomplishing the same end. But there is a vast mass of prejudice and ignorance to be overcome before the first beginnings can be made, and I ask you, who are my oldest and dearest friends, to tell me unreservedly what you think of the prospects of success in the proclamation of this simple gospel of reason and common sense."

After a short pause, my grandfather said:

"I am almost too old to understand ideas so contrary to all that we have grown to consider as the fundamental principles of society. We have been taught that the poor should be always with us, and that in some respects it is better to be poor than to be rich, 'For it is easier for a camel to pass through a needle's eye than for a rich man to enter into the kingdom of heaven.' I should be the last to discourage you in what you conceive to be your duty, but at my time of life it is difficult to conceive of a world where there should not be rich and poor, and the one appears to me the necessary complement of the other: the poor to perform all those tasks which are unfit for people of refinement and education, the rich to help the poor and, in doing so, develop those instincts of charity and benevolence which modify and excuse the selfishness of wealth. So far as I am able to see, the poor around us are contented and happy, and with fewer wants and cares, probably derive as much enjoyment from life as those in higher station."

"But, my friend," broke in the London rector, "you do not—excuse my saying it—you do not know what real poverty is. In the country the numbers of the hopeless poor are few, and their rich neighbors never allow them to starve or die from sheer neglect. And they have sunshine and pure air in abundance, and the glory and the beauty of nature all around them. And in your own parish in particular, where your daughter has worked such miracles, the pressure of poverty is unknown. But if you could see the poor in London, crowded together in filthy tenements, where a breath of pure air is unattainable, where vice and disease and poisonous drinks hold perpetual carnival; if you could see little children growing up under such conditions and becoming stunted and depraved, without the opportunity or the will to learn of anything better, and doomed from the cradle to a life of misery and shame, you could not think of poverty as a condition of things to be tolerated by good men and women, if there is any possibility of getting rid of it. What say you, Mr. Manson?"

"I feel as you do," said that gentleman. "The poverty we know—and having come into daily contact with it, we know it only too well—is a disgrace to our boasted civilization, and a curse which may be the ruin of England, unless some means are found to cope with it more effectually than any that have yet been tried."

"I see," said my grandfather, "that I am in no position to speak on this subject, and I bow to your superior judgment. But my grandson's idea, if I understand him rightly, is to do away with not only the vicious poverty of cities, but also the respectable poverty of the country. In this strange country he has just visited he found all the people educated and cultured to a degree that the best of us have not attained to here. Miners and fishermen, mechanics and wagon drivers, and household servants, too, have all been through college, and are able to hold their own in the most abstract fields of learning with university professors and statesmen. That is a condition of things which I am unable to comprehend. If we have no poor people to perform the drudgery of life I cannot understand how everyday life can be carried on at all. Then, if there is no class enjoying great wealth, but all reduced to one uniform level, what becomes of our noble palaces and the beautiful parks and woods which are the ornament of the country?"

"The noble parks and palaces will be there just the same," said I, "but instead of being inhabited by one or two persons for a portion of the year, they will contribute to the health and enjoyment of the whole people at all times when their possession is most desirable. As for bringing all men to the same level, there can be no objection to that, provided the level is constantly being raised higher and higher, and consists not in dragging down those who are above, but in raising those who are below. However, no such result will ever come to pass, for there will always be some who have greater ability to make money than others, and there will be enough for all to have sufficient, while some have a superfluity. All that is necessary is to guard against the extremes, which are harmful to all alike.

"I cannot agree with you in thinking it necessary that human beings should ever be compelled to live by drudgery. I understand the word to mean mere mechanical labor, without skill or the exercise of any intellectual force, and such labor in my opinion should always be performed by machinery and not by men or women, and so it is in Ionia. I went into the mines there, and in place of scores of men working with picks in painful and cramped positions, I saw machines that would perform the labor of fifty men directed by one. The ore was sawed out, broken into blocks, and dumped into wagons with a precision and speed that were perfectly astonishing. And so it is in every department of industry, even down to the housework of the women. They have cunning machines for sweeping, scrubbing, laundry work, and even for the washing of dishes. And the only thing that prevents us from doing all our drudgery by machinery is the lamentable cheapness and redundancy of human labor. The production of human drudges goes on without let or hindrance, and the poor creatures are jealous of the introduction of new machinery lest it take the bread out of their mouths. The trades unions are banded together against new inventions just because these tend to facilitate production and increase the returns of labor. But the moment you put a check on the unlimited production of laborers the keen competition amongst them will be reduced, the market value will rise with the skill of each pair of hands, and necessity will bring forth innumerable inventions for which, at present, there is no occasion."

"And this brings you," said Dr. Wolverton, "to the main question, whether it is practicable to limit the right of reproduction in a country enjoying the blessing of free institutions. The old commandment: 'Be fruitful and multiply and replenish the earth,' has been held until now to be binding upon all, and every man who takes to himself a wife and adds to the population by producing numerous offspring has been supposed to be performing a public duty. It may be that the earth is now sufficiently replenished, and that it is time to call a halt and pay some attention to the quality of the offspring, rather than to the quantity of it, but we old folks have been accustomed to think that nature's law and that of the Bible were in such perfect agreement on this point that any interference with them would partake of the nature of blasphemy and be foredoomed to failure.

"You see, I am speaking out plainly, as you requested, not from any wish to discourage you, but rather to indicate the reception which your new gospel is likely to receive at the hands of old-fashioned people. But I should be glad to hear what my old friend Calderwood has to say on the subject."

"The authority and example of the great apostle Paul," said the London rector, "is surely sufficient to justify us in regarding the commandment you have quoted as one which is not universally binding. When a man has work to do which demands all his energy, and all his thought, no one thinks any the less of him for declining to burden himself with family ties. The Roman Catholic Church, which for so many hundred years was the only church of the greater part of Europe, has sealed the custom of celibacy with its approval, and the system has undoubtedly produced many saints of both sexes. We Protestants do not approve of it, but at the same time, we think nonetheless of its priests or its sisters of charity as individuals, because they deny themselves the comforts of marriage. On the other hand, I confess that my parochial duties have brought me into contact with thousands and tens of thousands of children, yes, and grown up men and women, too, of whom it might truly be said that it would have been better if they had never been born. Now, if there be any means by which the state can prevent the birth of these miserable creatures, society would be the gainer to an incalculable extent. It appears to me that only good citizens should enjoy the rights of citizens, and that those who contribute nothing to the public well-being should be treated in such fashion as the health and prosperity of the community demand, consistently with the dictates of humanity and mercy. To that extent, at least, I am in entire sympathy with the law of marriage, which Mr. Musgrave assures us has produced such wonderfully beneficial results to the people of Ionia. Whether it is practicable in a free country like ours, is a question which requires the most serious consideration."

"Now, Mr. Manson," said I, "it is your turn to speak. I am sure that you have something to say on this momentous question, and I beg of you to give me your opinion candidly and without reserve."

"I shall do so with much pleasure," said he, "and have no occasion for reserving any of my thoughts, for my sympathies are entirely with you in the ideas you have imbibed from your noble friends on the other side of the world. To me their story is a revelation of hope and joy for humanity. I have long felt that our modern European society was the worst kind of sham and fraud; like a whited sepulchre above, but full of rottenness and dead men's bones below. Here in this island are thirty millions of people, of whom half a million revel in luxury, two or three millions enjoy a fair measure of comfort and such intellectual and artistic pleasure as make life tolerable, and all the rest endure existence without hope, and with little more of comfort than the beasts of the field. You speak of the rural poor as being well off compared to the wretched creatures who crawl through the slums of London. But, tell me, are my lord's horses and his dogs not vastly better off than the laborers who cultivate his estate? They are better fed and better housed; every precaution is taken that their health may not be injured, and that they are not injured by overwork. The laborers have to toil early and late in all sorts of weathers; rheumatism and ague work their will upon them, and they have no hope but in the grave. The workmen of our cities are little better off; their pleasures are few, and their hardships many, and if they can keep themselves and their children from pauperism it is the utmost they can expect. True, they are used to it, and their spiritual directors admonish them to be content with the station to which God has called them. But I protest against such canting hypocrisy. God never made this beautiful world to be peopled by a race of toiling slaves, and it is no wonder that our jails and our workhouses are filled, and that crime and vice and strong drink claim their victims by the hundred thousand.

"And what have we done for it all? We have built churches and schools; we have had temperance crusades and salvation army campaigns, but what does it all amount to? Some few have been dragged from the lowest depths of vice and misery, some few have been saved from falling into degradation and crime, but the cesspools of society are as foul as ever, and conditions which contribute to human guilt and misery remain unchanged. I have mourned over the prospect till my heart has ached with despair, for I could not see a ray of hope anywhere, and I have looked upon the condition of humanity in this world as hopeless. I have said to myself that, unless human nature can be changed, toil and hopeless misery must continue to be the lot of the vast mass of men and women. But now comes Mr. Musgrave with proofs that human nature can indeed be changed; that in one blessed spot of earth it has been transformed so that the inhabitants are more like the angels of heaven than the weak and wicked creatures which disgrace our great centers of population. And the means are so simple and obvious that the wonder is we never thought of them before. We have improved our fruits and our flowers, our dogs and our horses, and our cattle, so that they could hardly be known for the same by one who had not watched all the stages of the process. And why have we not applied the same methods to our own species, which needed improvement vastly more than all the rest? It can hardly be said that we doubted nature's power to help us in this as it has done in the case of inferior creatures. On the contrary, we knew it all the time; we knew that as we could not expect to gather grapes from thorns, nor figs from thistles, it would be foolish to expect the children of the vicious and depraved to be moral and virtuous. But we have never made the slightest effort to check the begetting of drunkards and criminals, and our feeble and paltry attempts to stop the tide of mischief at the flood were foredoomed to failure.

"It is strange that we have been blind so long, and I, for one, feel inexpressibly thankful to Mr. Musgrave for having opened my eyes. Tell your story to the world, Mr. Musgrave, and do not despair of results. Those who are interested in maintaining the present unhappy state of things may jeer and deride, for the redemption of humanity is a jest to them, but sooner or later the seed will bear fruit, and the path which the Ionians have beaten out will be followed by every nation which aims to rank amongst the leaders of civilization."

"I thank you, Mr. Manson," said I, "for these encouraging words. I have no fear for the future, but it is most comforting to know that others share my hopes."

"Behold the enthusiasm of youth," said Dr. Wolverton. "It sees no difficulties, and makes light of prejudices which are the growth of centuries; the future dream seems to it like the present reality, and the mirage on the horizon appears to be a smiling oasis but a few steps off. While we old fellows grope and stumble in the dark, the young ones bound forward with all the sanguine hopes of the morning. Your ideas may be all right, my young friends, and I sincerely trust that success may yet crown your efforts, but it is not easy to take the world by storm, and I confess that I do not see the way as clearly as you do. The changes that have been made in the physical world do not guarantee that corresponding changes can be accomplished in mental and moral fields. Your whole plan is based on the assumption that children will always resemble their parents—is it not?"

"In a general way it is," said I. "Every man and every woman is such as he and she are by reason of the qualities inherited from their parents or other ancestors, modified by education and circumstances. I think there can be no gainsaying that."

"Maybe not, but we have not all been accustomed to think so. It used to be considered that while physical qualities were inherited, mental qualities were not."

"Then how is it that an Englishman's brain is larger than a Hottentot's?"

"Oh, that is simply a matter of race."

"But a man's connection with his race comes entirely through his father and mother. If you bring a Hottentot man and woman to England their children will still be Hottentots. You may even adopt them into English families, and give them the training of English children, but they will never develop into Englishmen, and at the first opportunity they will return to the bush and throw off the varnish of civilization with their clothes, and become savages just like their ancestors. That has been proved repeatedly, and cannot be denied. On the other hand, certain families of Englishmen have shown the same mental qualities from generation to generation. Some have been prolific in statesmen, others in scholars, and still others in bankers and merchants. We do not expect the same mental ability in the children of laborers and those of lawyers, simply because the former inherit brains that are inferior to those of the latter."

"Then why is it that genius is so seldom inherited?"

"Because every man inherits the qualities of both his parents in greater or less proportion, and not only so, but he inherits some of the qualities of ancestors farther back than either. A man may be more like his grandfather than his father, or he may inherit some peculiar trait from a remote ancestor which has passed both his father and his grandfather by. But these instances are exceptional; as a general rule children resemble their parents mentally, morally and physically. Now, since genius implies a rare combination of qualities, and it is a very rare thing for a man of genius to marry a woman of genius, it would be unreasonable to expect his children to resemble him in the extraordinary conjunction of faculties which place him in his own particular sphere away above other men. And yet it happens sometimes: the two Pitts in statesmanship, the two Dumas in literature, the two Stephensons in mechanics, and the two Herschells in astronomy, are instances amongst many which might be mentioned."

"Pass that point, then," said my grandfather, "and let it be admitted, for the sake of argument, that children of intellectual parents resemble them intellectually; do you not think you are expecting too much of human nature to believe, that people who are defective either physically or mentally will submit to be deprived of the comforts of marriage for the benefit of future generations?"

"No right thinking man whose family is tainted with lunacy would seek to become a father," said Mr. Manson.

"Nor any sensible woman, who knows that she is positively ugly, to become a mother," said I.

"No man whose lungs are weak should ever wish to marry," said Mr. Manson.

"Nor any woman who is tainted with scrofula," said I.

"Cut the list short," said the reverend doctor. "We are not speaking about what ought to be, but what actually is. You know such people as you speak of do get married everyday, and pass on their infirmities and defects to their children."

"That is the very reason why we propose to have the state step in and prevent them doing what their own consciences ought to forbid."

"But we are discussing the case of a country like this, which is governed by the votes of the people themselves. If you can find another Timoleon and give him despotic power, no doubt you could accomplish all you wish, but how you can prevail upon a democracy to make such sacrifices I confess I am unable to understand."

"The greatest and most heroic sacrifices are recorded of democracies. Did not the Athenians leave their beautiful city to be defiled by the Persian host rather than surrender their freedom. Did not the Hollanders inundate some of their fairest provinces rather than submit to the Spaniards? But we do not propose such sacrifices to the people anywhere. The limitation of the right of marriage at anytime will only affect a small minority, and if the people can be persuaded that the liberty, or rather the license, permitted to that minority, is injurious to all the rest, there can be little doubt as to how they will vote. Each one will doubtless persuade himself that he is not to be counted amongst the unworthy minority, and in most cases he will be in the right in thinking so. The smallest spark of public spirit should be sufficient to make a man willing to run an insignificant risk for the sake of a great public good. If ten men were stranded on a desert island and the only chance of deliverance lay in the attempt by one of their number to reach a port three hundred miles away, in an open boat without a compass, none of the ten might be willing to undertake the voyage, and yet all might be willing to cast lots to decide who should undertake the perilous task, and to abide by the decision."

"Then," said my grandfather, "it is the selfishness of men that you propose to appeal to, and not any high sense of honor or public good."

"Undoubtedly," said I, "but it is to an enlightened selfishness. A hundred years from now we hope that the benefits of a far-seeing public policy will be so apparent to all that higher motives may have sway amongst the foremost nations. But today selfishness is the ruling principle, and we could not expect it to be otherwise."

"There, I am sure, you are not mistaken, but to come to another point: do you not think that your friends in Ionia were rather hard on their criminals? We are treating ours in England with more humanity than ever before, and I am told the results are very satisfactory. Why not experiment on that line a little farther before resorting to more cruel measures?"

"I have no doubt," I said, "that the most humane treatment of criminals is the best for them individually, perhaps, and it would be wrong to inflict upon them the smallest amount of unnecessary suffering.

　　　　　　　　　　　　　　　　ALEXANDER CRAIG

But in my opinion the case of the whole body politic is a desperate one, and if we can effect a cure by cutting off a diseased member, it is our manifest duty to do so. The existence of the criminal class is a menace to the moral health of the people, just as gangrene or cancer is to the living body, and to prove that this is true in a much larger sense than is commonly supposed, let me read to you a paragraph which appeared in a prominent newspaper only the other day:

"'Professor Sellman, of the University of Bonn, Germany, has been making a practical investigation into the doctrine of heredity, and furnishes some valuable data for the study of sociology. Frau Ada Jurke, for sixty years was a resident of the city of Cologne, and died there about a century ago. She was a confirmed profligate, addicted to all debasing vices, and frequently convicted of crime. She was the mother of several children, and six generations of her posterity, numbering altogether 834 persons, can be traced. Professor Sellman located and secured the biographies of 709 members of this remarkable family. One hundred and six were of illegitimate birth, one hundred and sixty-two were professional beggars, and sixty-four of them died in alms-houses. One hundred and eighty-one women lived lives of open shame; seventy-six were convicted and imprisoned for crime, and seven have been executed for murder. Professor Sellman calculates that it has cost the state an average of £2,400 a year, or a total of £240,000 to care for the paupers of this remarkable family, to protect society against them, and to punish their crimes for a hundred years.'

"Now this remarkable history finds a strange parallel in a book published twenty years ago by Mr. R. L. Dugdale, a gentleman connected with the penitentiary commission of the State of New York. It is called 'The Jukes and gives a minute account of several generations of a family so-called. Their common ancestor was a man of idle and profligate life, who was born about the middle of the last century. Seven hundred and nine of his descendants have been identified, of whom one hundred and eight were paupers, one hundred and twenty-eight prostitutes, and seventy-six convicted criminals, including a number of murderers. The writer estimates that the total number of this man's posterity must be something like twelve hundred persons, and that they have cost the state not less than a million and a quarter of dollars. He sums up the net results in these words:

"'Over a million and a quarter dollars of loss in seventy-five years, caused by a single family, twelve hundred strong, without taking into account the entailment of pauperism and crime of the survivors in succeeding generations, and the incurable disease, idiocy and insanity growing out of this debauchery, and reaching further than we can calculate.'

"Now there is not the slightest reason to suppose that these two cases are in anyway exceptional; on the contrary, we are justified in concluding that every criminal who arrives at maturity is the source of a stream of pollution which costs the state vast sums of money, and which spreads like blood poison throughout the lower ranks of society. It acts not merely as a moral taint, although that is undoubtedly its worst feature, but on account of the disregard by these wretches of all natural and moral law, it fills our hospitals with the most loathsome disease, and our asylums with the worst forms of insanity.

"The Ionian system would put a stop to all these horrors in the first or second generation, and in the light of the disclosures made by the American penitentiary officer and the German professor, who shall dare to assert that the system is too severe or that the unspeakable benefits the cost? The denial of existence to swarms of creatures who are a curse to themselves and a disgrace to our common humanity, whose lives are filled with misery and shame, and menace the happiness and wellbeing of all around them. This of itself is a great gain, and the community which can purge itself of its scum has made a mighty stride in the direction of true progress."

"There can be no question about that," said Mr. Manson. "If London could be freed from its professional criminals there would be but little need for the police force, and the honest poor could easily be dealt with. It has been forced upon my mind on many occasions that the children of criminal parents are not only a danger to the community, but a plague to themselves, and I have wondered what could be the purpose of the Almighty in creating such swarms of foredoomed souls. But now I see that the remedy is in our own hands, and I am satisfied that the maudlin sentimentality which would sacrifice the welfare of the people to the tender feelings of criminals can hold no place in the building up of a model state."

"You take the right view of the case, Mr. Manson," said I. "If the social organism is to be renewed by putting a stop to the creation of unsound members, where can we begin better than with those who sacrifice their rights by breaking its laws?"

"I am afraid," said Dr. Wolverton, "that the principle of mercy is to have but an insignificant place in your model state. I understand that you would inflict capital punishment in every case of felony by old offenders."

"When mercy would interfere with the public weal it must be sternly eliminated, but vindictive cruelty will have no place in our system. Crime must be rooted out, but it can be done without the infliction of agonizing pain. We do not propose to hang men like dogs as they do in England today, or butcher them with the guillotine as the French do. Capital punishment will be gently and mercifully inflicted by the drinking of a cup of mild poison in the old Athenian way, and no harm done at all. A mad dog hates to be killed, but it is better dead than living, and a determined criminal loses nothing that is worth possession when his career of wrong-doing is summarily ended."

"Well," said the doctor, "I suppose we shall have to surrender the criminals to your questionable mercy, but what do you propose to do about the land? Do you advocate the Ionian system of joint possession by the people?"

"The land question is, no doubt, a difficult one, but when all the people come to stand on an equal footing of intelligence and education, the injustice of a small number owning the soil from which all derive sustenance, will be universally acknowledged, and, in some way, it will be remedied so that equal opportunities may be afforded to all. The change cannot be made in a day, but will come in time; the government must ultimately be the universal landlord."

"And what, then, will become of our grand old nobility?"

"Your grand old nobility must improve itself very much to be accorded a place in the community at all. The people of the future will have all, and more than all the refinement which is claimed for the nobility of the present day, all their high sentiment of honor and much more than the average of intelligence which they possess, without the selfishness and vice which have always been so prevalent amongst them. I assure you that we can well spare your grand old nobility."

"And what about those who amass large fortunes by their skill in commerce and manufacturing business—do you propose to confiscate their estates when they die?"

"The men who contrive, by skill in manipulating the markets, or by superior fortune, or even by what might be called good management of business, to pile up vast hoards of wealth out of all proportion to their legitimate needs, are really public plunderers who have no moral right to their enormous gains, for it can seldom be said that they render any fair return for the millions they accumulate. It is not possible, and, perhaps, it would not be advantageous to set any limits to what a man may acquire by his own efforts, but if the public good requires an approximately equal distribution of wealth, it is perfectly legitimate to make the people at large the heirs of the millionaires, and to allow only a moderate competence to their children. The good of the whole people, and especially the welfare of future generations shall be the primary object of government, and all private considerations must give way to that paramount consideration."

"I see you propose to reform society from the root upwards," said my grandfather, "and, although I am too old and too conservative to appreciate and thoroughly sympathize with your radical ideas, I am sure I wish you all success, and I think your proposals, at least, worthy of consideration and discussion."

"Our day is nearly over, Doctor," said Mr. Calderwood, and we must confess that it has been to a large extent an evil one. We have known many good men and good women who have earnestly striven to benefit their fellow creatures, but their efforts have been over-balanced by the greed, selfishness and short-sightedness of those to whom the greatest privileges have been given. Neither high station nor wealth nor learning has accomplished much, nor, with a few honorable exceptions, has attempted much for the improvement of the condition of the masses, and the future is as dark as the past under the old regime. But our young friends propose to inaugurate an entirely different system, a system which has already been tried with wonderful success, and I trust their sanguine hopes are destined to glorious fulfillment. Surely it is permitted us to believe that a time may come when the woes of the widow and the orphan, and the sufferings of the destitute, may be prevented, and human life be as full of joy and sunshine as it now is of sorrow and gloom."

"I say amen to that with all my heart," said Dr. Wolverton.

"That such a time will come," said I, it is impossible to doubt, when we think of the mighty strides man has made in the extension of his dominion over nature within a few decades. The difficulties of time and distance have been all but annihilated; the lightning has been harnessed in man's service, and provides instantaneous communication with all parts of the globe; the oceans, which were the terror of our forefathers and the boundaries of their world, are dominated by swiftly-moving castles and palaces of steel; the land is covered with pathways of metal, over which, night and day, continually fly caravans of merchandise, and splendid vehicles in which numerous travelers are sumptuously lodged and fed; the creatures of the earth have been moulded to man's desires, and the waters bring forth their increase at his bidding; floods have been prevented, and the destructive havoc of whirlwinds foretold by his admirable prescience; worlds mightier than his own have been surveyed and measured; the great sun itself has been weighed as in a balance, and stars whose awful distance is measured by years of the unspeakably swift motion of light, have been analyzed as if they were present in his laboratory. Man has grasped the universe with the mind of a god, and failed only in the regulation of his own species, in which he has acted like a helpless imbecile. The human race has been allowed to spread like a noxious weed over the earth, growing wherever it can find nourishment, and propagating itself in uncultivated hideousness. This culpable recklessness must and shall be changed, and the powers of mind which have enabled man to bend all the forces of nature to the fulfillment of his desires will assuredly prove sufficient to deal with the maladies of his own race."

This ended our conference, and my two friends returned next morning to their arduous duties in London, but before they left, a wonderful piece of intelligence reached us. A cable message in the Times newspaper announced that a bill had been introduced into the legislature of the State of Ohio actually embodying some of the most important features of the marriage law of Ionia, and thus proving that the practical people of the United States have already grappled with the great problem of hereditary crime and disease.

The feelings which this glorious news inspired were those of exultation and hope realized, for the mere fact that such a law had been proposed appeared to us like the first ray of light heralding a glorious dawn.

All hail to you, Americans! You have been foremost in many great and good works. Follow up this noble beginning of a great reform, and you shall ere long give to the nations of the earth the splendid spectacle of a people with whom the golden age of poets' dreams has become a great and enduring reality.

A Note About the Author

Alexander Craig was the author of utopian novel *Ionia: Land of Wise Men and Fair Women* (1898). Little is known about Craig, and though his novel was published in America he shows a keen familiarity with England and English culture.

A Note from the Publisher

Spanning many genres, from non-fiction essays to literature classics to children's books and lyric poetry, Mint Edition books showcase the master works of our time in a modern new package. The text is freshly typeset, is clean and easy to read, and features a new note about the author in each volume. Many books also include exclusive new introductory material. Every book boasts a striking new cover, which makes it as appropriate for collecting as it is for gift giving. Mint Edition books are only printed when a reader orders them, so natural resources are not wasted. We're proud that our books are never manufactured in excess and exist only in the exact quantity they need to be read and enjoyed.

Discover more of your favorite classics with Bookfinity™.

- Track your reading with custom book lists.
- Get great book recommendations for your personalized Reader Type.
- Add reviews for your favorite books.
- AND MUCH MORE!

Visit **bookfinity.com** and take the fun Reader Type quiz to get started.

Enjoy our classic and modern companion pairings!

Printed in the USA
CPSIA information can be obtained
at www.ICGtesting.com
JSHW022330140824
68134JS00019B/1404

9 781513 291055